SPECIAL MESSAGE TO READERS

This book is published under the auspices of

THE ULVERSCROFT FOUNDATION

(registered charity No. 264873 UK)

Established in 1972 to provide funds for research, diagnosis and treatment of eye diseases. Examples of contributions made are: —

A Children's Assessment Unit at Moorfield's Hospital, London.

•

Twin operating theatres at the Western Ophthalmic Hospital, London.

•

A Chair of Ophthalmology at the Royal Australian College of Ophthalmologists.

•

The Ulverscroft Children's Eye Unit at the Great Ormond Street Hospital For Sick Children, London.

You can help further the work of the Foundation by making a donation or leaving a legacy. Every contribution, no matter how small, is received with gratitude. Please write for details to:

THE ULVERSCROFT FOUNDATION,
The Green, Bradgate Road, Anstey,
Leicester LE7 7FU, England.
Telephone: (0116) 236 4325

In Australia write to:
THE ULVERSCROFT FOUNDATION,
c/o The Royal Australian and New Zealand
College of Ophthalmologists,
94-98 Chalmers Street, Surry Hills,
N.S.W. 2010, Australia

Ann Brashares is the author of four bestselling young adult novels. This is her first novel for adults. She lives in Manhattan and spends her summers on Fire Island, New York.

THE LAST SUMMER (OF YOU & ME)

The long, hot summers spent on Fire Island have always been the highlight of the year for sisters Riley and Alice. Not least because it is there that they always see Paul: their next-door neighbour, Riley's best friend in all the world, and the only boy Alice has ever loved. Then Paul goes to university, and he leaves them both behind him. Three years later, as Alice in turn prepares to start college, Paul returns. The trick, he tells himself, is to have what he had without destroying it. But their world will change irresistibly, wonderfully and tragically, with every breath they take.

ANN BRASHARES

THE LAST SUMMER (OF YOU & ME)

Complete and Unabridged

CHARNWOOD
Leicester

First published in Great Britain in 2007 by
Hodder & Stoughton
a division of Hodder Headline
London

First Charnwood Edition
published 2009
by arrangement with
Hodder & Stoughton
a division of Hodder Headline
London

British Library CIP Data

Brashares, Ann.
    The last summer (of you & me)
    1. Sisters- -Fiction. 2. Friendship- -Fiction.
    3. Large type books.
    I. Title
    813.6–dc22

    ISBN 978–1–84782–609–1

Published by
F. A. Thorpe (Publishing)
Anstey, Leicestershire

Set by Words & Graphics Ltd.
Anstey, Leicestershire
Printed and bound in Great Britain by
T. J. International Ltd., Padstow, Cornwall

This book is printed on acid-free paper

For my dad
with love

No one ever gets over the first unfairness; no one except Peter. He often met it, but he always forgot it. I suppose that was the real difference between him and all the rest.

— J. M. BARRIE

1

Waiting

Alice waited for Paul on the ferry dock. He'd left a crackly message on the answering machine saying he'd be coming in on the afternoon boat. That was like him. He couldn't say the 1:20 or the 3:55. She'd spent too long staring at the ferry schedule, trying to divine his meaning.

With some amount of self-hatred, Alice had first walked out onto the dock for the 1:20, knowing he wouldn't be on it. She'd looked only vaguely at the faces as they emerged from the boat, assuring herself she wasn't expecting anything. She'd sat with her bare feet on the bench at the periphery, her book resting on her knees so she wouldn't have to interact with anyone. *I know you're not going to be on it, so don't think I think you are*, she'd told the Paul who lived in her mind. Even there, under her presumed control, he was teasing and unpredictable.

For the 3:55, she put Vaseline on her lips and brushed her hair. The boat after that wasn't until 6:10, and though Paul could miss the so-called afternoon ferry, he couldn't call 6:10 the afternoon.

How often she did attempt to process his thoughts in her mind. She took his opinions too seriously, remembered them long after she suspected he'd forgotten them.

It was one thing, trying to think his thoughts when he was close by, his words offering clues, corrections, and confirmations by the hour. But three years of silence made for complex interpolations. It made it harder, and in another way it made it easier. She was freer with his thoughts. She made them her own, thought them to her liking.

He had missed two summers. She couldn't imagine how he could do that. Without him, they had been shadow seasons. Feelings were felt thinly, there and then gone. Memories were not made. There was nothing new in sitting on this dock, on this or that wooden bench, watching for his boat to come. In some ways, she was always waiting for him.

She couldn't picture his face when he was gone. Every summer he came back wearing his same face that she could not remember.

Absently, she saw the people on the dock who came, went, and waited. She waved to people she knew, mostly her parents' friends. She felt the wind blow the pounding sun off her shoulders. She slowly dug her thumbnail along a plank of the seat, provoking a splinter but caking up mold and disintegration instead.

When it came to waiting, Riley always had something else to do. Paul was Riley's best friend. Alice knew Riley missed him, too, but she said she didn't like waiting. Alice didn't like it. Nobody did. But Alice was a younger sister. She didn't have the idea of not doing things because you didn't like them.

She watched for the ferry, the way it started out as a little white triangle across the bay. When it wasn't there, she could hardly imagine it. It was never coming. And then it appeared. It took shape quickly. It was always coming.

She stood. She couldn't help it. She left her book on the bench with its paper cover fluttering open in the wind. Would this be him? Was he on there?

She let her hair out of its elastic. She stretched her tank top down over her hips. She wanted him to see all of her and also none of her. She wanted him to be dazzled by the bits and blinded to the whole. She wanted him to see her whole and not in pieces. She had hopes that were hard to satisfy.

Her legs bounced; her arms clutched her middle. She saw the approach of the middle-aged woman in a pink sarong who taught her mother's yoga class.

'Who are you waiting for, Alice?'

Exposed as she was, the friendly question struck Alice as a cruelty.

'No one,' Alice lied awkwardly. The woman's tanned face was as familiar to Alice as the wicker sofa on the screened porch, but that did not mean that Alice knew her name. She knew the lady's poodle was named Albert and that her yoga class was heavy on the chanting. In a place like this, as a child you weren't responsible for the names of grown-ups, though the grown-ups always knew yours. If you were a child, relationships here began asymmetrically, and there rarely came a specific opportunity for reevaluation. You bore the same age relationship to people here no matter how old you got.

The woman looked at Alice's feet, which told the truth. If you were getting on the 3:55, you wore shoes.

Alice self-consciously straggled over to the freight area as though she had some purpose there. She didn't lie easily, and doing it now conferred an unwanted intimacy. She preferred to save her lies for the people whose names she knew.

She couldn't look at the boat. She sat back down on the bench, crossing her arms and her legs and bowing her head.

It was a small village on a small island with customs and rules all its own. 'No keys, no wallet, no shoes' was the saying that expressed their summer way of life. There were no cars and — in the old days, at least — nobody locked their house. The single place of commerce was the Waterby market, mostly trading in candy and ice cream cones, where your name was your credit and they didn't accept cash. Shoes meant you were coming, going, or playing tennis. Even at the yacht club. Even at parties. There was a community pride in having feet tough enough to withstand the splintering boardwalks. It's not that you didn't get splinters — you always did. You just shut up about it. Every kid knew that. At the end of each summer, the bottoms and sides of Alice's feet were speckled black with old splinters. Eventually they disappeared; she was never quite sure where they went. 'They are

4

reabsorbed,' a knowledgeable seven-year-old named Sawyer Boyd told her once.

Everyone's business came through this ferry dock, with rhythms and hierarchies unlike other places. You saw the people as they came and went and waited. You also saw their stuff piled on the dock until they loaded it onto their wagon and rolled it home. You knew what kind of toilet paper they bought. Alice still rated two-ply a luxury more subtle and telling than a person's bag or shoes. You knew that the people with the Fairway bags and the paper products were getting off here in Waterby or in Saltaire. The people getting off in the town of Kismet always had beer.

Cars were conveyors of privacy. Without them, you lived a lot more of your life out in the open. Where you went, who you went with. Who you waited for at the ferry dock. Who you brushed your hair for. You were exposed here, but you were also safe.

The carlessness of the place had always appealed to certain utopian types, even shallow ones. 'Get rid of cars and you get rid of global warming, oil wars in the Middle East, obesity, and most crime, too,' her father liked to say.

The ferry put an extra emphasis on coming and going. Adults went back and forth all the time, but there had been many summers when Alice and Riley had come and gone only once. They came with their pale skin, haircuts meant to last the summer, their tender feet, and their shyness. They left with brown, freckled, bitten skin; tangly hair; foot bottoms thick like tires;

5

and familiarity verging on rudeness.

She remembered the hellos, and she remembered the goodbyes even more. End-of-summer tradition dictated that whoever was last to leave the island saluted departing friends by jumping into the water as the goodbye ferry pulled away.

Now she heard the boat grinding up behind her. She loosened her arms and pressed her hands against the wood. She heard the slapping of the wake against the pilings as the boat came around. She untucked one leg and bounced her free heel on the plank in front of her.

Alice would have liked to do the arriving instead of the waiting. She would have rather done the leaving than the getting left, but that was never the way it happened. For some reason it was always Alice who waited and Alice who dove in.

★　★　★

The ferry was like a time capsule, in a way. A space capsule. It sent you and your fellow canvas-bag travelers through a wormhole, the same one every time.

Paul stood on the top deck in the wet wind as the monstrous coastal houses of Long Island's south shore gave way to dark, briny water.

The thick feeling of the air began when you stepped onto the ferry. The stickiness over every surface. His hair blew around and he thought of Alice, fishing in her backpack for an elastic. He could picture her anchoring various things in her mouth as she braided her hair. He'd had short

6

hair then, and though he admired her skill at braiding in wind — what boy wasn't mystified by a braid? — he'd thought it was needless. Now his hair was long.

The first sighting was the Robert Moses obelisk, and second was the gangly lighthouse. Well, it wasn't gangly really. In truth, this lighthouse set his standard for all others, and the others looked stout and dumpy by comparison. You loved what you knew. You couldn't help it. He couldn't, though he did try.

She would be there. If she was still Alice, she would be there. If Riley was still Riley, she would not be. He had called, so if Alice didn't come, it would mean something. If she did come, it would mean something also. He wished he hadn't called, in a way. The old staging unnerved him, but after all this time he couldn't just sneak up on Alice.

He could imagine that she hadn't checked the messages, but he knew Alice to be heartrendingly on top of the messages. As though she was always waiting for something good and something bad.

Now the sweeter, older, coast of the island emerged, coughed up by the bay in time for his arrival. He discerned the wide, curling arm of the dock. He saw the figures on it. He knew Riley would be the same. By the letters she wrote him, he could tell she would look and sound the same. But the idea of a twenty-one-year-old Alice scared him.

Would their parents be there? Could he

contend with the whole bunch of them on such a narrow tatter of land stuck out here between the ocean and the bay?

Now the shapes of the houses grew and sharpened, and the faces on the dock turned toward the boat expectantly — a bunch of circles without features at first. He unstuck himself from the bench, stretched his legs. He felt the chill sweat of his fingers knitted around the handles of his duffel bag.

Without quite giving himself the go-ahead, he started scanning the faces. The older ones were most familiar. The tricky doubles player with the comb-over — what was his name? The guy with the crooked shoulders who tended to the fire trucks, the brown lady with the dog under her arm. The club pro, Don Rontano, with the starched polo shirt, collar upturned, who got on so well with the lonely ladies. The children were impossible to identify, and the bodies between old and young he feared to scrutinize. Would her hair have gotten as dark as that? Could her shape have changed into that?

No and no, obviously. At this distance, closing in at this speed, you knew a person by her posture, by certain unnameable qualities, and those weren't and couldn't be hers. Maybe she hadn't come. Maybe she wasn't even on the island. But what could make Alice not come?

There was one other figure — a girl, it seemed — half-curled on the bench, one foot tucked under her. But her back was to him, and unlike the others, she didn't turn her face to the boat.

He scanned the small cluster again, resenting

the spasmodic activity of his eyeballs. What if she were different now? What if he couldn't keep his old idea of her?

As the ferry pulled around the hook of the dock, the sitting girl stood. Her hair blew around her face, obscuring it. Maybe that was the reason he continued to imagine her a stranger even after he got close enough to see.

For a few moments, both frantic and calm, he watched her carefully, feeling a tingle in the old, blocked-off passageways. He felt the neurons firing in the part of his brain responsible for present perception but also in the part devoted to memory.

Maybe that was why a strange overload took place just then, when he recognized her and didn't recognize her at the same time. Ideas and feelings rushed in that he might have rather kept out.

★ ★ ★

'Hey,' he said to her.

She hugged him, putting her chin on his shoulder and her face toward the lighthouse. It wasn't the kind of thing they did. It wasn't so much intimacy that provoked it, but the need not to look at him any longer.

She couldn't really feel anything of him or focus her eyes exactly. Her body was numb and her eyes confused her. In a moment of lucidity, she feared he could feel her heart pounding and she pulled away.

She put her head down and gestured to his

bag. 'Is that everything?' she asked his bag.

'That's it.' He sounded almost rueful. She wanted to check his face, but he was looking at her, so she didn't.

What was the matter with her? It was just him! It was the same old Paul. But it also wasn't. He was the strangest of strangers in that he was also her oldest friend.

'Is it heavy?' she found herself saying.

'No. It's fine,' he said, and she thought she heard the seed of a laugh in his voice. Was he going to laugh at her? He used to do that. He teased her and laughed at her without relent. But if he did that now, she would die.

She'd intended to feel cold toward him this time. For leaving for so long and forgetting her. *Did you forget me?* She was good at being angry with him when he was away, but in his presence she never could.

She forged ahead and he followed. Mrs. McKay was unlocking her wagon, and Connie, their old swim coach, was on the fishing side. If she raised her head, she would see others. They all knew Paul. Would they recognize him with his long, clumpy hair and his bristly face?

All the things she planned to feel, the way she planned to look and seem, the appropriate things she planned to say. None of them came to pass.

'Let's go find Riley,' he said from behind her, and her heart thrilled with relief. That was what they could do. That would make sense of it.

She offered him her mother's bike and got on her own. He balanced his duffel bag over the basket and maneuvered up the skinny boardwalk

10

ahead of her with the grace of a true islander. He used to ride three bikes at once. He could do a wheelie without his hands. He had been her hero of bikes.

They went directly to the ocean beach. He walked out of his shoes and peeled off his socks, barely slowing down. He stood on the stairs at the top of the dune, taking it in, and she lingered a few feet behind, breathless to see what kind of beach it was today.

As children, they had dozens of names for the beach, like Eskimos naming snow, and they were ever finding need for more. A placid, white-sand and sparkly turquoise affair was a Tortola beach after an island in the Caribbean that Paul had been dragged to with his mother. They scorned such a beach. The Riley beach, also known as Fight beach, was when the little grains of sand whipped like glass against your skin and the surf was ragged and punishing. An Alice beach was truly rare, and it involved tide pools.

Today Alice wanted the kind he used to want, the Paul beach, low-tide crunchy sand, a sharp drop-off to the water, and a close army of rough, green waves. How familiar it felt to want his wants for him. That much had not changed.

Once Paul told her that the beach was like him because it changed every day but it never made any progress. Later she remembered thinking that a normal person might have begun by saying that he was like the beach.

Alice held her hair back, acknowledging that this beach was yet another requiring a name. A Nervous beach. A Gnashing beach. The sand

11

was smooth and gradual, but the surf was wild, the waves coming in at a diagonal pitch. She was making up her mind not to swim as Paul set off down the decrepit steps. She looked east toward the lifeguard chair, with Riley sitting in it and the red 'no swimming' flag flying above her.

Paul didn't bend his steps toward Riley but rather headed straight for the water. Alice watched in muffled surprise as he walked into the surf fully clothed. He dove into an olive-colored wall. Alice watched eagerly for his head to pop out of the irritable froth crashing all around. She looked to her sister, who was now standing up in the chair, neck forward in her pose of lifeguard alertness, hands on her hips.

Paul's head did finally appear at least twenty yards out. He was beyond the breaking waves but bobbing and buffeted nonetheless.

Alice could see Riley muttering to another guard, who stood at the foot of the stand. She blew her whistle twice. 'Get out of the water!' she bellowed, pointing at the red flag. 'Asshole,' she muttered.

From far out, Paul lifted his arm and waved to her.

Alice could tell the moment Riley realized who it was. She whooped loudly enough for Alice to hear. She looked back over her shoulder and saw Alice there.

Riley's pose relaxed. Her whistled dropped. She shrugged and Alice smiled. Riley shouted to be heard over the fresh blast of wind. 'I guess Paul is back.'

'Just leave him out there,' Riley said to her backup guard. 'He'll be fine.'

She sat back down in her chair and watched Paul's bouncing head. She wasn't going in after him. Let him drown. He would never drown.

Paul had worked through every phase of lifeguard training alongside her, determined to best her every time. Though never to his face, she credited him with making her tough. She didn't just pass the challenges, she had to try to beat Paul. And then the day of the actual test — a formality by that point, their victory lap — Paul didn't show up. When she saw him later by the ferry dock, he'd just shrugged. It was the culmination of her life, and he'd acted like the thing had slipped his mind.

But on her first official day in the chair, when she'd nearly exploded with pride in her official red suit, Paul had turned up again. She didn't realize the dark-haired figure thrashing out beyond the surf was Paul. She'd leapt off the chair with all possible intensity, blowing her whistle, marshaling her equipment, shouting commands, her blood dashing with purpose.

When she got out to the deep water and saw who it was, she wanted to drown him for real. She called him a motherfucker and started to swim back to shore, her cheeks pounding red with fury. Then she saw the lineup of concerned citizens on the sand and the head guard apoplectic at the idea that she was abandoning the victim. And there was Paul out there, keeping up his act. What could she do? She went back and saved his ass. As she dragged him toward the beach, she gave a ferocious pinch on the back of his neck. It was the only time he writhed authentically.

When they were little, she and Paul were the same. She understood him without having to try. They fought sometimes. In third grade she kicked him to the ground. In fifth grade he shoved her into a doorway and she had to get six stitches in her eyebrow. They didn't fight physically after that, though she did try to provoke him. It was the scar, she thought, that made him stop. She liked the scar.

After middle school, he started making everything so complicated. He got quiet and brooding sometimes for no reason she could determine. She always thought he would have ended up happier if he'd just taken the lifeguard test. That was her true opinion. Later he joined weird political groups and tried to organize Central American fruit pickers who were too smart to take any of the crap he was trying to sell.

'I arrived with all my political ideas, but the poverty and sadness around here sort of nullifies them,' he'd written to her from a farm near Bakersville. 'Last night somebody stole my wallet from my pants while I slept. I am finding myself absurd.'

She couldn't argue. 'You should have been a lifeguard,' she wrote back.

And yet, she did love him. In that way, she hated his disappointments even if she disagreed

14

with the things he wanted.

'Can you take over the shift?' she asked Adam Pryce. He was her backup guard and her junior by six years.

He agreed, and she jumped down off the chair. With an old feeling of joy, she walked down to the waves and dove into an ocean that no sane person would swim in. She swam out to Paul with a few tough strokes.

And so they bobbed around together, skirting a riptide, taunting the waves while Alice looked on from the beach.

2

You'll Turn Out Ordinary
if You're Not Careful

In the old days Paul came over in his pajamas to fight for the good cereal. Alice suspected it was one of the few battles he could win or lose. The point was getting over there early.

His house was enormous and stood between their house and the ocean. The two houses were so close, you could hear each other's parents fighting at night when the ocean was calm. His house had seven bedrooms and a TV, and it was clean and had a shelf full of good cereal. But from Alice's earliest memory, nobody ever went over there to eat the Fruity Pebbles, let alone fight for it. Alice sensed that young children instinctively preferred the life inside a small house to a big one.

Paul did appear that morning, though not in his pajamas. He wore a pair of pants so yellow and stiff that they almost made Alice laugh. But she checked herself, wondering if that was the kind of thing they did anymore.

He came the customary way, from the back door of his house to the back door of theirs. If you went the regular way, it was at least a hundred and fifty steps on the boardwalk, more than that if you were Alice, and many fewer if you were Paul and you lied. But the sand passage through the phragmites was thirty steps at the most, and undetectable to the outside world.

'Did you eat yet?' Alice asked casually, caring too much about small things.

'No.' He looked mildly chastened. 'I'm fine, though. You don't have to feed me.'

She pushed the box of Rice Krispies toward him, along with a bowl and spoon. He seemed to forget his own words as he poured his cereal.

'Milk?' she said.

'Thanks.'

Her elbow on the table, her chin in her hand, Alice watched him eat. He never minded being watched.

'What's with the hair?' Riley asked, passing though the kitchen on her way to the laundry.

'It grew,' he said, crunching away complacently.

'Like that?'

'Yeah, like that.'

'Mine doesn't grow like that,' Alice pointed out.

'Because you probably wash yours and brush it.'

'I do, actually.'

'Well.'

'It doesn't look so good,' Riley said to Paul, a towel bunched under her arm. She stated it as a simple matter of fact.

'I know,' Paul said, feeling one of the clumps between his fingers. 'It's kind of itchy. I think I'll cut it off for the summer.' He put down his

17

spoon and looked at Alice. 'Do you still have your barber scissors?'

She was shaking the cereal box around to see if there was enough left for another bowl. 'Yes. Do you want to borrow them?'

'Can you do it?' he asked.

She put the box down. She uncrossed her ankles. She chewed the inside of her cheek. 'Can I cut your hair, you mean?'

'Yeah.'

She used to cut his hair sometimes, and Riley's, too. She'd cut other kids' hair once in a while. She'd removed wads of gum and nettles as a favor. Not because she was particularly good at it but because her Uncle Peyton had once given her a barber set with the good scissors. And otherwise you had to go off-island.

Could she cut his hair? If not, why couldn't she?

'Nothing fancy,' he said.

'Give him a bouffant,' Riley suggested.

'I guess I could do it.'

He stood, looking at her expectantly.

'Right now?' she asked. Now was not as good a time as later, when he would forget about it.

'Yes. Is that okay?'

Somewhat mechanically, she followed him up the stairs. They had just one bathroom, and she and Riley were locked in a long-term standoff about whose turn it was to clean it. Paul sat on the edge of the tub, just the way he used to do.

Riley stood in the doorway, a look of amusement on her face.

The scissors were there in the cabinet, still

18

rust-free in the original plastic case. She wished they weren't both watching her. It felt embarrassing to tend to one's scissors so well.

'Okay. So . . . ' she began. 'Just, uh . . . '

'Cut it off.' He pulled his T-shirt over his head, which didn't help put her at ease. She had to force herself into the orbit of his head. His face now related to her chest as hers usually did to his. He looked up at her, and she felt as though she were made of nostrils.

'Not all of it . . . ?' She couldn't stand to make him bald.

'The dreads, mainly. You can do it however you want.'

'I think you'll find wildlife in there,' Riley commented.

Alice nodded. That wasn't the thing she worried about. You couldn't grow up with Riley and be prissy.

It was funny the things the three of them talked about. Often it was the concrete things they hung upon. Concrete or metaphysical, and very little in between. That was another leftover, a child's prerogative, in a way. They talked about fish and they talked about God. But it was all the stuff in the middle that came to preoccupy you as you grew older.

The previous night, the rain had pelted against the tar shingles and they'd talked for hours on their sandy living room floor. They talked about the big storms, the houses that washed away, the old promenade that once lined the ocean beach and now lay deep under the waves. They'd talked about the sameness of their island in spite of the

19

fact that it was always changing shape. Alice had felt relieved that her parents weren't around so it was just the three of them, the way it used to be. It allowed them the freedom to let the conversation meander and stall. It allowed them to leave out large categories of discussion, such as what they'd been doing for the last three years.

Alice held up her scissors and snapped at the air a few times. She touched her hand to the top of his head for a start. It was warm and made her think of duck-duck-goose. She felt the stubble of his chin against her forearm. She had the feeling of crying creeping up her throat. How she had missed him. Sometimes you couldn't face the sadness of being forgotten until you felt the comfort of being remembered again.

'Well, here goes,' she said a little faintly. She grasped a clump of his brown hair and cut. Sharp scissors against hair made a wonderful sound: a soft, multitudinous zing. She remembered that she had always liked it.

Underneath the grime, Paul's hair was as fine as it had been when he was little, in spite of how he'd mistreated it. Each piece she cut at the base of the clump curled sweetly and lay down on his head. It was more docile, less complicated than the other parts of him.

'What do you think?' she asked, adverting to Riley.

Riley was standing still for longer than usual. She looked at the mess of tangles and clumps on the linoleum floor. 'He has to clean up.' She said it amicably, seeming to indicate approval.

Riley went back downstairs, and they heard the screen door slam and settle.

Alice held a clump at the nape of his neck and made him shiver. Delicately, she cut pieces around his ear, admiring the pale silky fuzz that sprouted along the edge. It wasn't just now. These things had always meant something to her.

'You are being very still,' she complimented him.

She didn't think he'd heard her at first, even though she was inches from his ear. 'I'm trying,' he finally said.

She came around to the front last, bold now in her barber persona. She held his chin to steady her cutting hand against his cheek, perhaps not strictly by necessity. She looked at his cheek, his jaw, and felt the reassurance of being near him.

She remembered when she'd first learned to knit from her Grandma Ruth after fifth grade. She'd spent a whole winter knitting Paul a hat. She'd wanted to keep some connection to him through the cold months when she didn't see him, when the distance between them and the awkwardness between their parents made him almost like a stranger. The next winter Alice had knitted him a scarf in green, gray, and blue to remind him of the ocean. She remembered sending it to him in his first year at boarding school. Her yarn was her proxy to touch him, to keep him warm, to make him remember her.

Alice fell into a meditative mood, lulled by the sound of her scissors. She evened, trimmed, shaped, and smoothed. She felt a fullness in her

21

heart and in her throat. She felt his head loosening on his neck, giving in to her hands, trusting her.

How long since she had felt this particular feeling in her muscles? She'd forgotten what it was like.

In spite of everything, she felt such pathos for him. She always had. Even though he was older than she. Even though he was mean to her, and dismissed her and even forgot her, she still ached for him. Maybe it was because his father died. Maybe because Lia didn't mother him in the regular way. Alice remembered her own mother telling her how at a few crisis moments when he was small, Paul had turned to her instead of Lia. 'I was touched when Paul let me take care of him,' Judy said, 'but it made me sad, too. A well-mothered kid doesn't have needs that fast, that big.'

'She's had a tough life,' her father used to say about Lia, even while acknowledging that she was a pain in the ass.

Lia grew up in Italy, orphaned by the age of fifteen. She called Paul *Paulo*, but only she was allowed. If Riley or Alice did, Paul would punch them. Apparently, his mother meant to name him after a heroic uncle, a spy supposedly, who died in World War II, but his father, Robbie, meant to name him after Paul McCartney. Alice did not know what it said on his birth certificate. She thought it was odd the way Paul acted as though he did not speak Italian even though they knew perfectly well he did.

Alice also knew that Paul's father's parents, his

grandparents, did not like Lia. They blamed her for everything that happened with Robbie. And though Alice felt that Lia deserved a lot of blame in the world, it was possible she didn't deserve that particular blame.

Paul was their only grandchild and supposed heir to the gigantic piles of money, which Lia was spending as fast as she could. She knew these things only from her mother and father, never from Paul. Paul's grandmother had once called Alice's mom in the hope that she would intervene on their behalf. Riley remembered it. 'You should be calling Lia,' Judy had advised, but the grandmother refused. Only the lawyers called Lia.

Paul stayed away from his grandparents. He did not get along with his mother but he would be loyal to her. It was the main way, as far as Alice could tell, that he managed to love her.

Lia spent most of her time in Italy since Paul left for college. When she was in the United States, she found endless faults with it — the food, the pace, the language, the music. Alice always imagined a happier Lia in Italy, but Paul once told her that Lia complained when she was there, too.

Alice did not remember Robbie, Paul's father, because he died when she was only a few months old. Riley did remember him — bits and pieces of him, like his beard and his rubbery sandals and his fingers knowing how to tie all kinds of knots.

It terrified Alice to talk about Paul's father, because she knew things she shouldn't have known. She knew things Paul had not told her, things he probably didn't know. Alice hated that and faulted her mother for having ever told her. Her mother was too keen on information, too quick to believe in the neutrality of facts just because they were true. 'It's the journalist in me,' her mother claimed, managing to praise herself even in apology.

Paul almost never talked about his father, and when he did, he acted as though he remembered him perfectly. But Alice noticed that he didn't talk about the small things.

Alice suspected Paul couldn't really picture him, just like she couldn't picture Paul when he was away. Maybe that was the case with people you wanted more than was good for you.

Alice let her scissors clatter into the sink. She stood still, her hands on his head, one over his ear, the other at the back. She let out her breath as his head sank slowly into her body, coming to rest just below her breasts.

She held him there, her head bowed to his. She felt the bones of his cheek and chin against her shirt, the bits of stubble catching in the weave of the cotton, his breath pooling in the wrinkles.

He was with her; he was here. She was scared to even breathe.

The screen door rattled in the kitchen. He lifted his head. She stepped back. And just like that, he wasn't with her anymore.

The air that had enclosed them reformed around them as separate bodies. He looked at her for a moment but said nothing. She retrieved her scissors and with shaking hands put them back into their plastic case.

He stood and regarded himself in the mirror. 'Nice job,' he said to her. And she realized he had completed the transformation back into the Paul she knew. They had done it together. From strange, foreign Paul, he'd returned to the beloved, exacting Paul of old.

But there was a moment in between, a moment flung free in the midst of the transition, when he had made contact. That was the moment she would dwell on.

★　★　★

For the first time in months, his head lay comfortably in his pillow and his scalp did not itch. But even so, Paul couldn't sleep, and this too he attributed to his haircut.

He pictured, or rather felt, Alice's toe kicking into the side of his foot. He could feel the pressure of her palm on his head and her fingers on his chin. When she bent over him, he smelled a new Alice smell, perhaps cleaner than the old Alice smell but still related and deeply stirring.

That was the thing that overtook him, when he'd pressed his head against her body. Why had he done that? What had it meant? It wasn't the kind of thing you did to any old girl. You couldn't take it back. You could try to discount it. You could pretend it hadn't happened. But it was there between them. Thankfully, though (he was thankful, wasn't he?), the rest of the day had seemed to constitute an implicit agreement to a mutual amnesia.

His distress and pleasure mixed and married, giving birth to several anxious children. Maybe he shouldn't have come back here. But what else did he have?

The trick was to have what he had without destroying it, if that was possible. Could you even do that? Every desire fulfilled was thus defeated. Could you interrupt the cycle? Could you make the world hold still?

There was nothing new in loving Alice. He had always loved her, even when he was mean to her. He remembered it, and he had been told so. He'd loved her before she even realized it. Wasn't that the easiest way to love a person? She was fat and wordless and comforting to him when she was a baby. He'd carried her around from place to place. His mother's psychiatrist had said that Alice was his transitional object.

He knew at the age of four when his father died that he wasn't going to be getting any brothers or sisters in the traditional way, and Riley had understood that, too.

'It's okay,' Riley had told him, 'you can share Alice.'

Riley was his equal, his rival, his flip side, and his best friend. In some ways, he found it hard to distinguish himself from her. They were the same age, and for years they'd been the same size. They'd worn the same pants. He felt disloyal for having kept growing after she had stopped.

Alice wasn't his friend, though he knew she'd always wanted to be. She was something else,

26

neither more nor less but not the same.

When he thought of Alice, especially when he was lying in this bed, he thought often of the summer when he and Riley were thirteen. Old friends and cohorts were turning vain and stupid everywhere they looked, losing interest in the things that had once mattered to them. Kids like Megan Cooley and Alex Peterson started up spin-the-bottle and truth-or-dare parties in the back room of the village library. Riley hated it, and Paul was afraid of it. What they'd witnessed from their parents made them only more determined to stay on the safe side of adolescence. Alice, at ten, copied her indignation from them.

As a band of children, they had laid a magical world over the topology of this skinny place, spread it from ocean to bay. It had places and creatures both evil and good, and part of the enchantment was their power to change sides whenever a good game required it. Both he and Riley realized this world was fragile. It would sink unmarked into the sea if they let it. It required believing in, and fewer and fewer people did.

In outward disgust and inward fear, he and Riley had established a mostly wordless covenant. Bodies were being snatched left and right, but they had each other to remind them what was true. If they kept each other honest, they decided, it would not happen to them. They would lash themselves to the mast of prehormonal bliss and sail through the storm that way. They'd had the prestige at that time to say, *This we know is true.* And if ever anyone said it was untrue, they would know that evil was whispered in their ears and the enemy was at hand. They would not talk. They would not give in. They'd carry the poison pill and use it if they had to.

But what would happen when they came out on the other side of the storm? They hadn't thought it through that far. They hadn't quite considered that by trusting one part of your life, you could undermine all the others. By siding with an early version of yourself, preemptively, you would doubt all future selves that conflicted with it.

Alice had been easy to enlist at the age of ten. Alice, who would grow breasts at thirteen and attune herself to the broader and subtler frequencies of human interaction. She hadn't known what she'd be giving up.

The rest had been looking backward. Trying to remember what was true rather than seeking it. They were holy men divining the ancient book, judges interpreting their constitution. They harkened back to a calmer, more just time.

But time went on, as it will, and the seasons changed. What did not accord with the covenant Paul did not tell Riley and Alice. The ambitions, the petty preoccupations, the sex he'd finally had with the laughing girl in his history class junior year. He went ahead and lived those seasons, all the while feeling that his real life lay here, on this beach in the summer, with Riley and Alice.

What was powerful at thirteen and even seventeen should have grown quaint by twenty-four, and yet the covenant, by its nature, had durability. It still existed between them. He could feel it even now. You could go away for months or years, but it was still here, bound to what you loved, binding you to it.

Alice kept it out of loyalty, he suspected. For Riley, it wasn't so much like a choice. And for him?

For him, what he'd had here on this island with Riley and Alice was the best and most lasting thing in his life.

3

Bottles and Stones

For nine years Paul had not called her by her name. She had been 'Shorty' or 'Kid' or 'You' to him since she was twelve. It wasn't until her first night working as a waitress at the yacht club that Alice realized this.

It was a Friday night, so she was not stunned to see her parents turn up. Since the end of high school, Ethan and Judy had left the girls at the beach on the weekdays and come out on Friday's noisy and social sunset ferry. Ethan was a history teacher and coach at a private school in Manhattan during the school year and taught summer-school courses and tutored through July and most of August to boost his income. Her mother copyedited and proofread textbooks and pitched articles on child-rearing and related subjects to a handful of editors she knew. Judy talked about her articles a lot during the conceiving and pitching stage, but after that they often disappeared, uncommissioned and unwritten.

'I'll take the bacon burger. And what have you got on tap?'

Alice had her arms crossed, pen in her teeth, pad tucked into her armpit. It seemed typical of her life experience that her sole table on her first shift was taken by her parents.

'Dad, you know what they have,' she said in an undertone. Within moments of being near them, she felt her eyeballs rolling skyward. Even if she kept her eyeballs still, she could hear the tone in her voice.

'Okay, make it a Bass.'

Her father's hair was a mix of black and gray, and as full as a soap opera star's. Most people tread lightly over what they have and dwell heavily on what they have not, but in that sense her father was original. He thought as often about keeping his hair as balding people thought about losing theirs, and the extent of his pleasure easily matched the extent of their distress.

Her mother was blond. Though it was dyed blond, she felt as though she had a right to the color because she had once been blond. She spoke out against blondes who had no natural claim to it. 'It really doesn't look right,' she'd say.

Alice had inherited this blond hair, though a rustier, wavier version, and the color was holding steady, though Alice suspected it would turn dark when she had to stop spending summers at the beach. Next summer, for example, when she'd be working at a law firm. And all the seasons after, when Riley would keep teaching her outdoor leadership courses during the year and lifeguarding through the summers, and Alice would be working endlessly at a law firm. Alice had begun to picture herself in the future with dark hair.

Though Riley spent most of her life outside, she had never been blond. She had dark hair that tangled easily, as Alice knew from her attempts to trim it. Even when she was little, she never let Judy brush it. It was always cut straight around to a length somewhere between her chin and her shoulders, often tucked behind her ears. Her hair made her look younger than she was, and her freckles made her look even younger than that.

Since about the age of thirteen, Alice had grown used to being mistaken for the older sister. That was fine. What got tiresome were the protests of disbelief when Alice corrected the mistake. She felt awkward about it sometimes — more for Riley's sake than for her own, she thought. But in truth, she wasn't sure if Riley cared.

'You sure there are no specials?' Her mother smiled mischievously.

'Mom,' Alice snapped. Her mother was asking only because she wanted to make Alice recite them, not because she cared what they were. Year after year, the food at the yacht club was bad. Only first-time customers ever ordered anything more ambitious than a hamburger. Alice walked back to the kitchen. If she got the order in fast, she could get them out faster.

From the back, she saw the second of her four tables fill. It was the Kimballs and some friends of theirs she didn't know. They watched her expectantly, beaming like parents as she came over.

'Can I get anyone a drink?' she asked self-consciously.

It was strange the things you knew about people here. She knew, for instance, that the

Kimballs had lost a child when it was still a baby. For everything Mrs. Kimball did or said or wore, even the way she served a tennis ball or ordered a glass of wine, Alice felt her loss.

She knew that Mr. Barger, who settled in at table four, had left his wife the very day their youngest kid, Ellie, went to college. Now he had a new house right on the beach and a new wife who had fake-looking teeth, and every hostess knew the perils of seating the old Mrs. Barger too close to the new one. Alice resisted the urge to return the new wife's friendliness in deference to Ellie, who really hated her.

'Don't you look cute!' the new Mrs. Barger erupted.

Alice knew, upon taking the job, that she'd have to wear the royal-blue polo and the jaunty sailor's cap, but she didn't realize how much they would mortify her.

How else was she going to earn money here? She was taking out massive loans for law-school tuition, and still she needed more for living expenses. You had to work twice as many hours here, because the pay was bad. The pay was bad because most of the families were prosperous and the kids were working for show. By day she had her regular babysitting jobs, but by night . . . what else was there?

It was hard to get hired to wait tables at one of the good restaurants in Fair Harbor or Ocean Beach, because there people actually tipped. You couldn't keep professionals, so the staff was a rotating cast of island kids, playing at working, serving their parents. The two other waitresses on her shift were two of the flakiest girls she knew.

It brought to mind the problem of babysitting for the children of family friends. They underpaid you because they felt they bestowed a favor by recognizing you as something other than a child yourself. Friends and favors made a mess of commerce, in Alice's opinion.

When she scuttled to the bar to put the Kimball order in, she realized she'd forgotten about her parents' drinks. Well, there was little tip to be had or lost.

By nine o'clock, her parents had moved on to a friends' get-together and Alice's feet were throbbing. Now the bar area was filling up with her friends, and eventually Paul appeared, as she both hoped and feared he would. It took all of her courage to face him with the sailor hat on.

'Oh, Alice,' he said.

Something about it startled her, and she realized, as she fled to the kitchen to catch her breath, what it was: He said her name. In one way, she loved that he had bothered with all the nicknames through the years (though she was sad when she heard him call other kids by the same ones). In another way, she wondered what the problem of saying her name was and whether perhaps he had forgotten it.

She thought of his cheek against her body. How close he came and how far he went while she just waited.

Now he had said her name and she couldn't decide whether it shortened the distance between them or lengthened it.

★ ★ ★

Paul wandered with his beer to the recreation room at the back of the yacht club. He could practically smell his old adolescent sweat. The floor had a patina of spilled soda and sticky bare feet. Paul remembered how black his feet were throughout his childhood summers, and the approximate moment when his mother started to notice and care. At Riley's house, nobody made you wash your feet before bed. The filth of the yacht-club floor lived not only atop the thick coat of polyurethane but also inside the layers. The paint on the walls was the same. They didn't sand or clean the surfaces here but simply slopped on another coat.

He loved how dirty and ramshackle their yacht club was. He loved the scummy, giddy air and the cheerful slap of the screen door. He liked the degree of exclusivity: If your check cleared, you were in. He liked that it had no yachts, that in fact the harbor was too shallow to host any.

It was his father in him, he suspected. A rich boy trying to cultivate his liberalism. But his father had lived it deeper and more vividly, hadn't he? He'd taken the drugs, posed for the mug shots, made the journey to India to bend his mind. Robbie had grown up in a better age for radicalism. And more than that, Paul knew, when it came to unmoored self-destruction, his father hadn't been faking it. After a three-day disappearance when Paul was four years old, Robbie had died alone of a drug overdose in Bellevue Hospital.

The green felt on the pool table by the windows was scratched and hopeless from years of play by small amateurs. The Ping-Pong table on the other side of the room was given its proper use only sporadically, when someone remembered to get balls on the mainland. The balls always got lost, dented, or crumpled in a matter of days. Paul remembered playing games with super balls and even tennis balls. Summer days stretched out so long you could easily spend a whole rainy afternoon adapting the Ping-Pong table to a game involving tennis balls. Riley was good at inventing games like that. She liked creating the scenario. Some kids got too attached to the rules, even ones that hadn't existed five minutes before. Riley wasn't like that. She liked rules but she always saw the larger promise.

The stage with the tattered blue curtain was the venue for the talent show held at the beginning of each summer and the Labor Day show at the end. Paul and Riley did a magic act one year and a boomerang demonstration the next, but both had ended badly. Later, they scorned the shows. As the years passed, it became a chance for girls to wear makeup and sparkly Lycra outfits and lip-synch to bad pop songs. By the time they were fifteen or sixteen, Paul and Riley didn't perform; they didn't even bother to go. They made like they forgot it was even happening. They'd hear the charitable applause or the thank-God-it's-over applause make it all the way to the ocean beach and they'd say, 'Oh, yeah.'

This room was the home of the kids' movie

every Thursday night. The combination of darkness and noise and the crowd of kids, their faces lit up by the film, combined for an almost unbearable excitement. He could never remember the plot of a single movie he watched here, but he remembered the feeling of all of them. When they got older, the kids would gather at movie night but not stay for the movie. It was a big party night for the parents, so the kids ran wild while they were supposedly watching the movie.

Paul lived with a housekeeper during those summers, while his mother spent most of the time visiting friends in Europe. He lived with a different housekeeper every summer from age twelve to age eighteen. He suspected that his mother didn't want him to get too close to any one of them for fear it would seem like she was losing her job. Paul spent all his time next door anyhow.

Kids got their independence younger here than in other places. The main predator of children and deer was the automobile, and there weren't any cars on the island, so the children and the deer were mangy, plentiful, and free. 'It's the one place in the world where I don't have to worry about abductions,' he remembered Judy, the news junkie, saying one time.

'What about alien abductions?' Riley had asked.

There had been alien abductions. Or so it had seemed to them. Rosie Newell, for example. He remembered the fateful night when she'd made a lot of noise about organizing the whole group into a circle. The movie projector was busted for the third week in a row, so most of the little kids had gone home. There were probably fifteen or so kids left between the ages of eleven and fourteen. And then there was Alice, of course, who must have been ten at the time. He remembered sitting on one side of Riley, with Alice on the other. He remembered that Riley was wearing the T-shirt they had tie-dyed for an arts-and-crafts project at camp the year before. They had no idea what was coming until Rosie, surrounded by her gum-chewing, belly-baring posse, produced a bottle from behind her back with a flourish. It was a clear glass beer bottle, Corona, Paul remembered.

'I'll go first,' Rosie had declared.

'Go first at what?' Riley asked. She looked suspicious.

'Isn't it obvious?' Rosie replied, looking to her friends, girls like Becca Fines and Megan Cooley, for backup. She went ahead and spun the bottle. 'If you're a girl and it lands on a girl, you spin again,' Rosie explained, all business. 'If you're a boy and it lands on a boy, same thing.'

'What if you're Riley?' Becca said.

Immediately Becca's gang of friends were giggling and making a show of trying to cover it up.

Paul remembered staring straight ahead as the shame and agony unfolded. He wanted to pretend like he hadn't heard it. He wanted to pretend Riley hadn't heard it, either. He couldn't even turn his head to look at her. He remembered the feeling of blood pounding in his temples.

'Shut up, Becca,' Alice said through her teeth.

'Go away, Alice,' Becca shot back.

Paralyzed, Paul stared straight ahead as the bottle spun slower and settled.

'It's on Paul,' Rosie declared, even though it was really closer to Alice. Riley was already on her feet. Rosie stood, too, looking mischievously at him.

'It has to be on the lips,' Jessica Loomis shouted.

This broke Paul's paralysis. He remembered Rosie walking toward him straight through the middle of the circle. He stood up and took a step back.

'You have to, Paul. It's the rule,' Becca declared, chomping her gum aggressively.

'He never said he was playing,' Riley said in an even voice.

'I'm not playing. It's a stupid game,' Paul said. He'd wished he'd had half of Riley's dignity. 'Let's go,' he said to Riley.

'Chicken,' Rosie taunted.

Riley cast a look at the part of the circle where their friends sat, Alex, Michael, Jared, Miranda. Paul expected them to get up and follow, but none of them moved. The girly-girls had always resented Riley for being the leader, for being the one girl all the boys wanted to play with. Paul expected nothing good from them, but he was surprised about the other kids. Only Alice tagged along after them.

After that, he remembered, they'd broken into

the market and stolen 3 Musketeers bars. They'd skipped stones at the bay, where Riley crushed all previous stone-skipping records. They'd crossed to the ocean side and swum in a sea so wild that Alice had nearly drowned. And even that hadn't been quite enough of a distraction.

★　★　★

Alice was reading on the beach Sunday afternoon when Riley approached. She dropped down onto Alice's towel and lay beside her on her side, bouncing her toe against Alice's calf. Companionable as it was, Alice knew she wouldn't be there for long. Riley never held still on the beach unless she was sitting in the lifeguard chair. She swam constantly, she surfed under the right conditions, she was a wizard with a boogie board in shallow water. She liked volleyball, and in the old days, she loved building sandcastles. Even now Riley gave no thought to sunbathing, and she never read a book or even a magazine, as far as Alice knew.

Alice was a reader and Riley was not. Alice remembered long ago sitting in the kitchen at the little table across from her mother in their apartment in the city. Judy was doing a big freelance proofreading job for an educational publisher at the time. Alice remembered all the proofs piled on the table. It was winter, she recalled. It was already dark in the late afternoon, and Alice wore thick socks around the apartment instead of bare feet.

They'd lived in the same two-bedroom

40

apartment on West 98th Street between Amsterdam and Columbus avenues since Alice was a baby. It was near the school where Ethan taught history and coached wrestling, and where Alice had gone since kindergarten. Riley had gone there, too, until fifth grade. It was a good private school, and Judy and Ethan paid half-price for them, which was partly why they were so slow to switch Riley to a school that specialized in teaching kids with learning problems.

It was after Christmas, Alice remembered, because Riley had gotten the dolphin book wrapped up under the tree. Riley had left it on the kitchen counter, and Alice had picked it up and started reading it for her mother. She was showing off, she knew. Her brain did not turn any of the letters the wrong way, and she felt guilty for it in retrospect. In first grade she could already read books meant for fourth-and fifth-graders. She blasted through all the words, hard and easy, until her mother noticed and came around the table to admire her. Alice hadn't realized Riley had come into the room until Riley was moving toward her, her mouth in a contortion.

Riley had reached out and snatched the book from Alice's hands with such force that Alice just sat there, blinking. 'That's my book,' Riley had said angrily, and strode out of the room. Alice always had an easier time being bad at things than Riley did.

Now Riley leaned into Alice, so their arms and shoulders were pressed together. She leaned over to see the title of Alice's book.

'*Middlemarch*. Is it good?' Riley asked, as though she may or may not read it herself.

'Amazing.'

'George Eliot is a woman, right?'

'Yes,' Alice said. It felt nice, Riley's body leaning into hers. Whatever their differences, their physical closeness was never awkward or strained. The body of her sister was not quite like a separate body. Riley's limbs felt to Alice practically like her own, like they were partly bound into her central nervous system and vice versa. Like if she thought hard enough, she could make Riley's knee bend. With an old feeling of tenderness, Alice rested her head on Riley's shoulder. She used to do that when she was smaller.

'Do you want to walk to Ocean Beach?' Riley asked. 'They're having the sandcastle contest today.'

'Today?'

'I saw the flyer in the market. The judging's at four.'

'I'll go,' Alice said. It was one of the milestones of early summer. Riley jumped up and offered Alice two hands.

Together Riley and Alice had made tremendous sandcastles. They had won the contest the second year they'd entered — not the kiddie contest but the real one. Alice still had the ribbon hanging over the door of her room in the city and a photo of it stuck to her bulletin board.

Riley had the bold design ideas and the ambition. She was a vigorous builder and a naturally gifted engineer. What Alice offered was the patience of execution. She was focused and good at following orders. 'Alice never gets bored,' Riley had bragged to one of the judges as Alice skim-smoothed a wall for the thousandth time.

Their winning castle was a cloudlike fantasy, a feat of design. It didn't have the bottom-heavy look that most big sandcastles have. But the greater triumph they built the following year, when Alice was fifteen. The Barnacle Tower was modeled loosely on the Chrysler Building. It was so tall the girls had to build scaffolding out of sand to construct the top. It had the most gorgeous surface design made out of barnacles, gathered by Riley and painstakingly applied by Alice.

But here they'd built too close to the sun. So magnificent in size, finish, and beauty, it put the others to shame. The irritable and sun-burned judge disqualified them on account of not being residents of Ocean Beach. Instead, he gave first prize to the Pody brothers, who'd built a totally conventional medieval-style fortress. Worst of all, Barnacle Tower was mysteriously destroyed before Ethan arrived with his camera. And so it remained an edifice in memory only — growing thereby larger and more skillfully built with time.

'I wonder if the Podys will enter,' Alice mused as they headed east, along the edge of the surf.

'They suck,' Riley said, galloping lightly along. She would habitually run and circle and weave all around Alice, who tended to walk in a straight line.

'They don't suck.'

'Yeah, they do.'

'Well, they beat us.'

'Unfairly.'

'Jim Brobard sucks.'

'That's true.'

'He's the one who kicked down Barnacle Tower.'

'You don't know it was him.'

'Yes, I do.'

Alice leaned down and picked up a piece of a horseshoe crab's shell and examined it. 'Do you want it?' she asked. It was a vestige from past walks when they used to help each other with their collections. Riley's collection was always easier. Hers included any and all detritus from sea creatures: shells, claws, egg cases, starfish, an occasional bone or tooth. Once she'd found a piece of a shark's jaw and stunk up the whole house with it. Never sentimental, Riley dumped it all at the end of the summer and began collecting anew at the start of the next season. Whereas Alice collected only one kind of thing: smooth, semi-transparent stones of a particular pink-orange shade. She looked for them summer after summer, and never dreamed of throwing any of them away.

'No, thanks.' Riley tossed the piece of dark brown shell into the waves.

They saw the bathing suit-clad crowd as they drew close. There were about a half-dozen castles up for consideration, and the sisters examined each of them through expert eyes.

'That thing's more cave than castle,' Riley remarked about one of them near the middle of the group.

'That one's kind of nice. Very classical.' Alice pointed to a castle modeled roughly on the Pantheon.

'I think it's about to fall down.'

Alice pointed to an elaborate construction at the outskirts. 'The Podys are back, and they've been watching the *Lord of the Rings* movies again.'

Riley laughed. 'Where are they? Which was the one who asked you to go skinny-dipping with him?'

Alice rolled her eyes. 'The younger one.' He'd had the nerve to proposition her after the Tower incident, even with his blue ribbon hanging around his neck.

'Let's keep going.' Alice didn't feel like being ogled by the younger Pody. Anyway, the competition still left a slightly bitter taste.

They walked out onto the jetty, Alice picking her way along the slippery stones and Riley bounding around like a goat. They sat at the end with their feet dangling, mist hung like a net over their shoulders, wind and water indistinct.

Later, on the walk home, Riley leaned down and picked up a stone. 'Alice, look.' She washed it off in the surf and held it up to the sun, her fingers glinting water.

'Oh.' Riley put it in her hands and Alice studied it.

'Perfect, right?'

Alice nodded excitedly. 'It could be the best one.'

It was a see-through stone of the most perfect pale orange-pink color, almost exactly in the shape of a heart. A rare addition to Alice's collection.

4

The Talent for Being a Child

Alice's babysitting charges went unexpectedly off-island the following Tuesday. She should have swept the sand out of the house or mailed the things her mother had left on the desk, but instead she bought a bacon-and-egg sandwich at the market and wandered up to the beach. She finished her sandwich sitting on top of the stairs at the dune, so that Riley wouldn't give her a hard time about eating on the beach. The sister of Riley had to be above reproach.

Sitting there, Alice had a wide and quiet view of things. She saw the squad gathered *Baywatch*-style in their red bathing suits, listening to weather reports and other lifeguard-related briefings. There was always a solemnity to these proceedings, which tickled Alice a little and was probably the reason she hadn't become a lifeguard. That and her inability to do the devilish butterfly kick.

She finished her greasy sandwich and hunched down to wash her hands and face in the foot wash. The shower would have worked better, but it was broken. It had been broken for so long that it might have been fixed, but Alice wouldn't know because she never tried it anymore.

She didn't walk down to the sand as she

planned but settled again on the top step, her chin in her hand. Maybe it was because Paul was back, but the world had shifted and everything looked as if it were a bit farther away.

Riley was standing in the center of the group, and Alice saw that she was small. Alice knew her sister was small — at least four inches shorter than she — but she didn't usually see it.

Her mother said Riley turned out small in a tall family because of a disease she'd had when she was a toddler. Alice couldn't remember the name of it, but she knew that Riley had nearly died. She also knew that her mother got pregnant with Alice not too long after. Her mother also blamed the disease for Riley's dyslexia. She always called it that: 'Riley's dyslexia,' as though it belonged to her, like a sweater or a pet. Her mother was oddly protective of her genes, it seemed to Alice. Maybe it was just another way to keep the tally straight between her and Ethan.

Alice always felt proud of her sister because she was tough and nervy. She never showed girly weaknesses like cellulite or crushes. She never laughed if she didn't think something was funny. (Alice did do that.) She wasn't afraid of the water. She never lingered on injustices committed against her.

Alice felt proud of her today also, but from this wide angle, she felt herself slipping toward sad. Riley used to be the youngest lifeguard in Fire Island history, and now she was possibly the oldest. Few twenty-four-year-olds could afford to take entire summers at the beach anymore.

These other guards were flirting and preening, Alice saw, and Riley was not part of that. These new guards did not appear to be there for the same reasons Riley was there. Did Riley used to fit in better? Or was Alice usually too close to see?

She felt protective of her sister, she realized, and it made for an uncomfortable reversal.

Some people had gifts that made them great at being kids. Riley had those gifts. She was fearless, and she was fair. She was effortlessly expert at skateboarding, sailing, running fast, coaxing a fish off of any line. She was the pitcher on the winning corkball team for seven years in a row. She was the first kid up on a surfboard. She was even good at indoor things, like card tricks and video games. She didn't believe in hierarchies — not even mothers. She was the one kid every other kid wanted to befriend, and she never used her power for ill.

Riley led them to the creation of worlds — ancient burial grounds, unseen reefs, valleys, mountains, treasures under the sea, and the things that lurked under the boardwalks too vicious to discuss, except when they occasionally turned nice.

Riley made it seem like they were all gods of their world, but Alice knew that Riley was really the god. She just gave them turns sometimes.

So great was Riley's imagination that she did not bother with the distinction between what was real and what wasn't. The older the other kids got, the more they wanted to keep track of that, but Riley never cared.

Alice remembered the first season Riley pitched the corkball team to victory. They were playing the Ocean Beach team in the tournament finals. It was the ninth inning, they were up by one, and Ocean Beach had their best hitter, a strutting character named Brian something, on deck. Mr. Peterson, Alex's dad and Riley's coach at the time, took Riley aside and told her to walk the guy — just roll the ball four times in a row and get on to the next batter, he'd said. Riley got a fierce look and struck Brian out in three pitches to end the game. They carried Riley off the field in victory. After that, Ethan took over as coach and led them to many victorious seasons until the team disbanded years later. Ethan never told Riley to walk anybody.

Alice remembered the two trophies Riley got at the awards ceremony that night. When they were going to bed, Riley came into Alice's room with the bigger one, the MVP trophy, and handed it to Alice. 'You can have this one,' she'd said. Alice was thrilled with it and added it to her shelf, towering as it did over her small cluster of participation trophies. She remembered the feeling of incipient transformation.

But the transformation did not occur, and as the days passed, the gigantic trophy seemed to mock Alice's other meaningless trophies on her shelf. Early the next summer, Alice snuck it back into Riley's room and deposited it in the middle of Riley's groaning shelf. She didn't say anything to Riley about it, and she wasn't sure if Riley noticed that it had been returned. As generous as her sister was, Alice understood that Riley couldn't share the thing that mattered.

As they all grew up, the qualities that defined success changed. Girly-girls had been customarily shunned by the central group, but the summer after eighth grade they got their moment. The boys turned their attention to the girls who grew breasts and wore lip gloss.

And as they all got older still, academic prowess started to matter — who was applying to what college, and then who got in. And after that, their old friends started to think and talk most urgently about prestigious jobs and money.

It seemed wrong to Alice that the child-gifts became trivial — hobbies at the most. It seemed wrong that what made Riley a superstar among them had so little currency anymore and that she was so distant from the things that did matter.

Alice exalted the gifts that her sister possessed. She worshipped Riley, and Riley remained a benevolent and uncorrupted idol, always looking out for Alice, no matter how far down she had to reach. And Paul, in his way, looked out for her, too. In return, Alice put her energy and her meager talents into doing whatever Riley and Paul did, loving what they loved, disavowing what they hated. She tried her best.

Alice felt disloyal to Riley when she began to realize, much later, that her natural talents, her ability to communicate and observe, her caution, her empathy, her love of knitting, suited her better to the grown-up world.

And then there was Paul. He not only had the gifts that equipped him for childhood, he had a natural aptitude for adulthood, too. He was a

51

capable student and a subtle writer. He had a cunning sense of irony and a handsome, masculine way of being. He had lots of money and a prestigious name, though he disrespected both of those things. He had talent enough to march victorious from age to age, and yet he didn't seem to fit comfortably in any part of his life.

Alice didn't like this feeling, but she sat there watching her sister and prodding it like a sore tooth, trying to gauge how sore it was. It was unsettling to feel sad for a person you respected. It was doubly unsettling when you knew that person didn't feel sad for herself. Alice didn't want to see more than Riley saw. She didn't want the alignment to shift.

But Alice had the sense that, like these shallow, pecking lifeguards, she was moving through her life, and Riley, true to her core, was staying who she was.

★ ★ ★

'The wind is up and nobody's taken out the Hobie,' Riley reported from high on the seat of her bike, catching up to Alice on her way back from babysitting at the Cohens'.

'We should go,' Alice said. She was never as good a sailor as Riley, but she did love it. She had ribbons in her bedroom from when Riley let her crew.

'I'll get Paul,' Riley said.

'I think he's doing his paper.'

Riley looked back and smiled. 'Who cares?'

Alice was struggling to pull the boat into the bay when the two of them arrived, white knights on rusty bikes. They took over in their old way, fast-moving and competent with the sails and the knots. They pushed it deftly into the water.

'Hop on, Alice,' Riley called to her. Alice crouched down on the trampoline as the boom swung violently. Paul gave a last push off, and he and Riley jumped on board. The water was rough, and Alice felt glad for her life jacket. Riley would no sooner have worn a life jacket aboard than she'd have worn a hula skirt.

'*Wheee*,' Alice shouted into the wind as they headed to open water and the boat picked up speed. The boat was already heeled over onto one pontoon. Alice clung to the other pontoon, but Riley was darting around the trampoline, setting the sails as though she and gravity had a separate arrangement. Even Paul got out of her way and let her do what she did best.

'Here's a day you wish for a spinnaker,' Riley said happily. Only Riley would want to go faster than this.

They flew along on the edge of one pontoon, the other high in the air.

'Alice, you steer,' Riley ordered.

'Paul, give us some ballast, would you?'

The wind came in bursts, each threatening to push them over. Paul leaned off the edge as far as he could go without a trapeze system in place, trying to keep them upright.

'Ha!' Riley shouted with glee when the boat heeled so far over that the boom splashed up bay water. She loved to sail on as much wind as she could. She'd push it to the edge and sometimes, Alice knew, she'd go right over.

'Okay, fall off, Alice,' Riley yelled at her.

For a moment, Alice forgot which way to fall off and instead came right into the wind. The sail lost wind instantly and the boat came down hard, hurling Paul off the edge.

Alice screamed, partly from alarm and partly from pure thrill. Riley let the sail luff and held the boom so Paul could get back on. She laughed. In Riley world, it was a boring sail if nobody went overboard. And though Riley never made those kinds of mistakes herself, she didn't get mad at Alice for them.

Not so with Paul. 'Alice!' he shouted. 'Do you know what 'fall off' means?' She could see how mad he was as he hoisted himself back onto the boat. She saw he was coming after her, so she shrieked and stood up, teetering on the canvas.

'Sorry!' She tried to get away from him, but where could she go? She backed up to the edge of the tarp, trying to find purchase on the pontoon.

'You're going in,' he told her, shaking off the water. He never swam in the bay by choice.

'Paul!' she screamed, laughing.

He was laughing, too, as he put a wet hand on either side of her. 'Sorry, kid.'

'No!' She shrieked again. She hated when she sounded so girly. She felt his hands on her hips, holding them gently and then hard.

'Paul! You better not!' She was laughing so hard she couldn't breathe. 'Paulooooo!' she shouted as he pushed her in.

Riley sat cross-legged in the chair, ten feet up from the sand, and looked over the water. Here was a comfortable seat and an orientation to the world that pleased her. At this moment, there were no swimmers to watch over. That was often true of her time in the chair, and she didn't mind. She loved the freedom to let her mind rove out and out over the sea, with nothing for it to bump into until maybe the Azores. In the early morning, there were usually just a few veteran ocean swimmers. They typically swam far out and passed through her jurisdiction without incident. Sometimes there were surfers, but she didn't watch them in the same way she watched the regular wave jumpers. She knew the surfers, and they knew her. She surfed with them sometimes, and she knew they respected her abilities and her courage. They'd rather drown than be saved by her.

It was a custom held over from long ago, she guessed, but when she gazed out over the water, some part of her was always looking for dolphins. She'd seen them about ten times in her life from this beach, and each time it was a matter of breathless joy, but also it left her with a strange feeling she hardly knew in any other context. It was a feeling of incompleteness, of wanting more or different than she had.

According to her father, the first word she said as a baby was 'jump,' and the second word was 'splash.' She put them together quickly to describe the dolphins at the Coney Island aquarium. All she wanted to do was visit the dolphins — the prize pair of them, Marny and Turk, came to be spoken of as members of the family. Riley loved to watch them jump and splash. She remembered throwing pennies into the toilet, pretending. Partly she remembered it, and partly it was what she had always been told. They went to the aquarium every Sunday for years when they weren't at the beach. It was an outdoor aquarium, which was part of what she loved about it. 'You were a handful' was the way her mother described her constant demands.

Her books were about dolphins, the pictures on the walls of her room were dolphins, on her bedsheets there were dolphins. The single thing she liked to watch on TV was a documentary her father found of dolphins — bottlenose, spinners, Atlantic spotted — swimming fast through open water, jumping, and splashing.

For years she begged to be allowed to take the subway by herself, and the first day she got permission, at the age of eleven, she took it to the end of the line, all the way to Coney Island. She went to the aquarium to watch Marny and Turk. They didn't do the shows or the tricks anymore, so she just watched them swim. And then she went around and admired the sharks and rays and whales and narwhals, too. The furry things, like otters, seals, and walruses, she also enjoyed, but they didn't capture her imagination in the same way. Like her, they were bound to land.

When she'd seen all that she'd liked, thrilled with her freedom, she made her way out to the

56

famous beach, vacationland of old. Along it was the boardwalk, all lonesome honky-tonk. In back of it was a desolate, dilapidated theme park and a number of dodgy neighborhoods, but still it was one of the widest and most beautiful natural beaches in the world.

And to her astonishment and delight, like a gift from nature itself, she looked out with her best eyes, and just beyond the surf, they were there. A school of them, jumping so high in the air you could see the water and sunlight streaming off their backs. Back and forth they swam with speed and agility to make you weep, and suddenly Riley wondered whether they knew about their compatriots just across the water, captive in their tanks. She wondered if they could hear each other, maybe at night, when the world was silent and the ocean was calm. What would a free dolphin say to a captive one? How could one possibly understand the circumstances of the other?

And after that it made her sad to think of those dolphins, her old friends, pent up in the aquarium, swimming in their narrow confines. It pained her to recognize that without the inducement of the shows, the dolphins never jumped or splashed.

After that she only ever wanted to see them in the wild.

5

Not Getting Ahead

'Alice! Alice?'

Riley was grabbing her foot and yanking on it.

'What?'

'It's an Alice beach.'

'It's — ?'

'Get out of bed. Come on.'

It was depressing how radically your priorities shifted when you were tired. Alice was so deeply in sleep, she might have slept through a fire if she could have died without too much pain.

'Are you sure?' she said groggily. According to her bedside clock it was 2:21 a.m.

'Alice!'

'Okay.' Yes, she'd forget what she loved when she was tired enough, but lucky for her, she had Riley to remind her.

Alice shoved herself out of bed before Riley could do it for her. She followed Riley, shivering in her T-shirt, boy underwear, and socks. Riley was still in her pajama pants and a T-shirt. When Riley was inspired, Alice learned to get going.

'Oh, my gosh,' Alice breathed when she saw the moon reflected in four different places. 'When did they come?'

'High tide, earlier tonight,' Riley said, face full of wonder. Only one beach was an Alice beach,

58

but all beaches, in a way, were Riley beaches.

'Oh.' Alice took off her socks so she could wade into one. It was fine, even sand, not the kind that normally sat under still water.

'I'll get Paul,' Riley said, racing back up the beach toward his house before Alice could make any complaint. Riley didn't care when or how Paul saw her. She didn't package herself for him or anyone. When the water looked like this, she didn't care how she looked, how silly and stick-up her hair. She wasn't hiding any part of herself, whereas Alice sometimes felt she wanted to hide all her parts.

She heard Riley banging thoughtlessly on Paul's door. She wondered if Paul thought they had gotten too old for that. What a sad thought that would be.

People like Alice, and possibly Paul, got overfond of sleep during adolescence, but Riley did not. She respected it no more now than she had in nursery school. A magical beach, an orange moon, a chance to see a dolphin always trumped it.

Alice remembered the time Riley had dragged her out of bed in the early dawn to see dolphins. When Alice had finally stumbled onto the beach, all signs of the finned, arcing backs were gone.

'I'm sorry,' Riley had said, uncharacteristically solicitous.

'That's okay, I'm happy to be up early,' Alice replied.

'No, I mean about you missing the dolphins,' Riley said solemnly.

Now a groggy Paul appeared on the beach,

59

exposed in his boxer shorts and nearness to sleep.

'Hey, kid, it's your beach,' he called to Alice, a look of joy building on his face.

Alice waded into a shallow tide pool and sat in the middle, surrounded by the full, bright moon. She shivered and broke it up, and then she tried to be very still as it gathered around her again like an inner tube.

Paul and Riley sat at the edge with their feet in the water.

'I'm in the moon,' Alice said beatifically.

Paul gave the water a kick, and the bright droplets splashed and rained down.

'Look at the ocean,' Riley said. It was storming the beach, seemingly put out by the fact that it had left part of itself on the land and eager to take it back. But the moon had other ideas.

'The tide is going out,' Paul said.

'We should swim,' Riley suggested.

Alice feared this would happen. She was ashamed of the fact that she'd never really loved swimming in the ocean at night. She didn't want them to know.

'Hey. Let's.' Of course, Riley was already on her feet and halfway down to the surf.

Alice was happy in her tide pool. But as she watched them pulling off T-shirts and wading in, out seeped the old fear, the younger-sister fear, that they would leave her out if she couldn't keep up. It was a fear more basic than that of sharks and wrenching currents and all the unnameable mysteries of the ocean at night, though it did not exclude them.

She saw their heads bobbing. Riley was telling Paul something funny. She stood to follow them, pushed by the dread that if they got too far ahead, she would lose her place with them.

Riley and Paul raced over the seams and junctures of life, and she always got stuck on them. Should she take off her shirt? She wasn't wearing a bathing suit or even a bra. She'd be swimming in her underwear. But otherwise she would have nothing dry to put on when she got out. Riley didn't care and Paul probably wouldn't notice her either way, but her doubts seeded other doubts. Most people here were so easygoing about casting off their clothes and jumping into the ocean, but Alice cared too much about everything. Could she rush back to the house and get her suit on? Did she have a dry suit? She pictured the ball of suits she'd left on top of the machine. Had her mother done laundry?

There were Paul and Riley, radiant in a calm sea, faces turned up to the stars, and her mind was with the laundry.

Some people have no magic, Riley used to say.

Alice cast off her shirt and dove in. She tried to catch up, but they were already off in the direction of the lighthouse. She swam after them, her normally neat strokes seized by insecurity. Effortlessness was not one of their things she could hope to match. She heard the dark water in her ears, felt the volume of it under and around her, felt her heart smashing along in time with her kicks and her pulls.

She made for the lighthouse, swimming out

past the surf, but she felt herself pulled from her path. She struggled against the tide carrying her back into the beach.

She kicked harder. She drew rough breaths. When she looked up again, she realized she was making almost no progress. And with the sweep of the beam from the lighthouse, she also realized that Riley and Paul were no longer in the water but on the sand. They weren't wrestling the tide but simply walking along the beach toward home.

She came in after them, fighting to catch her breath several yards behind them. She hurried along, covering her chest with her arms, feeling the cross she wore on a chain around her neck tapping against her sternum.

She recognized that unlike her, Riley had some kind of suit on, and Alice felt doubly self-conscious. Riley always clothed herself with the idea that there might be a swim involved, whereas for Alice it came as a revelation for which she was never prepared. Paul's back was bare and his boxers hung drenched. She studied his back, a man's back, gracefully shaped by nature plus all the years of outswimming everyone.

Riley was several inches shorter than Paul, but her stride was long. Her shoulders were wide and her hips were as slim as a boy's. There was no nonsense in the way she shook out her wet hair.

With agitated strides, Alice caught up to their easy ones. She joined them, full of doubt and attention. She wanted Paul to notice her, and she also wanted to find her T-shirt and put it on as quickly as possible. She wanted to submerge herself up to her neck in the moon, just revel in her Alice tide pool and allow herself to think thoughts about Paul that gave her an anxious pleasure and a calm sort of pain.

She knew the fear of being left behind. But she was also afraid of getting ahead.

★   ★   ★

Alice came to keep him company the next day while he worked on his paper. He was surprised at first, and unsure of what to expect. He was thrown by the way he had seen her the night before, so much of her shivering in the moonlight. He was thrown further by how his body had responded to the sight of her body. He was ashamed now, in that morning-after way, of all the pleasures that his sleeping mind had come up with.

He was suddenly concerned that she would recover from their post-haircut amnesia, and he stood on the verge of telling her to get lost, ready to rebuff her questions as to what he was writing or why. So prepared was he, in fact, that he was almost disappointed when the questions didn't come. Instead, she yawned like a cat and settled on the top of his unmade bed, facing away from him to look out the window at the ocean.

'No more Alice beach,' she murmured.

'It never lasts long,' he said.

She looked over her shoulder at him, stricken.

'But it comes back.'

'I guess.'

He returned to his notes, or made it seem so. He thought of her last night on the beach, arms crossed over her breasts. Now on his very bed where he'd had his dreams, she lay. There were her same arms, her same back, but less provocative now that they were covered by a faded brown cotton shirt.

Sunshine came in the window. She rolled over to watch him. She looked so beautiful, it was hard to look away.

'You should go, Alice. I need to work.' He felt irritated at her, and it was obvious in his voice. *I can't work with you here. I can't make any of my thoughts go the way I want.*

She looked hurt as she left. Her eyes were shiny, and he felt guilty.

And even after she was gone, he didn't think about Kant. He thought about Alice. One thing that made her so beautiful was her colors: her reddish gold hair, her green-yellow eyes, her pinkish freckles, her black eyelashes. *She comes in colors everywhere. She combs her hair. She's like a rainbow.* When she was tiny and he carried her around, he thought she was the best possible person to look at.

For some reason he thought of the cross she wore. He'd forgotten about that until he saw her last night, otherwise bare. It reminded him, guiltily, of how fervent she'd been in her faith when she was small and the times he'd tried to talk her out of it.

He remembered lying with her one night. She was probably about eight and he was eleven, and he was fleeing his house in the customary way and for the usual reasons. She couldn't fall asleep, and when he crawled under the covers he found a rosary in her hands. It made him mad for some reason, and he told her there was no such thing as God.

'Is there a devil?' she had asked.

They were quiet for a long time, and he assumed she'd long since fallen asleep when he heard her stirring again. He remembered her little face, full of shiny-eyed pondering. 'Well, is there such thing as Jesus?' she'd asked.

He'd laughed at her meanly. 'Alice. You can't have the one without the other.'

Looking back, it was the thing in his life that shamed him the most: the times he was purposefully, calculatingly mean to Alice. It was those moments, and there had been many of them, that indicated to him that he was not a good person. He got mad at her for many things, but it was always really for the same thing: that she possessed his love and he couldn't seem to get it back.

She didn't deserve it, which was to say she deserved better.

★　★　★

In past summers when the beach was calm, Riley sometimes let him sit beside her up in the chair. The following day, Paul was inexpressibly gratified when she scooted over to make room for him.

'What's up with you?' she asked.

'What do you mean?'

'I don't know.'

Paul tried to relax and make his face go into the normal shapes, but it wasn't easy. He felt strain in every muscle. You couldn't be artificial around Riley, but sometimes you couldn't be honest, either.

He felt guilty toward Alice, but that was by no means the worst of what he felt. He wished guilt were the principal emotion, because that would mean he had the upper hand, and he did not. He only pretended.

It was a strange way to love a person.

What was the matter with him? Why couldn't he just get over her? Or at least be nice to her. He'd done this for too long, alternating between loving her and punishing her for being loved.

'Trevor spotted a shark out there this morning.'

Well, one reason was sitting next to him, bouncing her legs. Paul nodded. 'Did he really? What kind?' He tried to work up enthusiasm. Sharks had been a sacred fascination of theirs. Not like dolphins for Riley, but still big.

'Probably a nurse shark.'

He nodded. 'Not big, though.' The fantasy was always a big shark. He always drew back from his fantasies.

'Not so small, actually.'

'Huh.'

He was glad to be near her, because Riley was a touchstone. For him and for Alice, too, he knew. Her outlook was simple, and when you looked at the world through her eyes, you could see it simply, too. Like those Magic Eye pictures. You looked and you looked and suddenly, almost miraculously, the random chaos of all the flat little shapes turned into a three-dimensional picture. But then you blinked or you looked away and it was lost.

Riley had certainty. She was how she was, and while the rest of the world teased and shifted around her, she stood firm. He had once thought he could be like that, too. She discarded whole chunks of life that obsessed other people. She didn't torture people she loved, nor did she hunger for them. She kept it simple. She trusted what she had.

She thought he was still like that. She didn't realize how far he had drifted. He was always grateful that Riley could not see into his brain.

'Do you remember our deep-sea fishing trip on Crawford's boat?' he asked.

'Which one?'

'The first trip. I think we were twelve, when you caught the tiger shark?'

She looked eager, but not necessarily because of remembering. 'Was it a tiger shark?'

'You don't remember that?'

'Tell me. I'll try to remember.'

'It was flipping around like crazy on deck. Remember? Crawford was shouting at us. The shark was bigger than you were. It freaked him out.'

'What happened?' she asked. She loved this kind of story.

'You found a ball-peen hammer below deck,

and you smacked that poor shark in the side of the head.'

'That worked, right?' she asked.

'Like a charm,' he said. 'Don't you remember?'

He could tell that she didn't. It was an odd thing about her that she loved these stories, she loved her own acts of derring-do, but she couldn't remember them very well. She'd had so many of them.

He looked at her feet, her braided anklet she'd had since before she was a teenager. Her same bathing suit. Her same hair tucked behind her ears in the same old way.

That episode with the tiger shark was in the past for him — thrilling, but never to be repeated. It represented a particular time, a particular feeling. He marked it as he passed it; that was the way he recorded it. But in some sense he knew Riley had not passed it by. She was still there.

'We should go again,' she said. 'Crawford still does the deep-sea trips.'

And though Paul heartily agreed, he felt sad about it. He couldn't do it again. If he did, he would arrive as a different person, only playing at their old way, and he hated to disappoint her.

6

God Made Alice for Alice

Alice nearly fell over when she saw her sister in bed the following morning. 'What are you doing?'

'My throat hurts.'

Alice went to sit on Riley's bed. Her sister was wrapped up in her old quilt of primary colors that had grown fragile with age. She could hardly think of another time that Riley stayed indoors while the sun shone. She put her hand on Riley's arm and then on her forehead. 'You're hot.'

'Thanks.'

'I can't believe you are in bed.' Riley had no respect for illness, especially her own. She'd swim in an icy September ocean, get a head cold, and do the same thing the next day.

'Well.' Alice could see that that one syllable took effort.

'Have you taken anything yet? I'll get you an Advil and some juice,' Alice proposed.

'Juice would be good,' Riley said.

Riley never took anything. Alice suspected she didn't like swallowing pills.

When Alice came back with the orange juice, Riley's quilt was tucked tighter around her neck.

'The warm feeling is not so bad,' Riley said,

69

her freckles standing out on her skin. 'I'm having a lot of dreams.'

'Nice ones?'

'Some. All kinds. I don't think I could divide out nice.'

'Do you want me to stay with you?' If it were Alice, she would have wanted Riley to stay home with her or for her mom to be there making her tea, but Riley never took pleasure in being babied.

'No. I'm fine. I'll be back out by tomorrow.'

'You think? No calling Dr. Bob?'

'No to Dr. Bob.'

'How about toast?'

'No thanks.'

'Bowl of Rice Krispies?'

'No.'

'Tomato soup?'

'Alice, would you go away now?'

When Alice went back to check on her after babysitting the Cohen kids through lunchtime, Riley was not in her bed, which made her feel relieved. Riley was no doubt back in the lifeguard chair. Alice went to Paul's house the back way.

'Hello?'

'Come on up,' he called from his bedroom.

He was at his desk with his notes spread out and his laptop sleeping. She noticed a strand of his hair she'd left too long, but she didn't offer to fix it.

'Do you want to walk to the lighthouse?' she asked him.

He shook his head.

'Do you want to go get a salami sandwich?'

'That's tempting, but no. I have to finish this.'

Sometimes she felt she was always offering people things they didn't want. 'What page are you on?'

'Last night I was on page seven. Now I'm on page three.'

'I think you are going in the wrong direction.'

'I erased it because it was bad.'

'No sandwich for you, then.'

'Will you bring me one?'

She looked at him, insulted.

'Right. Never mind.'

She looked out the window at the gray water and noticed a figure on the beach wrapped up in a blanket. Then she realized it was Riley's faded quilt and that the figure must be Riley.

She walked out of Paul's room and down to the beach. When she got close to her sister, she saw Riley curled up on the dune, face pointed to the water, but her eyes were closed and it gave Alice a scare at first. But Riley's eyes opened and she smiled.

'How are you feeling?' Alice asked.

'Good.' She sat up, keeping her quilt tight around her.

Alice could tell by her eyes and her cheeks that she was still feverish. 'Are you sure?'

She looked around her. 'These dreams I am having sure are nice.'

★ ★ ★

'So, Paul, how's California?' Judy asked eagerly.

Alice chopped tomatoes for her mother's customary Saturday-night salad and felt a bit sorry for Paul.

'I left.'

'For good?'

'I think so,' he said.

'Really?'

'I think so.'

The price of tonight's dinner was parental inquisition, but in a way, Alice was kind of enjoying it. These were questions Alice wouldn't ask but whose answers she wanted to hear. Just as in high school she'd never ask a friend where he was applying to college, even if she was curious. Alice felt bad letting her mother do the dirty work.

'Riley said you were working on a farm.'

Paul gave a bemused smile. 'Many farms.'

'Oh?'

'I was working on a project — it had to do with a state referendum — but it didn't end up getting on the ballot.'

'I'm sorry to hear that. We really appreciate your idealism, you know?' her mother said with a smile that revealed orange lipstick on her teeth.

Alice winced.

'Yeah, well.'

'You're reminding me of your father,' Ethan said. 'In the good ways.'

Paul's face remained closed. 'I guess he also specialized in political failures.'

Alice saw the obvious emotion in her father's expression. Her father had felt true pathos for

Robbie, and he'd loved Paul. Riley sometimes joked that she was the son her father never had, but really that was Paul. And Alice was reminded now of how stony Paul was to him.

Once, Paul had loved Ethan in return. He'd attached himself to Ethan like a staticky sock, mirroring Ethan's gestures and opinions. But some time later he pulled away. Alice couldn't pinpoint the time exactly. She'd ascribed it to adolescent cheek. She'd figured it was part of Paul's endless rebellion.

And it continued even now. She wondered why. She looked from one of them to the other.

'Do you know if Riley's joining us for dinner?' Judy asked.

Alice ran up to her room to check on her and found Riley in bed, doing something on her laptop computer. Riley often kept odd hours and made herself scarce when her parents were there. Alice understood Riley hadn't told Judy she was feeling ill. 'Do you want to eat with us?' Alice asked.

'No,' Riley said.

'How are you feeling?'

'Fine,' Riley said without looking up.

Returning to the kitchen table, Alice looked around, seeing it though Paul's eyes. Her vision changed when he was around, and she couldn't say if it warped or if it improved or, for that matter, whether accuracy was necessarily an improvement.

Nobody had a regular seat at this table. It was round and made of a warm-colored wood, so scratched and ringed that the damage had

73

become the surface itself. The chairs were reproduction Windsors from a sale at Macy's a decade or so ago. Alice remembered the shopping trip, running up and down the aisles of the huge store on 34th Street, delighting in all the little room setups with their prop TVs and fake plants. She sat on a couch in one, lay on a bed in another, trying on a different life for each. It was funny how all the different rooms existed in one gigantic room, how you didn't need walls to divide space. She couldn't remember her family shopping for furniture any other time.

The window over the sink was big but showed only phragmite stalks and changing slivers of Paul's house. The cabinets and counters were a scratchy white Formica that warped in places, showing the swollen, pulpy wood fiber underneath. Alice knew how much her mother wanted sleek cabinets and stainless-steel appliances like their friends had. But her father always said, 'Judy, it's the beach,' as though that were the reason and no other.

How staunchly people rationalized the things they had, even (especially) if they didn't choose them. Her father went to rhetorical lengths to support the philosophy of a simple house at the beach and to assail the grossness of extravagance. But she wondered if he would change sides if he had a million dollars.

Paul espoused the same philosophy, and he presumably did have a million dollars. But Paul had his principles, whereas her father had his feelings. Pride was what they had in common.

Their house was built in the seventies with

little generosity in material or design. The flimsiest wood, the most vomitous linoleum, the cheapest fixtures. The doorknobs felt light and wobbly in your hand. Even the aluminum windows peered out oafishly and with a look of apology. Alice often wondered aloud if the builder made it ugly on purpose, but Riley wouldn't hear a word against it. And though Alice judged her home strictly, it was the place she loved most, and she wished for it when she wasn't there.

There were three small bedrooms upstairs and one truly tiny bedroom downstairs. This had been a darkroom, a painting studio, and a recording studio, and briefly housed a loom for weaving. All this was in accordance with her father's changing hobbies and delusions, the delusions requiring more radical renovation and expensive equipment than the hobbies. By now the room had vestiges of all of these, plus a plastic crate of free weights. By now it was a storage room and an archive.

Alice suspected that if it was her mother's father who'd died in the spring of 1981 and left them a hundred thousand dollars, then the little room would have been a guest room or a den or, best of all, a writing studio for her private use. Alice's father did not make much money in his job as a private-school teacher and a coach, but his father, Alice's grandfather, had been a successful lawyer. And though Grandpa Joseph had been a notorious gambler at the horse track, he had provided the windfall that bought them this house and, moreover, bought them entry into this world of plenty where they did not otherwise belong.

The single great luxury of the house was the trumpet vine that grew around the arbor and fence, an extravagance of orange flowers and attendant hummingbirds. It was a mystery to all of them. Their potted tomato plants yellowed, the vinca rotted, and the basil plant withered. Their cultivation failed, but their accident prospered.

Sometimes the vines got to be so much that you could feel the fence straining under them. So Alice and her father took to the vines with giant clippers, laying violent siege to their one glory. But the flowers always came back more and more, like disappointed children or thwarted desires.

Every south-facing second-floor window, including the two in Alice's bedroom, looked directly at Paul's family's grand three-story shingle. She thought of Tolstoy when she considered its generic, platonic beauty, compared to the unique homeliness of her house. The outside of his house was part of her landscape, but the inside she hardly knew at all. The windows stayed dark at night, so you couldn't even see in. It was more an idea to her than a place. For every thousand hours Paul had spent at her house, she'd spent one at his. Paul's empty house looked at the ocean, and they at it.

You would have thought Paul's house had been built after theirs — islanders were always grabbing up one another's views. But in fact, his house had been standing since the nineteen-twenties, though it had to be picked up and moved shortly after the hurricane of 1938. The builder of their meek house had actually chosen to lean it into the shadow of a great and substantial one. It seemed to Alice further proof of the builder's poor self-esteem.

'So, Paul.' Judy reinvigorated her line of questioning over Ethan's grilled pork chops, as dense and hard as roofing tile. 'What are you planning to do in the fall?'

Paul did not throw his plate to the floor or suggest that Judy leave him alone. He was always more patient with Judy than her daughters could manage to be.

'I have to finish up an old incomplete from Cal-Berkeley this summer, and then I'll hopefully be starting a graduate degree in philosophy and political science.'

Judy nodded with obvious approbation. She always had high hopes for Paul.

'Where are you planning to go?' Ethan asked in his careful way.

Alice looked back and forth as though taking in a tennis match. It was more like Canadian doubles, though, and she found herself rooting for the lone man.

'I have a provisional acceptance from NYU. One of my professors at Cal joined the faculty there, and he's looking on my application kindly,' he said. 'So I guess that's where I'm headed.'

Alice opened her mouth to speak, but her mother got there first.

'Well, that is wonderful!' Judy nearly shouted.

'You and Alice will be there together. You can see each other all the time.' She turned on Alice with a look of pride. 'Only Alice will have a pretty rough schedule. You know how the first year of law school is.'

⋆   ⋆   ⋆

'You are going to law school?' Paul pulled her out of the house and down the boardwalk as soon as they had done a respectable job of eating her father's pork chops.

She blinked at him, unable to say anything. The directness and urgency of the question was startling, the subject matter far outside their usual bounds.

'Why didn't you tell me that?' he demanded.

Why didn't she tell him that? Why didn't he ask? Since when was she supposed to tell him anything about the life she led or, God forbid, ask him any questions about his? She wished she could say one of these things aloud.

'Paul,' she said in protest. What was he doing?

'Law school?' he said again.

'Yes. What's wrong with that?'

He shook his head as though too many things were wrong with that to even say. He was leading her to the beach, but then he turned around and led her toward the village instead. This was not a conversation to be had on hallowed ground.

'You think you are going to be a lawyer?'

'You say that like I'm going to be a bank robber.'

'I'd rather you be a bank robber.' His jaw

muscles clenched and his eyebrows came down to his nose. Here was that intensity that scared most people off.

'Anyway, lots of people go to law school and don't become lawyers.'

'What a pile of shit. Did you really just say that?'

She turned and walked away from him. He couldn't treat her that way anymore.

He pulled at her hand to make her stay with him. 'Alice. Hang on. Please? I'm sorry.'

Her chest ached. She wished she could help herself. Why did he care so much? Why was her life suddenly his to arrange? And if he cared so much, why had he left her for so long?

'A lot of people go to law school, you know. It's a pretty normal thing to do.'

'But not you.'

'Why not me?'

'Because!'

His disapproval stung in her eyes. She chomped down on her cheek so she wouldn't cry. Worst was the memory of how she imagined she'd impress him when he learned. She always wanted him to think she was smart. How stupid she felt now.

'You're not exactly normal.'

'Thanks.'

'You're not. Anyway, normal is the problem. Why would you waste yourself like that?'

'Waste myself?' She kept her face incredulous. 'Do you know how hard it is to get into a good law school? You have no idea how hard I worked.'

'You're right. I don't.' He still held on to her hand in a conciliatory way but a little too tightly. They walked past the post office and the village hall. He was still thinking she might turn around and go.

'What if I want to be a success at something? What if I want to be able to make some money?'

'That is crap.' Even when he was trying to be nice, he was mean.

She snatched her hand away. 'Crap to you, maybe. But other people actually need money. You'd like it a lot more if you had less of it.'

'I'd take less, but I don't want to like it more.' He was following her now, down along the bay promenade and to the ferry dock.

'Listen,' she said, walking briskly, her face turned away from him. 'Not all lawyers are the guys who work for your grandparents, writing you checks and harassing your mother.'

He was quiet for a minute. 'I know. I know you won't be one of those guys.'

She nodded awkwardly. She hardly ever got anything off him.

'But they will try to suck you in. You know that, too. You'll wear those suits and those shoes, and you'll never get out alive.'

'Paul.'

'I'm serious. They'll give you money to fight with people. You'll spend your days distrusting people and thinking of what will go wrong. You're an optimist. You'll get crushed by that.'

'I won't,' she said defensively. 'I'm not so fragile.'

He managed to get her hand again. He pulled

her to a stop. 'Everyone is fragile. Everything beautiful is fragile.'

She chewed on her cheek. She stared at her feet. She tried to blink the water back into her eyes before she looked at him again. 'You want to fish for crabs?'

She walked to the lamppost at the edge of the dock and pointed to where you could see the leggy shapes gathering. Crabs were so dumb, how they loved the light, how easy they made it for you to capture them at night.

'Okay,' he said. She could see that he was hesitant to leave this conversation, strained and foreign as it was. But his face also showed relief to be back in their regular world. 'I left my net at your house.'

'Three years ago?'

'Yeah. I'll get Riley.'

'Don't. She had a fever all day. We should let her sleep.'

* * *

Alice had her purple bucket. Her brown legs. He watched her hanging out from the lamppost with one arm, ready to stab her net — his net, actually — into the water. And the poor, stupid crabs clacked around in her bucket.

How much could he say? How much could he tell her?

That he believed in her? That she had her special Alice-ness and she shouldn't just ruin it? That he knew her from the day she was born and he had faith in her? She was his avatar, his better

81

angel. He knew he asked for too much.

'I think they mate for life,' he mumbled into his hand, gesturing to her bucket.

'You're thinking of lobsters,' she said. She had supernatural hearing. She always heard everything he said. 'You're such a wuss.'

He was a wuss. Riley could gut a fish and forget to wash her hands. Alice would smash a three-inch silverfish with her bare heel. He was ashamed of the fact that he didn't like to kill things.

'I will never eat another one of Ethan's crab cakes. Hey, there's one.' He was pretending to be her spotter, but his heart wasn't in it.

'That one's tiny.'

He felt sorry for the crabs, but suddenly he felt happy for himself. Here he was on a calm bay with his feet dangling off the dock. Here was Alice with her predatory expression and her large glow-in-the-dark gold eyes sweeping the bay floor. He would be happy if she kept crabbing but didn't catch any more. It was no wonder he couldn't come up with a better life to lead.

'So, you'll be back in New York,' he said. Now that he had broken down the wall to this other part of her life, it was tantalizing to go in and look around a little. He'd have to fix the breach soon enough.

'Yes. Did you see that one? It was huge.'

'Do you know where you are going to live?'

She squinted her fox's eyes at him. 'Two of my high-school friends are getting a place in Greenpoint. They said they have room for a third.'

'Which friends?' Now he was getting comfortable in here. He liked picturing her in her life. Did she wear shoes there?

'Olivia Baskin and Jonathan Dwyer. You don't know them.'

It was true that he did not know Jonathan, but he was able to hate him nonetheless. In a fit of hypocrisy, he hated the idea of a man claiming to be her friend and planning to live with her. It seemed wrong. And yet, how many nights had he shared a room with Alice? How knowingly and willfully did he claim to be her friend, even feeling what he felt? Maybe this was why they didn't talk about their other lives.

Could he tell her not to go to law school and also not to live with Jonathan? He couldn't stand her doing things like that in close proximity with him knowing about it. Maybe he was better off in California.

He once dreamed that his soul took the shape of the mottled moon, but in miniature, and that she held it up to the sky and then put it on her tongue like a Communion wafer, and afterward he could see it glinting in her eyes.

She let go of the lamppost, seeming to grow weary of her war against the crabs. Her netting arm hung down by her side. She looked at him, unsure of how to be, of whether they were allowed to be here like this together.

'What about you? Where will you live?'

It was only fair, when you took the liberty of asking questions, that you also answered them. 'I have to get into the program first — officially. I have to finish up the incomplete, so I'll have a BA. They get hung up on that kind of thing.'

'That's the paper you're writing.'

'Yes.'

She surrendered his net and sat down next to him.

'And then . . . I guess I'll find a place. Maybe Brooklyn,' he continued. He hadn't thought of Brooklyn before now. He hadn't thought of where to live at all.

The smell of crabs trailing from her bucket tricked his unconscious mind into believing that no time had passed and nothing had changed. But this person sitting next to him, with her plans and her intentions, was not the same. The way they talked was not the same. There was the future unfolding here where it had not been before. He felt as though he was living the past, present, and future at once.

She peered into her bucket of crabs. Then he watched her carefully as she stood, steadying toes curled over the edge of the dock. She picked up the bucket, pulled aside the white handle, and tipped the captive crabs into the water, where instantly they scurried back into their circle of light.

7

Red, Red Wine

When Alice was about eight years old, she learned that her father was having an affair. She learned it from her mother. She didn't really understand what it meant until a few years later, when the affair was presumably over. If it hadn't ended or if another had begun, at any rate, her mother didn't tell her about it.

It was just one of those things. It didn't fill Alice with righteousness or anger exactly. When you learned things young, you just stuck them into your haphazard pile of life and went along.

There was one piece of information that stayed with Alice more than the others — the fact that the woman with whom her father had the affair was on this island, in this town. 'Right under my nose' was how her mother had put it. Alice knew this, but she didn't know who the woman was. And though she didn't really want to figure it out, she made a strange practice, at certain moments, of trying to figure it out anyway.

It was moments like this, even all these years later, when she was sitting in front of the market on a Sunday morning, for instance, watching people stream in and out with coffee, newspapers, bagels, donuts, when she would study each woman. *Are you the one?* she'd wonder, waving hello to Cora Furey in her running pants. *What about you?* she silently asked Mrs. Toyer, reading her *Wall Street Journal*, who was quite wrinkly now but might have been appealing many years ago. She thought of Sue Crosby, who was parking her bike. But it couldn't be her. Ethan referred to her as 'that large woman.'

Was it someone she knew well? Like Mrs. Cooley? That thought made her cringe. Or someone she knew barely or not at all? Like the lady who made gypsy jewelry and sold it from her house on Mango Walk? She wore pink, gauzy clothes and made a tinkling noise when she walked. Depressingly, she was the kind of fake exotic woman Ethan probably would have really gone for.

Sometimes Alice tried to tell by the way the various women looked at her, the wronged daughter. Were they guilty perhaps? Evasive? A little nervous? Alice was like an amateur detective, but she had no serious intention of solving the mystery. It was just a peculiar spectator sport.

She tried to talk about it with Riley once, not long after she'd heard. 'Did you know about Dad?' she asked one night when Riley was lying in her bed.

Riley had nodded but not said anything.

'Do you think that means Mom and Dad are going to get divorced?' she'd asked.

Riley had shrugged, looking troubled. 'What did Mom say?'

'She said that they were trying to work through it.'

'What did Dad say?'

'He got mad that Mom told me.'

Of course, their parents hadn't gotten divorced. Neither had they quite worked it through. Her mother remained in a perpetual state of umbrage, and her father in constant contrition. Her father was a naturally guilty person, though, and her mother was naturally drawn to umbrage, so it suited both of them to have a reason.

Riley had turned to the wall and said nothing more.

Both her parents had an oddly theoretical relationship to children and child-rearing. In her mother's ardor for both gathering and sharing information, Alice flipped and flopped between subject and audience. When she was older, it got worse. Her father began teaching a puberty class for sixth-graders when she herself was in sixth grade. Alice was mercifully put with a different teacher, but still she found the whole thing embarrassing and terrifying. Only later could she find it funny. She knew how little her father knew, how completely clueless and tone-deaf he was to kids her age. If he was the authority, what did that mean? She tried not to extrapolate from that bit of inside knowledge. Unlike Paul, she wasn't naturally prone to doubting the things you were supposed to believe in.

Alice stretched and got up from her picnic-table perch and went into the market for more coffee. When she came back out, her father appeared as though she'd conjured him, wearing his customary too-short running shorts made out of a silky material. It seemed more clueless than vain in the case of Ethan, but it was sometimes hard to tell. Just as some people believed that every person had one natural age, Alice believed that every person had one natural fashion moment, and her father's had occurred in the late seventies.

'Heya, Allie-cat,' he said, waving to her as he stretched his calves by the wooden fence.

On Saturdays and Sundays, her father ran around the island waving at friends, jumping ceremonially into the ocean at the end of it. He ran the same loop every time, not faster or slower, not longer or shorter, whereas her mother was all about progress.

He kept his tan all year round, it seemed to Alice. At one point she thought for sure he was visiting a tanning salon, but she never actually caught him doing it. 'It's the beta-carotene,' he told her, rather inexplicably, when he discovered her following him down Columbus Avenue. He teased her about it for months and bought her a Christmas gift certificate to Portofino Sun. He had that way of making you laugh and also of turning the tables.

'Your father enjoys himself too much,' her mother used to say. Until she learned about the affair, Alice hadn't understood the trouble with that.

★　★　★

On Monday morning, Alice sat in the waiting area of Dr. Bob's office. She'd forced Riley there when she saw that Riley was sick enough to miss her lifeguarding shift for the second time in a row, but she couldn't reasonably force herself inside the examination room when Riley clearly wanted her to get lost.

'It's strep throat,' Riley announced, coming out of the doctor's office, fluttering her prescription in her hand.

'You had that before, didn't you?'

'Everybody's had that before.'

'You'll have to swallow pills.'

'So says Dr. Bob.'

'Did you request the chewables?'

'So funny,' Riley said, but Alice could tell she didn't have enough spark for a fight.

'I'll pick them up for you at the ferry. Go back to bed.'

'Are you Mom?'

Alice was instantly hurt by this, not because it was outrageous but because it was quite plausible. She wanted to be Riley, but she feared she was her mother.

'Sorry. You are not Mom.'

Riley didn't take well to being mothered by one mother, let alone two. Alice tried not to be grudging. Riley never was. Her anger flashed and then vanished, and afterward she had no memory of it at all.

'If you get them, that would be great,' Riley said gallantly.

'Fine. On the ten-fifty?'

Alice patiently waited for the 10:50, but she

felt strangely out of sorts. Two nights before, Paul had lifted the veil between two worlds and she felt a strange wind blowing through, carrying unexpected things back and forth. They had let the veil fall again, she thought, but now she wasn't sure. The wind still blew, and she found herself mixing. She was mixing Paul into New York. She was mixing New York into here. She was mixing the past into the future.

She'd tried to shake herself out of it by doing familiar things that did not include Paul. The night before, she'd gone with a bunch of friends to The Out in Kismet and tried to keep up her end of flirting with Michael Hunte, but she wasn't really there.

The feeling pervaded, against her efforts. It made her feel like she was not really present on this ferry dock. It made her feel only half-visible to the people waiting alongside her. It made her feel strangely guilty for not really being there to pick up Riley's pills, even though she was and she did.

★　★　★

Paul appeared at the yacht club the following night. His grown-up face was a strange one to see in this caramel-lit place, amid the knotty pine and the faux-yachtish paraphernalia. He didn't sit at one of her tables, but he arranged himself at the bar so that she passed him on every trip to the kitchen and helplessly offered him the opportunity to tease her about the sailor hat.

He was too familiar to her to make her

nervous, but his presence there provoked something similar. Maybe it was because he was drinking red wine. Maybe it was because Riley was still sick in her bed. Maybe it was because he drank glass after glass and ate only goldfish crackers and popcorn from the bowls on either side of him at the bar.

And as her shift drew to a close and he stayed on, she was fearful of what the night might bring. She trusted that if Riley were there, they would stay firm on this island, but Riley wasn't, which left her afraid of where they might go.

It reminded her of the time, years before, when he'd drunk red wine, nearly a whole bottle of it. She was fifteen, and she'd followed him to the beach because she'd felt worried about him. His mother had been at the house with her boyfriend at the time, and Paul had seemed reckless and angry. More than usual. At first he'd avoided Alice, and then he'd told her to go away.

'I'm not bothering anyone,' Alice had said, and sat down at the edge of the surf. 'Anyway, it's not your beach.'

Eventually, he'd come to sit next to her. She wondered if he had been crying. They sat there in silence and darkness with no moon at all for a long time. For hours it seemed to her. And when she got tired, she'd lain back on the sand and he'd put his head on her stomach. She'd been startled by it, but she hadn't pushed him away.

He was drunk and tired and sad and a little bit sick. She could imagine even now the heavy, warm feeling of his head lifting and falling with her breath. 'You are the only good thing in the world,' he'd said to her.

'I don't want to be the only good thing in the world,' she'd answered at last, but her words floated upward and she suspected he was already asleep.

★ ★ ★

What was he waiting for? Why was he doing this? What had he in mind? He wouldn't let his mind spool forward. He wouldn't be dishonest with himself. He would, apparently, be evasive.

Alice, in her sailor hat, was killing him.

She made a meager waitress, but not out of vanity or ennui like the other two. She was as diligent and generous as ever. Her mistakes favored other people.

He was getting into trouble here. He should go home immediately and erase some more of his paper.

And yet he stayed. He ordered another glass of wine. The cute girl behind the bar refilled his popcorn bowl for about the fiftieth time. She was too young to know who he was.

Alice had one table left in her section, and they didn't look like lingerers. The kitchen was closing while the bar filled up. That was the rhythm of the place. First the families with the kids came and went, then the older couples whose kids didn't eat dinner with them anymore. Once they'd gone, the third wave arrived — those same grown kids stealing their parents' chit books and drinking at the bar until all hours. He'd been in the first category and he'd been in the third. It was hard to imagine he would ever be in the second.

But Alice. What would she be? Not a lawyer, please. Did she have a boyfriend in her regular life? Was the so-called Jonathan playing that role? Did she want to get married? Did she want to have children?

He didn't believe she had a boyfriend. He would somehow know if she did. Not that it was his business.

He remembered the hard time he'd given her when she was sixteen and seventeen. She'd dress up for a yacht-club dance or wear makeup to a party on the beach and he'd tease her and torment her for it. He'd wanted her to think she looked silly or ungainly, but it was the pure opposite of the truth, and that's what made him do it. He'd pretended he was doing her a service, keeping her head size in check.

He'd been ruthless about the boys who hung around her. He saw only their worst intentions, because he also saw them in himself. He'd tried to dignify it as something other than jealousy. He'd never tried to kiss her.

He saw Alice glance at him as she cashed out for the evening. What was he thinking? Would he let her go home? That's what he should do. Let her go home and let himself do the same.

He thought of his house waiting. The gleaming kitchen no one ever cooked in. The perfectly posed couches where no one sat.

There was one room in the house that had any real character, any life, he might have said. The room with the stuff and clutter, the old LPs, posters, and photographs, the endearingly terrible shag carpet, and the chair you'd actually want to sit on, was the room that housed his father's old things. It had escaped the sterilization process because no one could bear to move it or touch it. It remained the altar to his father that nobody visited. It was enough that it was there.

If Paul wore ink on the soles of his feet, you would see a simple pattern to his use of the house. There would be the path from the back door up the back steps and into his bedroom, and a path into the bathroom. That would be it, and even that was too much. He would rather have slept at Alice and Riley's as he used to do, but he was twenty-four years old, and a sleepover was hard to rationalize.

How strange that he'd slept on both Alice's and Riley's bedroom floors literally thousands of times. Longer ago, he'd slept in their beds, too, even though Riley kicked and Alice had nightmares.

How could you think about a girl whose bed you'd slept in until you got an Adam's apple? And the thing was, he hated the onset of puberty most urgently because it made him know he had to sleep on the floor, or worse, on the couch. Later, he'd thought to hate it because it gave him an ever-strengthening desire to sleep in Alice's bed, but for reasons he felt ashamed of. And the stronger that desire, the more he knew he could not do it.

You couldn't slip from one kind of sleepover

to the other. You couldn't. You had to go away for a while. Maybe even years.

★   ★   ★

'I guess I'm going home,' she said to him, a question in her eyes. *Were you waiting for me? What were you doing this whole time?*

She'd hung up her apron. She'd ditched the shoes. She'd cleared her tips. She'd washed her hands and face in the bathroom. She'd put something on her lips, if he wasn't mistaken.

And what had he done? He was such a bastard, the way he purposefully ignored her questions. He gave her expectations and then he pretended not to notice them.

'Okay,' he said. 'See you later.'

'Okay,' she said. He saw her hesitate. *Just go,* he wanted to tell her. He was perversely proud of her when she walked out the door of the yacht club. He saw her sailor hat wadded up in her hands.

He loved her for being so beautiful, and he hated her for it. He loved how she put shiny stuff on her lips for him, and he also reviled her for it. He wanted her to walk home alone, and he wanted to run after her and grab her up before she could take another step.

Let me love you, but don't love me back. Do love me and let me hate you for a while. Let me feel like I have some control, because I know I never do.

★   ★   ★

She told herself she wasn't hoping when she walked onto the beach that night. She felt angry at him in a familiar way, but she could assemble no case against him. What kind of lawyer would she be?

Why did he make her feel this way? She couldn't retrace the moves that left her here. Why did she continue to want him, regardless? Why did she spend so much time trying to understand what he felt? Talk about a waste. That was the true waste.

She sat on the sand, just out of reach of the finger waves. She felt moisture creeping from the sand into her pants, but she didn't really care.

The moon was a sliver. As old as she was, Alice didn't see the moon as round. She saw it as the shape of the light, no matter that she knew better.

She lay back and rested her head in her hands. Her bed would be sandy tonight if she didn't take a shower. She started upward and felt frustrated at the murk of constellations. She secretly suspected that all those people who claimed to see them were making it up.

When the moon got lost in a cloud, Paul showed up. Or perhaps it was the red wine that showed up.

She was too tired and he was too drunk to make a show of surprise. He went ahead and sat close by.

'Nice watching the waitress in action,' he said.

She didn't feel like parsing his words, weighing the sarcasm against the affection.

'I hate that job,' she said.

'I like it.'

'You don't do it.'

'I like watching you,' he said.

'Better a waitress than a lawyer, you'd probably say.'

'I would.'

'Well. I think I stink at either,' she said.

He sighed. 'You try, though.'

It sounded to her like an insult, but he said it nicely, so she let it go.

'Alice.'

'What.'

'Nothing.'

She closed her eyes. She heard his breathing. A wave made it as far as her toe. The tide was coming, but she was too tired to move. It seemed okay to be swallowed up.

He lay back beside her. She liked him there, but she didn't turn her head to look at him.

When she was nearly asleep, she sensed him moving beside her, and then she felt his head on her stomach. This was what she wanted, wasn't it? He let the weight of it settle on her gradually, asking permission in his way.

Was he giving in to her or getting ready to torture her some more? Maybe both.

She felt a sad longing for her sleep as it ebbed away. It was just like him to wait until she'd given up. She felt the sad acceleration of her heart, a misbehaving organ if ever there was one. She knew he could hear it, too.

She felt the weight of his head as she had years before. Heads were heavy. She breathed it up and down. She freed a hand from under her head and let it rest on his ear, his forehead, his cheek. She wasn't sure if he wanted more from her or if he wanted less.

Maybe it was both. Maybe it was always both.

★ ★ ★

When Riley's afternoon shift had ended at six, Adam Pryce had the idea of doing a sunset run to the obelisk with a couple of the other guards.

'Are you up to it, Riley?' he'd asked.

If she hadn't been before, she was then. She was feeling almost completely better from her sore throat.

When she got back from the run, it was nearly dark and the house was empty. Alice was working at the yacht club, she remembered. She thought of going over there and giving Alice a hard time, but she was hungry and tired.

She didn't remember until it was late and she was falling asleep in her bed that she'd left her bag on the beach. She forced herself out of bed and back into clothes. She went to the top of her walk and down the dune. It was a beautiful beach, a peaceful night. The sky was black on blue with a sliver moon that came and went. She saw the silhouette of the lifeguard chair and tried to see the shape of her bag in the dark. But as she padded down toward the water, she saw two figures in front of her. Immediately, she was stopped by the intimacy of their position. It wasn't the first time she had come upon lovers on the beach. But there was something about these two that struck her. She walked away from them, giving them their space as she walked toward the chair on the soft, uphill sand. Her brain seemed to process slowly and unwillingly, yet it would not let go. She cast another look toward them, not quite able to help herself.

It was almost certainly Alice. She could see very little of the second person, but she knew, somehow, that it was Paul.

She stopped. She didn't want to go closer, but going up the dune would only put her on higher ground, giving her a broader view of things and making her easy to see.

Her surprise was physical. She was astonished, and at the same time she knew. There were many things in life like that. You couldn't imagine it, and then it happened and you couldn't really imagine it hadn't.

She turned around and went back toward the house. She felt a distressing shift under and around her. She felt the wind blowing the loose sand, as though the world was trying to reshuffle to accommodate this discovery. Riley resisted it. She would wait until the storm settled.

Anyway, what did it mean, really? What did it necessarily have to mean? Her impulse was always the same: to protect the past. To shield the future. To keep things the same if she could.

She tried to clamp down, to steady her heart. Not to feel or think too much. She didn't like people's secrets. She didn't want to find out things she shouldn't know.

She had once gone to the school psychologist in the beginning of fifth grade. It was her father's idea. She remembered the woman telling her about the way the mind dealt with distress. 'It has an immune system of its own,' she'd said. 'It surrounds the offending element like a germ and stops its spread.'

'I have no idea why you are making me do this,' she'd said to her father, angrily, as soon as she came out.

'That's why I'm making you do this,' he had said.

She was tired. Her legs began to ache. She stopped feeling the sand under her feet. She no longer saw the sky. She kept her eyes straight ahead as she let herself into the house and climbed the stairs to her room.

She relished her quiet, empty bed. It wasn't that she wanted what they had. But nor did she want to feel separated from them. She was happy to be alone, but she felt suddenly apart.

She closed her eyes and wished for sleep. She thought of the total time of her run that evening. She'd worn her stopwatch. She tried to divide it into nine miles, to calculate the average, to the second, of each mile.

It was a complex calculation that saw her all the way to sleep.

★　★　★

Riley woke early the next morning. When she thought of the beach, she thought not so much about what she'd seen but why she'd been there in the first place. She'd left her bag, and it had her pills in it, her penicillin.

She put on her suit and sweat clothes over it.

She turned inland and jogged along Main Walk to the big beach entrance. It was early and still deserted. She headed immediately to the chair, but the bag was not where she had left it. She had an uneasy feeling as she looked at the texture of the sand. The winds had been strong overnight, and the sand had shifted. The tide had come in unusually high.

She sat down on the sand. She thought fleetingly of the shadow shape made by Alice and Paul. She thought of her bag, thrown around on the waves, drawn out to deeper water. She thought of it growing waterlogged and heavy, sinking to the bottom. She pictured her towel, her extra suit, her goggles, her pills. Had the bag been zipped, or was each of her belongings finding a separate place underwater?

It was easily possible that it hadn't been swept out by the tide. Somebody might have found it. It could have washed in farther down the beach. She'd check the lost and found. She always wrote her name in permanent marker on her suits. Maybe somebody would find it and call.

That could easily happen, she told herself, several times over the course of the day. But every time she thought of her bag, she pictured it at the bottom of the ocean.

8

The Kind of Person to Be

'So, how is it being back?'

Paul sat on a picnic table outside the market early in the morning, drinking coffee and waiting for Riley. He got Ethan instead.

'It's all right,' Paul said. He looked into his coffee cup.

'It's been a while, hasn't it?' Ethan sat on the end of the table, in spite of the fact that Paul offered no welcome. He was tanned and confident, but just underneath his tan, he wasn't.

'A few years.'

'Makes a big difference at your age.'

What was Ethan trying to say? 'It does and it doesn't,' Paul said evasively.

Ethan was the first grown-up Paul had ever been purposefully rude to, and now it was habitual. It had been strange, when he was ten, starting to uncover the weaknesses and mistakes of the grown-ups in his life. Riley understood them, too, but she was quick to forget, whereas Paul always remembered. As a child he'd liked the feeling of power and he'd also hated it. He abused it, but he didn't want it.

'Riley said you two were going to fish for blues this morning.'

Paul nodded. It occurred to him that Ethan

was probably hoping to be invited.

Ethan was handsome, and he was funny. He did accents and impressions. He would speak for a whole day in his Russian accent and another day in his Scottish burr. Riley and Paul and Alice screamed and yelled in protest, but they really loved it. Ethan cooked badly, but he prided himself on it nonetheless. He cried easily and forgot things. He gave them third scoops of ice cream when Judy wasn't home. He taught his daughters to skateboard, fish, and windsurf.

There was a time when Paul used to look at himself in the mirror and wonder if his hair would look like Ethan's when he grew up. He practiced his accents in a room by himself. When he thought of being a man, he tried to picture his own father, but he usually thought of Ethan.

Ethan did know how to be happy, but over the long haul he wasn't the guy to pin your ideals on. He wanted to be more than he was. That's what Paul came to understand about him. Dead men made better idols than living ones.

And yet, in spite of Paul's principles, he found it hard not to love Ethan. While in the case of Paul's mother, it was the opposite.

Paul thought of the beach the previous night. He thought of Alice, and then he felt ashamed. He didn't want to think like that. It was a weakness that could make him too able to understand a desire-driven man like Ethan, and he did not feel like understanding Ethan.

Ethan looked at him hopefully. He wanted to be man-to-man, now. He thought they could be friends.

103

There was something about his bedroom that made Alice do it. That's what Alice told herself the following afternoon. Not the bed itself, though that was something. Maybe it was the unfamiliarity of it; neither of them had spent time there in past summers. It was on the island, but it had a sort of embassy quality. It stood in one country but belonged to another.

A part of her, a big part, just wanted to know. It didn't matter so much what the answer was, she just needed to know one way or the other.

It took a moment of righteousness to get her in the door. When had he ever knocked at her house or waited to be let in?

'Paul?'

'Up here.'

She pushed her hair back with clammy fingers. Her legs had a goose-bumpy feel, though it was easily eighty degrees. She climbed the back stairs slowly.

'Hi,' she said, feeling suddenly shy in his doorway.

He turned from his desk. Not his whole body, only his head.

'How's it going?' she asked.

He leaned back in his chair. 'I'm trying to write about Kant's *Critique of Pure Reason*. I'm focusing on a section that's about a page and a half long. I think I understand it about as well as my mother's dog understands *The New York Times*.'

She laughed cautiously. His self-deprecation

104

used to charm her senseless, but she'd begun to realize it was also a form of self-acceptance. He enjoyed the qualities in himself that he complained about. The truly tender things he didn't bring up.

'So, are you writing or erasing?' she asked.

'Writing. I erase by night.'

She looked at him carefully. He indicated no knowledge of what had gone on at the beach the night before. 'I think you erase by day, too,' she said.

His face had a cautious look. He liked to break the barriers between them, but he had to be the one to do it. She was supposed to go along with him unquestioningly, to explore when he wanted to explore and forget when he wanted to forget. 'You can't erase what isn't there,' he said.

She felt tremulous. She should have kept her mouth closed. 'Is there nothing there?' she asked.

He considered his computer screen. He shook his head slowly, turning to look at her. 'Nothing new.'

She glared at him, feeling the old frustration. Sometimes in his presence she felt the deepest connection to him, and other times she felt completely alone — as though any bond to him was her own bitter imagining.

'You'll just have to live with your incomplete, then, won't you?'

His forehead wrinkled toward the middle. 'Maybe so.'

'Anyway, college degrees are for the little people.'

'Alice, stop.'

She was going to stop. She was going to leave and get away from him and avoid him for the rest of her life if she could. But she couldn't make herself go yet. 'What did it mean?'

His back was stiff. He looked uncertain. What a joke that she had come here with the thought of seducing him. 'What did what mean?'

'You don't know?'

'Why don't you tell me?' His expression said the opposite of his words. He didn't want her to tell him anything at all.

Was the torture intentional? Did he despise her? And if so, for what?

She felt desperate enough to raise the ante. She needed to see where it would go. 'Was it me and you on the beach last night? Or was it just me?'

He was uncomfortable. He would have left, clearly, but it was his own house. She was beginning to see the trick of staging your scenes at someone else's house.

He shrugged. 'I drank too much wine. I was wrong if I gave you any ideas.'

'Any ideas?'

'Yes.'

She felt like throwing his computer at him. The angrier she got, the worse it would be. She knew that perfectly well. But sometimes what you knew made no difference to what you did.

'You are an asshole, Paul. Either that or stupid, and I don't believe you're stupid.' She slammed the door behind her, remembering that it had been open when she walked in.

★ ★ ★

When Paul heard the noise downstairs the next evening, his heart leapt and sprang open with the dazzle of a firework. He'd been working on his paper, hating his paper, wishing and wishing that Alice would reappear. He wished that she would appear at his door in those cutoff shorts she sometimes wore. He wished she would stretch out like a cat on his bedspread like she had days before. Even if she just looked out the window the whole time. Even if she asked questions, he wouldn't mind. He would answer all of them — and honestly this time. Even if she said nothing at all, he wouldn't mind. He wished they could go back to how they were.

If she would just come to him, he would feel all right. Whatever she said, he would respond differently this time, he thought, if she would only come. And then he heard the door open and the wind blow into his house.

'Paulo?'

And still like a firework, his heart fell back to earth as a spent gray ember. She always arrived with little warning. That was one of the reasons he distrusted this house; trouble always arrived with very little warning.

He saw when he walked downstairs that she came alone. That was the best that could be said of it.

'Paulo.' She kissed him twice on one cheek and three times on the other.

'How are you?' he said, hoping the strain didn't sound as clear to her as it did to him.

'The traffic was awful. The LIE doesn't move, you know. The water taxi stopped in Fair Harbor first and then Saltaire before it came here. You pay them a fortune and they don't take you where you say to go.'

'Right.'

'Look at you.' She managed to get in a sixth kiss. She was pleased. The last time she'd seen him was in Fresno, California, and his hair and beard had been in full bloom. 'You are so handsome, *caro*.'

He heard her cellular appliances buzzing and dinging as he carried her bags upstairs. He tried to think of what her hair would be like if she left it alone. He pictured it dark and curly from a long time ago. It was long and wild and probably one of the many things her parents-in-law hated about her. If they could see her now, wouldn't they be surprised. She was as blond and bobbed as any Park Avenue lady. She could easily be a lady lunching among his grandmother's circle. If only they'd had faith. But it was too late for that. They hated her now more than they ever had then. And by now she had given them reason.

How long would she stay? That was the single question that interested him. She didn't like the beach. She no longer liked this town or virtually any of the people in it. She didn't like the sea smell or the mold or the corrosive salt in the air. She was never quiet about it. There was nowhere to get a good meal. There was no place to buy a pair of shoes. All the things he loved were the things she hated. He knew that. And still, he couldn't help but feel responsible for her pleasures.

'*Come sono le regazzi?*' she asked, looking out the window at Riley and Alice's house. 'They are here still?'

'Yes. They're here.'

'*La madre? Il padre?*'

Paul cast his eyes to the window, where majestic waves flattened themselves into a framed seascape on the wall, like a thing you could buy. 'They're fine. Still the same.'

'You've seen them?'

'Of course. They're right there.'

'I would like to see how your little one comes out,' she said. '*La bella.*' His mother had a personal and vested interest in beauty. She would not be disappointed in Alice, he thought with sorrow and pride at the same time.

He watched his mother clank around in search of something on a kitchen shelf.

She was admirably turned out, he recognized. She had things stuck or hung on almost every part of her person. Necklaces, pins, bracelets, scarves, elaborate earrings, large gems on her fingers. But it struck him how weighted down she was by them. All of her privilege, her self-gratification, she wore conspicuously on and about her.

And yet nothing much went inside her. Her thinness was a triumph to her, but it looked to him like deprivation. She would bedeck herself, but she wouldn't feed herself. Whatever self-care she had stayed on the outside.

'Paulo, the telephone directory? Do we still have it?'

He knew she wanted the number for the market, and more specifically the annex of the market that sold the spirits.

'You want the store number?' he asked.

'How did you know?' she asked coyly, rhetorically.

'Don't worry about it. I'll go pick up some things for you. I need to go there anyway.' He didn't need to, but it was a good excuse to get away for a while.

She jotted down her list, but he could have shopped for her without it.

'And also the water taxi number. I need to call them again about picking me up.'

'You could take the ferry.'

'Tomorrow is Saturday. It's too crowded on Saturday.'

'You are going tomorrow?'

He was happy with this news but vaguely outraged as well. She was planning her exit before she'd even unzipped her suitcase. But this was how she was. She went to great effort to find him anywhere on the globe. And as soon as she'd succeeded in reaching him, she turned her attention to leaving.

He walked down the boardwalk, his back to the ocean, longing to see Alice. It had been more than a day. He could survive years without her on the other side of the country, but here he couldn't survive a day. Not, certainly, when his mother was in the house.

His mother did not fit here anymore. It was

hard to picture her here, even when she was standing right in front of him. She had fit once, hadn't she? She'd made an effort once.

She spent little time in New York now. She'd gotten an apartment in Rome, but she complained of the noise. She went many places, and spent less time in each of them. Only the places she hadn't yet visited met her expectations.

In some sense, she was never really anywhere. She was happiest, Paul suspected, in transit, where the past was untouchable and the present negligible. And she would be, he guessed, for as long as she kept believing that the future would be better.

★　★　★

'Paulo, they are such *assholes*.'

He should've called it a night after the first bottle. He should've.

He couldn't now remember whether she was talking about her most recent boyfriends, his grandparents, or the staff of a hotel where she'd recently stayed. It could have been any of them. It could have been anyone in the world.

Except his father. His father was the only one permanently excluded from Lia's roster of assholes. Maybe it took dying to exempt yourself.

It used to be that she'd speak in English until she got really angry or really drunk and then switch to Italian. Now it was reversed. He wondered if she knew that about herself.

111

'I mean, Paulo, you don't know. You have no idea! None! Why do they never do what they say?'

He shook his head. He didn't know.

'Assholes,' she spat.

How he minded her weaknesses: her brittleness, her anger, her haughtiness, her grudging memory, her fear. Her tendency to drink too much wine. He recognized them too well.

'Paulo, I think of your father. He would not do these things. He was a good man and he loved me.'

Paul suddenly knew her tears were going to come. Her angry drunk changed into sad drunk in a predictable way. But he never really prepared himself. Even if he could have, he didn't.

'I just — I just wish — '

'I know, Mama,' he said.

'If he just could have — '

'I know.'

'In this house, you know. I think of him.'

'I do, too.'

'We were happy then. We had each other and you. And we didn't care about the other things. Do you even remember?'

'Some of it,' he said. The overlay of what he'd been told was so heavy it nearly suffocated his few little sprouts of real memory.

He wondered the same things again and again, but they weren't questions he liked to follow around the corner. *If we were so happy then, why did it end? What happened to him? How could he let it happen?*

112

And he wondered of his mother, *If you were so good at being happy once, why have you never been happy since?*

As a child, Paul believed what he was told. But he also believed what he saw. He couldn't help it. And what did a person — a child — do when the two things did not fit together?

His mother lay back on the couch, her chin squashed into her neck at a graceless angle. Tears gathered in her eyes and flowed down her face as the black eye makeup flowed with them. Her lipstick smeared and feathered at the edges. Her face looked tired, slack, and old. Her nose ran, but she had not the self-possession to stop it. She would fall asleep here on the couch. At some point, in a stupor, she would bring the television to life and he would have to listen to it all night.

'Why did she let him do it?' Paul had once asked Judy, when he'd begun to grapple with the idea of his father's drug addiction.

'I think she was doing it, too,' Judy had answered.

He hated when Lia got like this, though he knew she would. He felt disgusted by her and ashamed of her. And ashamed of his own disgust.

Worst of all, he felt responsible. He could take care of her better. What would his father have to say?

He tried to feel sorry for her. It seemed like the generous thing. He knew she was a victim. She was widowed at twenty-nine, hated and rejected by her late husband's family. She had no family, no real support of her own. Yet he couldn't do it. He saw her as a person who brought her troubles on herself. Maybe if she had been less adept at feeling sorry for herself, he could have done a better job. But as it was, there were no gaps to fill.

Lia didn't have to spend all that money. Paul didn't care about the money itself, whether it came or went, but he hated the way she wore it and drove it and drank it and flaunted it. He hated the proportion of it that went to spas and suites and jet fare.

Paul's father hailed from an extraordinarily rich family, and the fact that Lia had ended up with millions of dollars drove Paul's grandparents half mad. They spent the waning energies of their lives trying to take it from her. They stuffed as much as they could in large trusts for Paul. But what had belonged to Robbie during his lifetime — a significant pile of money landed on him when his last grandparent died in 1980 — belonged to Lia when Robbie died. Paul's grandparents sent whole corps of lawyers into battle with the most severe instructions. And Lia fought back by spending.

Partly it disturbed him for the sheer hostile waste of it, but also because he took it as a betrayal of his father. His father was an idealist, misguided though he may have been. He was a free spirit — or as free a spirit as you could be coming out of St. Paul's. Robbie hated the culture of money and the money itself. He embraced underdogs, starving artists, and hopeless causes. He'd never supported a political candidate who'd been elected. He wore the same sandals every day, winter, spring, summer, and fall.

Paul knew most of these things from Ethan, not from his mother, but he remembered the sandals himself. In the full anger of his adolescence, he'd confronted his mother with these and other grievances. He didn't try anymore.

Anyway, what was to be done? The money was what Lia had. The money and Paul. And though the money was more obedient than Paul, she managed to use both in the fight against his grandparents.

Lia snored. Paul took the glass from her hand and brought it to the kitchen. Blearily, he found a blanket and put it over her. What a sorry pair they were.

It shouldn't have been disappointing. He knew how it was with her. But his capacity for hope, like hers, was irrational and unending. That's what it was to be a son. If he resigned himself to the truth, he wouldn't belong to her at all anymore.

9

La Bella

Paul left the house with his mother sleeping in front of the television and passed through the phragmites soon after dawn. He could pretend to himself that there was no premeditation, but he also knew that Riley left for her shift just before six. It was a reckless sort of premeditation even so, as he let himself in through the screen door in the kitchen and walked up the stairs. He didn't know what he would do when he got to Alice's bedroom, but neither did he stop long enough to make up his mind. He opened her door and went in, knowing he had no right to.

'You don't own me,' she had said to him once when she was about twelve. She was climbing onto a motorboat with a friend whose father, the driver, was visibly drunk, and Paul had forbidden her to go.

'I never said I did,' he'd snapped at her sternly. But as she'd walked away from the boat, neither of them believed themselves.

She was sleeping. Her hair pointed in a hundred directions and her face was turned away. She'd kicked off half her covers, giving him a long view of her left leg.

La bella. He didn't want his mother to see her. He sat on the edge of her bed and she slept

116

on. It was lonely when she was mad at him. He was miserable.

'I'm sorry,' he leaned and whispered in her ear. He could still smell the wine in his breath. He touched the tip of a strand of her hair. 'I know what you meant,' he said. 'I don't know why I acted like I didn't.'

He needed the feel of her, just like when he was a child. What would she do? He couldn't say what he wanted or what he was prepared to offer. But he loved her. Could he tell her that? It was simple to love her and simpler still not to have to acknowledge it.

Even after all he'd done, he trusted her to be kind. He crawled onto her bed and flattened himself out next to her. He pulled the sheet over the top of the two of them. Very carefully, he scooted closer to feel her warmth. Tentatively, he put his arm around her waist, barely touching her but yearning for the feeling of embrace. He nearly groaned aloud when her leg came around his. She was warm from the covers and from being a good person, he supposed. He wanted to put his face into her neck and braid his limbs with hers.

'I love you,' he mouthed into her hair. He could say it when she couldn't hear.

He lay there, gradually relaxing. His heart slowed; he let himself breathe again. His mind settled.

He'd imagined that if he ever made it into Alice's bed as a grown person, it would all be different than it was in childhood. And he did regard her differently this time. The feel and smell of her struck parts of his body that he hardly knew he had back then. If he were to let his mind run free, it would conjure possibilities he hadn't known existed back then. But he wouldn't let it run free even if it pulled and strained like an untrained dog. He'd be dragged around the block by it. He might even lose it altogether for a moment or two, but he wouldn't let go.

There was one thought, and it tangled him up like a repetitive, half-awake anxiety dream. *Could love be continuous? Could you carry it unbroken from childhood to adulthood, wrestling it over the crags and pitfalls of adolescence? Could it come out the other side as the same kind of love, just expressed in new ways? Or were those two kinds of love disjunctive and creepily at odds?*

Maybe it wasn't simply the answer that was baffling. Maybe the question was wrong. Maybe there weren't two kinds of love. Maybe there were a trillion kinds. Or just one.

But now he held her. He forgot to worry as much about waking her up. She turned her body to his, eyes closed, and curled herself around him. She pressed her cheek to his chest, and he felt the tickle of her hair in his neck and under his nose. Though he was too big for the bed, she made him fit.

Trust and love went together. He understood that. But how did desire work its way in? How did it fit? How, if at all, could it be kept out?

He didn't know if she was awake or asleep, but he felt her heart beating and the further pulse of it in her hands when he held them. He felt the ridge of her shin against his, the softness of her thigh. He didn't know what it meant, but he felt deeply comforted by her skin, her warmth, and the way she always let him in.

Maybe it wasn't so different now. Even with her breasts and her long, curving limbs, she was still his same Alice. Maybe the things he most loved about holding on to Alice were exactly the same things he always loved. The end of loneliness. The hope of ease. The feel of a body he trusted.

★   ★   ★

Alice woke from her dream into her dream. It made it hard to keep straight sleeping and waking, but she didn't feel any need to distinguish as long as the dream kept on.

She'd been so angry with him when she'd fallen asleep the night before, and now his lovely body was all around her, and the anger was nowhere to be found. With Paul, she could never remember where she'd mislaid her anger, even the times she promised herself she would go back and look for it later.

She kept her eyes shut. She'd grant him the power of deniability. So what if by lunchtime he'd erased the entire thing? Right now there was something, and she wanted to keep it going, that was all. For all she knew, she had Don Rontano, the tennis coach, here in her bed, but, oh, he felt good.

Still with her eyes closed, she found the hem

of his T-shirt and lifted it over his head. He could disclaim her if he liked, but she wanted his skin. She snuggled deeper into his chest. She felt the warm passage of his back and shoulders.

Could she kiss him? Would he allow her that? Was that something he could pretend was nothing? What about making love? Could she just open up her legs and pull him inside her and have him all she wanted and later give her assent that it was nothing?

She pressed herself closer. She boldly matched her pelvis to his, though his shorts and her underwear came in between. Maybe the top half of him didn't want that, but the bottom half did. She moved with him a little. What body could help it? She kept her eyes closed.

I was asleep, he could say. *What even happened? I thought you were sleeping, too.*

If she could have him this way, really, would she take him? Was it worth it? And, God, if she ended up losing her virginity to Don Ron, wouldn't she feel stupid.

She opened her eyes. She snuck a look. It wasn't Don Ron and his eyes weren't even closed. No fair that he got to look and she didn't.

He caught her looking. She felt his hold loosen. His pelvis unstuck from hers.

She discovered a bit of last night's anger. It was there, rather plainly, in the crook of his stiffening elbow.

He sat up in bed and she sat up, too. He looked as though he was surprised to see her there.

You were the one who snuck into my bed, not the other way around! she felt like shouting at him. But she didn't want to kill the mood. It wasn't dead yet, was it?

She looked at him there in her bed. Shirtless and tangled in her sheet, with his uneven haircut and his tortured face. At least it looked like they were doing it. Perversely, she wished one of her parents would walk into her room right now. What would he say then?

He put his two feet on the ground. Damn him, he was already erasing.

You can't erase when there's nothing there, he'd say.

'My mother's here,' he said. She could smell the wine on his breath.

She nodded. That explained something. She was back to being Alice the security blanket, but she wasn't as good at the job anymore. She'd grown too needy. That was the problem, wasn't it?

'For how long?'

'Just till today.'

'Oh.' Alice suddenly felt mildly exposed in her bikini underwear and her undersized T-shirt, talking about his mother. 'How is she?'

'The same.'

She nodded. She crossed her arms over her chest. 'Do you want me to come over and see her?'

'No,' he said immediately. 'I mean, you can if you want.' He stood.

God, he was going to leave again, and they'd be right back where they started. The dream was gone. The mood was dead.

She watched him find his shirt under the covers and pull it on. In despair, she opened her mouth. 'Is there really nothing?' she asked. She fixed him with a glare, daring him to ask her what she meant. If he did, honest to God, she would punch him.

He looked pained, but he didn't worm away. 'Alice. There isn't nothing.'

What was that supposed to mean? She needed to count the negatives to see where they came out.

'Is there something?'

'There was always something, wasn't there?'

She closed her teeth hard. He could be dishonest and cowardly if he liked, but she didn't have to play along. She fixed him with another look.

'You know what?'

'What?'

'I want to be with you. You pretend there's nothing, but I know there is. You may say there isn't for you, that it's all in my head.' She was getting a little ahead of herself. She cleared her throat. 'Is that what you'd say?'

He was frozen. He didn't answer.

She made herself plunge forward now or she never would. 'But I've never done it before. I want it to be you, but I don't want an unwilling partner.'

He looked both shocked and stricken. He didn't know which part to answer. 'You've never done it before?' he said finally.

Of course not! I've been waiting for you my

whole life, you stupid idiot. She didn't say that. 'No,' she snapped instead, cutting off avenues to further questions.

'I — '

'You don't have to answer now,' she said. 'If you want to, come to the west beach tonight at midnight.' She could hardly believe the things she was saying, but she was rather impressed by them. 'If you don't, then don't.'

'Alice.' He could hardly believe her, either.

'If you don't want to, I fully understand, and you should consider yourself forgiven.' She said it more grandly than she felt. *But don't come crawling into my bed anymore.*

'Alice.'

'I'm serious,' she said, even though it was hard to feel serious in purple underwear and a tiny shirt. 'But if you do come, bring Paul. And expect to see Alice, okay?'

He nodded.

'And don't be drunk.'

She would have liked at that moment to have turned on her heel and marched out in the glory of her conviction. But because it was her room, she had to just sit there and watch him go.

★ ★ ★

She'd never done it before.

Well, did he really think she had?

He didn't like to think about it much at all. If he forced himself, he might have thought she'd gotten it over with in a quick and meaningless way. Much as he had.

He'd done it meaninglessly many times. Sometimes quickly, sometimes slowly. He'd enjoyed it, sometimes a lot. he thought of the buxom Mexican girl, Maria-Rosa, sneaking off with him into an empty field in the middle of the day. It never fit into the broader context of his life. He'd never done it under the premise of expectations. He'd never even promised a girl he would call.

She hadn't done it at all. *She's waiting for you. Oh, lord.*

But of course. He would hate it if it were any other way.

His entire body was pounding when he saw his mother off in her water taxi. He was too preoccupied to abhor a single thing she said. That was a new experience. Excitement, desire, anticipation, and the strong need to pull it all back again.

'Are you okay?' his mother had asked him in a rare perceptive moment, as she jangled along next to him on the dock.

'Yes.' His voice was choked. It came from somewhere near his midsection.

Could he possibly meet Alice on the beach, knowing what she expected? Could he freely, openly admit that it was what he wanted, too? Weren't they above that? Wasn't he, at least?

After he left his mother, he walked. He walked to Lonelyville and beyond. He walked to Ocean Beach, Seaview, Point O'Woods, all the way to the Sunken Forest, where the mosquitoes, drove him away.

His feet hurt and his shoulders turned red in the sun.

Alice was asking something of him. She was offering him a gift. Demanding and giving. He handled neither of those commitments well.

Could he possibly meet her at midnight?

Could he possibly make it without her until midnight? What if he went to her now? Could he?

Suddenly, he felt as though she was his bride, and he had to wait until the wedding to see her.

What a thought that was! The places his mind began to roam!

Wasn't this what he always wanted? He was finally plunging into his life, the one he dreamed of but didn't deserve.

Step up! Take your life. It is waiting for you! a part of his brain told him.

But how could he? What if he wrecked it? What if he destroyed the best thing he had?

It was what he lived for. He would rather protect it for a lifetime, like the curator of a priceless object, than contemplate losing it.

He wouldn't go to meet her. He didn't even want it.

How could he wait until midnight?

10

Take Your Life

She waited. Again.

Why had she set it up this way? Did she hate herself as much as he hated her? She and Paul, they were a working tandem. A one-two punch.

She looked at the moon. She'd fantasized that it would be full, but it was gone altogether.

'Whose stupid idea was this?' she asked a mussel shell before she threw it into the water.

She hadn't brought a watch. She hadn't thought it would come to that.

I'll give him five more minutes, she decided.

What a lunatic she was. She was waiting for him in her prettiest bra, her fluttery underpants, her one good sundress, totally exposed and humiliated. She felt like a mail-order bride whose groom-to-be hadn't bothered to show up at the post office. Why did she put herself in these situations?

It was certainly after midnight by now. He wasn't coming. She was such a turd. Such a loser. How easy it was to reject yourself when you felt so thoroughly rejected.

She looked at the assortment of stones the high tide had laid out for her. She could be like Virginia Woolf, pack her pockets full of stones and walk into the sea.

But the pockets on her dress were flimsy and fake. You couldn't get a suicide load into them, no way. She wished she'd worn a big old slicker and a pair of waders. Her attempt at sexiness was for nobody.

'I think I'll die,' she told the water.

'Alice?' Her misery had been of too noisy a variety to allow her to hear the footsteps behind her. She'd already given up.

'Hey. Alice.'

She didn't even feel like turning around. She'd given up.

'Am I late? I'm sorry,' the person behind her said.

She did turn around. She didn't want to, but she couldn't help it.

'I'm so glad you didn't go,' the person said.

Was this Paul who was saying these things? It looked like Paul, but it didn't sound like Paul. She tried not to get her hopes up.

'I was just leaving,' she said robotically.

'Please don't. I was just coming,' he said.

She expected hesitancy and contortions. She expected excuses. Why did he look so relaxed? Was it really Paul?

He came up very close, but he didn't try to touch or kiss her hello. They didn't know how to do those things casually, as they were intended.

'I realized we probably needed one of these,' he said. 'I should have thought of it earlier.' He held a strip of small plastic square packages.

He'd brought condoms. She instantly flushed. She hadn't been as pragmatic as he. She hadn't really believed this would happen. She was so surprised she wondered if she had been bluffing. Was he calling her on it?

'The store was closed, you see. I thought I could order them from the mainland and have the ferry bring it over, but they were closed, too. I should have thought of it earlier.'

'Then how did you get them?' she asked, dazed.

'From Don Ron at the yacht club.'

'You did not.' She was suddenly giggling like a twelve-year-old.

'I did. Why not?'

She giggled some more. 'No reason.'

'I brought a few other things,' he said. His voice was steady but forceful, forceful but light. Was it really Paul?

He placed his armload on the beach. He unwound a blanket. 'I brought this,' he said. 'To lie on.' She expected furtiveness, but his gaze was unwavering.

'Good idea,' she said breathlessly. Did he mean this? Was he really going to go through with it, or was he using some kind of tricky reverse psychology? She scanned his face for indications of strategy, but she did not see it.

'And this,' he said, 'for after.' It was a bag of fancy chocolate chip cookies.

For after. She couldn't speak. She couldn't say a single thing.

'And this,' he said, 'for you, not me.' It was a bottle of wine.

She was touched. She felt like she would cry.

'Are you nervous? Do you want some? I brought a corkscrew, too.'

She touched her fingers to her eyes. 'I think I'm okay,' she mumbled.

He touched her shoulder. He put his face close to her ear. 'After all this, we need to do it right. Don't you think?'

★ ★ ★

He spread out the blanket. Usually it was a battle, but the wind was calm tonight. He made their place in the no-man's-land between villages, in the cradle of two dunes. Nobody would bother them there.

Now it was she who looked scared. Now it was he who was sure. But he didn't want his certainty to scare her away.

He arranged their things. He sat down. 'Come sit,' he said, and she sat down beside him. The moon arrived to show how lovely she looked in her fitted dress of tiny aqua and purple flowers. He thought of a gift, wrapped to please, and only being able to think of what was inside of it.

He allowed himself to feel the joy of her beauty and not the pain of it. Hers was a benevolent power. He knew that, even though it was hard to trust it.

'If you're nervous, don't worry,' he said in a low voice. 'No pressure.'

'Who are you, and what did you do with Paul?' she whispered back.

'I brought him,' he said. 'He's right here with Alice.'

He was. He was finally here. He was taken back by his own certainty, but he was certain now. Enough for the two of them and for anyone else who might come along. This was what he wanted. Now that he'd decided it, the future could not come fast enough. *Beware the power of the converted*, he thought.

At the same time, he knew he was at the edge of a great and rare pleasure. A pleasure you got only once in your life, and if you didn't make the most of it, you were stupid. He was weary of being stupid.

'Are you ready?' he said. He could barely see her gold eyes, it was so dark. He wanted to see. He wanted her to see him. Now that he had decided.

'Am I forcing you into this?' she asked timidly.

'Do I appear to be forced?'

'No. But honestly. You don't have to. I won't be mad. You can still sleep in my bed.'

'I want to sleep in your bed,' he said. And he leaned over and kissed her. He kissed her cheek at first. And then her jaw. 'I want to do a lot of things.'

As long as he had loved her, he had never kissed her before. Maybe he was afraid of what it might let out.

He kissed her neck and the place just to the left of her cross. He kissed her collarbone and her ear. This was Alice! These were places he knew so well but had never touched.

He waited to kiss her mouth. Because when he did, it was almost too much to take. As he knew it would be.

She kissed him back, and the intimacy was almost intolerable. He lost himself and made no effort to find himself. He kissed her like it was his first. It was his first, in a way. He was a virgin, too.

He thought of telling her that and other important things, but he was in a rapture of kissing, and talking would have meant stopping the kissing, which he would not do.

He let his fingers and his mouth discover the parts of her known only by his eyes before this. How could he even have known how much was pent up?

Then there was this dress to consider. There were the parts he hadn't seen. His heart pounded and he felt like a fourteen-year-old. It was different when it mattered. The ramifications went forward and backward forever. But when she pulled her dress down over her hips and kicked it off her feet, forward and backward rolled into the middle, into now.

Her fluttery, intent fingers got rid of his shirt, went about the button of his jeans. Despite the care he'd taken with dressing, he was also quickly unwrapped for presentation.

He pulled her on top of him and felt the sand remolding under his back. The beach was the place where this couldn't happen and where it had to happen. She'd known that, of course.

He was hard as could be as she pressed against him. Joyfully and miserably wanting. It was a painful pleasure. A hurting want. It tapped all places along the spectrum from agony to comfort.

Her eyes were wide open and so were his. There was a certain convention of coyness that

131

had no place between them. Her two eyes squeezed into one Cyclops eye as he kissed the bridge of her nose. Neither of them was going to miss this.

Her legs were around him. She was strong, as he well knew. They were barreling ahead at the speed where you couldn't stop. You had no road left and you had to fly, no matter what, even if both of your engines fell off.

She was shaking. Or was it him? 'We can wait,' he said, in part because it wasn't true. He had a scary feeling of oblivion, and maybe she did, too, because she said, or at least he thought she said, 'It's not the only time. Only the first.'

Entering her, he felt taken apart and then remade almost at the same time. He clutched her, probably too hard. His eyes swelled with a different kind of tears than he had cried before.

He kissed her on the mouth and she kissed him back as he pushed deeper. He had never done that before.

'You're Alice,' he said to her when he lifted his head. It was hard to believe.

Here she was, here they were, after all this time. It was the joy of joys.

He was not just making love to Alice, though that was elation enough. He was making peace with himself.

★   ★   ★

Afterward she lay with her head on his chest. She might even have fallen asleep for all she knew. So many sensations carried on below, she could no

132

longer keep track of them.

He had folded the blanket over them, so they were naked to each other but not to the rest of the world. She felt warm and content lying between his legs, four arms a sweaty tangle.

She was afraid to make sudden movements or even make words for fear of puncturing this fragile state. She didn't even want to think too hard. It felt too sweet to exist, to be allowed, to be good for you.

What if the world took no notice? Maybe they could just stay like this. But she heard the turn of the waves and she could mark the progress of the moon as it freed itself from a heavy band of clouds. The world was still rotating, and they were still on it. Dawn would come, and it would be a different day. If this was real, if this was true — if some unseen force did not snatch it away, if the man in her arms didn't try to erase it — then tomorrow would not only be a different day but a different life.

They ate cookies. Alice felt crackling grains of sand in her teeth from her sandy fingers. It felt familiar and not totally unpleasant. She remembered her mother saying that sand had no nutritional value but that it had been her childhood staple.

Each time she looked at Paul she expected him to disappear, or for his eyes to evade, but he did not. He stayed with her. He matched her, cookie for cookie.

They fell asleep for some amount of time, and she woke up to the feel of his mouth on her breast. And they made love again, longer and in some ways sweeter. The sky was lightening and he was on top of her and she could see his face. She could see his pleasure, unequivocal and unguarded in a way she had not seen before.

'I love you,' she said, when he bent his head down to hers at the end and they stuck together all the way up and down, cheek to cheek, her toes reaching just above his ankles. 'I always have. I always will.'

She knew she was getting far out ahead, and maybe saying too much, but so it was. Because it was true and it couldn't be helped anyway.

* * *

Alice wanted to be in bed before Riley realized she was gone, and that meant hurrying. Neither of them wanted to be greeted by the early-morning surfers and joggers. She was grateful that her parents were in the city.

So many things were thrilling and strange. Dressing in front of him, watching him do the same, feeling some sense of right to him now. Feeling not just that she belonged to him, as she always had in some way, but that he belonged to her, too. They held hands back from no-man's-land and up the short bit of boardwalk to their houses. He was the one who'd reached for her hand.

They kissed once more before they separated. She tried not to watch him go, but she did anyway with a sense of pleading in her heart. *Don't leave me*, she thought. *Stay like this.*

In her room, she sat on the bed and stared at

the wall and watched the memories of the night replay themselves.

Memory was a force. Already it was editing, reordering, creating a narrative out of raw feeling. This was how it would go down for her. How would it for him? She wondered.

She was reluctant to shower, for fear of washing the experience away, but she did. She was afraid of falling asleep, for giving her unconscious mind a chance to rearrange everything. But she did that, too.

When she finally woke up, it was into a joyful remembering. Usually, she calculated how her dream related to her waking life, but now it was turned around. It had really happened, hadn't it? The sensations around her body told her it had.

She was starving. She ate three bowls of cereal, barely stopping to breathe. She got dressed, noticing the strange way she felt in her underwear, then she hesitated at the door. She was afraid her state of magic would dissipate in the regular world of people and things. But how was she going to get an egg sandwich if she didn't risk it?

The market was thankfully empty. Camp was in swing, and her babysitting obligations did not begin until after lunch. She ate half her sandwich in relative peace, looking for Paul in every direction, even ones by which he could not possibly come.

She wanted to see him, but she was afraid to. She wanted to keep her version of events for as long as possible. She didn't want to give him a chance to remember it all differently, to tuck it away in a package that was easier to seal off and easier to forget.

He was standing at her door when she ambled back home. She was nervous and overjoyed to see him. She was scared to look too long at his face. *Did it really happen?*

Why was she searching his face for the answer? She knew it did! Wasn't that enough?

But, really, it wasn't. The chief frustration of romantic love was that you couldn't make it go by yourself.

He motioned for her to follow him, and she did — through the secret path, into his house, and up the back stairs. The windows in his room were opened so wide that the ocean was practically inside it. The wind blew right through.

She offered him the remaining half of her egg sandwich and he wolfed it down. He balled up the foil and tossed it high up and into the garbage can.

'Nice,' she said. She would be his cheerleader. She would establish a tone of agreement.

They sat side by side on his desk, none of their feet touching the ground. They didn't say anything, but they shared a glance every so often.

Hey. Did that really happen?

Finally, she asked it out loud. She girded herself. She clenched her hands. *Don't say, 'what?' Don't equivocate. Don't say anything wrong this time, please,* she begged him silently.

He smiled a smile she did not recognize. He slid off the desk and reached for her, picking her

136

up with one arm under her shoulders and his other arm under the bend of her knees. He carried her to his bed and laid her down on his bumpy bedspread. His hands were instantly tugging on the waist of her shorts.

'Let's just make sure,' he said.

★　★　★

Alice walked home from her shift at the yacht club two nights later full of excitement and impatience. She had the feeling of eating up her life in big bites, so voraciously she could hardly remember to chew. She'd washed her face and put on a little makeup in the bathroom before she cleared out. She had the idea she would go straight to Paul's. He would make a show of surprise, but she knew he'd be waiting for her.

The bay was calm as she walked along the promenade. There were no big party boats out tonight. She saw a kayaker cut through the path of the moon, and she thought of Riley. Her blood slowed as a different mood stole in.

Alice looked back at the yacht club, the bar still lit up for the drinkers. She remembered a night six years ago along this same walk, the night of the annual Memorial Day Social.

'We don't want to go,' Riley had said to Judy early in the evening. She'd figured she could speak for herself and Alice, too, because usually she could. Usually, Alice agreed. They would do something together, just the two of them, like go for a night boat ride. Alice had long been conditioned to feel lucky when she got Riley to herself.

But that was the year Alice was fifteen. She'd finally gotten her braces off the winter before, and she'd discovered some goop that tamed her hair as straight and uneventful as the other girls' hair. She'd gotten a new pair of jeans, and she was proud of them. She hadn't wanted to admit these things to Riley.

'I think I might go,' she'd said timidly to her mother.

Riley had turned on her in astonishment. 'You want to go?'

Alice had felt embarrassed to want it, but she did. 'Just for a little while maybe. Just to see a few people.' Alice had the extra secret of knowing that Sean Randall liked her. Janna Green had told her so on the ferry the first Friday night. Alice didn't know if she liked him back, but it was exciting to have somebody look at you in that way.

Riley had watched her in confusion half an hour later when Alice had walked downstairs in her new jeans. Alice had packed eyeliner and lip gloss in her purse to put on in the bathroom when she got there. She always seemed to primp in secret.

'We can still go kayaking if it gets boring,' Riley had offered.

That made Alice feel worse than any criticism or judgment Riley might have come up with. She'd felt bad leaving Riley alone. She'd remembered feeling sorry that Paul wasn't there, that his mom hardly ever opened up the house

138

until the Fourth of July. The lifeguards Riley hung out with were mostly local kids from Bay Shore or Brightwaters. They didn't start coming out until the end of June, and though some of them lived in the barracks in town, most went home on the ferry at night.

The way Riley had looked at her, Alice knew there was no part of her sister that wanted to go to the social. There was no part of her that could even fathom why Alice would go. Alice felt it a weakness inside herself to want to look pretty and have a boy like her. Riley was eighteen years old at the time, and then as now, Alice had never known her to go out with anyone or kiss anyone, boy or girl. *It was Riley who was strange, wasn't it?* she remembered thinking defensively, with an ache of betrayal and the coldest of comfort.

Alice remembered so clearly walking along this same bay front, the feeling of her stiff new jeans, her shame, her stealthy excitement.

11

Look at What You Could Have

'Paul! Come on! What the hell are you doing up there?' Riley shouted at Paul from the back door of his house the next day. The ocean was huge and they'd agreed earlier in the day to go surfing if it kept up. Riley was impatient because she knew the quality of the waves could change in an instant. Her temper was short for Paul these days.

'Come in. I'll be down in a second!' he shouted back.

'No. I'll be on the beach,' she said, and she pulled the door shut behind her. She didn't like his house. She never went in there.

It was the kind of house she not only disliked but felt threatened by. It seemed to her that in the old days, the houses were full of sand and the windows and doors stayed open, the cereal got stale in its box, and you could smell the sea. Even this house had been that way once. Now the houses were professionally cleaned and the openings were sealed off. The air conditioners labored in the windows or behind the shed, and the dehumidifiers hummed and shook. It was like a virus that swept over the island, infecting one household after another. Renovations, dishwashers, first-string furniture, and fancy curtains for privacy. It made for a bunch of stage sets, in Riley's opinion, where people posed and believed but did not live. Only her house was still good.

Lia, Paul's mother, was beautiful in a way similar to her house: ruthlessly.

Riley had developed a distrust of very beautiful women, and she supposed it probably started with Lia, who was the type to use it against people.

Riley was forced to make an exception for Alice. She'd sort of hoped that Alice wouldn't go completely that way, but it seemed she had, and not as the result of trying, either. Alice didn't have a tyrant's beauty, though she could still manage to hurt you with it. But she was Alice, so she would be forgiven.

Looking up at the house from the beach, she allowed herself another view of her discomfort. When Alice was gone at night and crept back in the morning, so early she thought nobody noticed. When Paul failed to show up at the usual times for meals or poker games. Riley didn't want to think those thoughts to their logical end. But really she knew they were at Paul's house. Lia's house.

It made Riley sad that Paul didn't employ his old tricks to live at their house anymore. He didn't pretend to fall asleep on the couch so they wouldn't send him home at night. Now he stayed in that big, unfamiliar house. He waited for Alice.

★　★　★

141

Alice had a dream that night in which she was stuck inside her house and she knew in that dream-way that she couldn't get out, even though she hadn't tried the doors. The house had the queasy feeling of not quite having its postings footed in the ground. She wanted to see the sky, but you couldn't see out of the windows. They were no longer openings to the outside but rather pictures of the same kinds of things the windows would normally show — sky and reeds and even Paul's house.

But suddenly she wasn't looking at the pictures but found herself looking through piles of laundry, looking and looking for Riley's red lifeguard suit, because she knew that Riley needed it, and in the dream it was Riley's only one.

Alice woke up in the early morning with a cold start and a tingle straight down to her toes. She tried brushing her teeth and washing her face, pacing around her room, but it was hard to get out from the feeling of the dream.

Without thinking much, she threw on a pair of shorts and a T-shirt and ran barefoot down Main Walk to Riley's beach.

She felt comforted by the sight of Riley in her red suit, perched and alert in her chair, looking over the ocean, same as she ever was. Alice tried to shout to Riley. Not that she needed to tell her anything, just to say hello. But the wind blew her words back at her and Riley didn't seem to hear.

★　★　★

When the FedEx woman rang the bell at the front door in the late morning of the following day, Paul felt almost as though he was being served papers. He was standing at the door, so he couldn't realistically pretend he wasn't home.

He knew it would be something from the law firm. He didn't need to look to know. It would doubtlessly be urgent and require a minimum of three signatures, and he would most likely toss it in the garbage and not think about it again. His grandparents delegated the dirty work to the lawyers, and he delegated it to the trash can. He signed Paul McCartney and took the package.

They always found him. One uniformed delivery person drove straight into Kings Canyon National Park after him. In certain paranoid moods, he suspected his grandparents had surgically fitted a GPS into his anklebone while he was asleep.

He went back to his desk, dropping the package on a pile of papers. He stared at his screen and thought about Alice until the real Alice appeared in his door, stealthy and windswept. 'Have you seen the beach?'

'Just from the window.'

'You'd like it today.'

'Come here,' he said. The trouble with their new arrangement was that he wanted to be touching her at all times.

When she got close enough, he pulled her onto his lap. Immediately, her lips were on his and his hands were under her shirt.

'Are you done working?' he asked hopefully.

'Until two.'

'I missed you.' Oh, the things he found himself saying. He used to imagine that people made themselves say these kinds of things when they were in love so as to demonstrate their status. He didn't realize they would just come out of you without you even being able to stop them.

'I love it when you wear the little skirts,' he told her, hiking hers up. He had a condom in his pocket. He had them all around now. He had one in his shoe. He was prepared to make love to her in the deli aisle of the market if no one would object.

In just over a week of nearly solid lovemaking, he was getting good at navigating her trickiest bras and bikini tops, while she was an ace at freeing him of his pants. They hardly needed to pause or change position. Still on his lap and facing him, she put his arms around his neck and helped him find his way inside her. He groaned in contentment. He used to voice his sounds of pleasure as a kind of service to his partner, but with Alice he couldn't hold them in.

What if he couldn't do another thing in his life besides make love to Alice? It was all he thought about and all he wanted to do. Maybe after things settled down, he could work on his paper in this position. What could she do? Maybe read or write or grade papers. He'd have to try out that idea on her. Maybe they would be the first couple to achieve career success while having sex. They couldn't really teach classes or go to meetings, but maybe they could do conference calls. The lawyer route would be out of the question, which was all the better.

He kissed her hair and her ear and her eyelid. He was happy.

And after she came and he came, they slumped together for a long while.

When it was time to go, he watched her sitting on his desk, fastening her bra and braiding her hair. She was so good at that.

She was telling him about Gabriel, the four-year-old who tried to flush his older brother's electric train down the toilet, and Paul was listening, he really was, but he was also admiring her. Love made you admire funny things about a person, like how good she was at remembering to return her library books and at slicing cucumbers very thin. She was a veritable wonder at pulling a splinter out of her foot.

How could you feel this way? How could you just let your life spread out in front of you, with no plans other than making love? It just didn't seem possible. Or at least not allowable.

Had they stumbled into some existential loophole, where you could just be happy all the time?

He knew it couldn't be, but what did he know anymore?

It was unbelievable. It was impossible. It blew the hinges straight off his mind.

He would believe that the world could contain any amount of suffering, but somehow not this. This was the thing he had not foreseen. He was like an experimental rat, conditioned for suffering, confused and half wanting to find his way back.

Alice stood up and kicked his toe affectionately. He didn't really want to find his way back.

'What's this?' she asked.

'Something from my grandparents by way of their lawyers.' Not even that could take him down. He thought the package looked pretty in her hands.

'You didn't open it.'

'I know. It will be a document I'm supposed to sign that transfers some pile of money from my mother to me.' He shrugged. 'I'm hungry. Do we have time to make scrambled eggs?'

'Maybe quick ones. Are you going to sign it?'

'No. I never do.'

'We have time for scrambled eggs, but not the scrambled-eggs special.'

He looked disappointed. The last time they'd made scrambled eggs, they'd also made love in the pantry and burned the toast. 'Please? That's the kind I like.'

She checked the clock in the hallway. 'Oh, okay.'

He watched her crack the eggs (like a downright genius) and he sighed again. He couldn't help it. He found himself thinking that if the story of Alice and Paul ended right here, it would be happy.

★   ★   ★

'I heard Lia was here,' Judy said.

'Right. Yes.' His life had undergone such a conversion since then that he'd almost forgotten about it until today.

146

'How is she?' Judy had her nosy face on, her nosy cadence, but Paul tried not to let it get to him. He saw her faults almost as clearly as if he were her child, but he forgave them as though he lived next door.

Paul cast a look at Ethan. 'She's the same.'

Alice sat across the table, one foot up on the chair. He would not let his mind wander under her skirt, but the act of forbidding it also made it so. He wasn't getting better; he was getting worse.

'I didn't see her,' Riley said. 'I didn't even know she was here.'

That's because I've been avoiding you, Paul thought but did not say.

'Had enough of the pasta?' Ethan asked, getting up from the table, starting to clear it.

'Yes, thanks,' said Paul. He'd finished the pasta but was still hungry for Alice. But even though Alice had insisted he come to dinner, she wouldn't look at him.

'If you don't come, it will be weird,' she'd said, spinning by his room before dinner but not letting him take off any of her clothes.

'You don't think it will be weird if I do?' he'd asked.

'When have you ever not come over when we were cooking?' she'd asked, and she did have a point. So attuned was his nose to their kitchen that he managed to detect even a microwaved meal, even when the wind was blowing in the other direction.

'Am I supposed to keep my hands off you the whole time?' he'd asked.

'Unless you want them to know.'

'Maybe I do,' he'd said.

She looked at him as though he'd lost his mind, and essentially he had. He didn't know what he thought about anything anymore. His principles were deflated and flattened. He pictured them somewhere else, like in a Rolodex under his desk, and he would have to thumb through them to see what he thought.

'How did she feel being back here?' Judy persevered.

Paul thought of the FedEx letter on his desk. He had a history of honesty with them. 'No better than last time.'

He heard Ethan singing along to a Bruce Springsteen song on the radio and noisily washing the dishes.

'Is she going to keep the house?'

This was the thing Judy couldn't square with. She could fathom the dead husband, the strained family, the life lived around the globe. But having a house on this island, a house much more valuable than hers, and neither using it nor renting it out nor selling it. Judy's efforts at understanding the mind of Lia came to a halt here.

'Well, it turns out she's not.'

For a moment, Alice's face gave them away. 'What?'

Riley caused her tipping chair to smack four legs to the ground. 'She's selling it?'

'Well.' He could feel Alice's eyes gouging into him. 'She's giving it to me.'

'She's giving it to you?' Judy repeated.

'I'm not sure why. But she signed the papers. I thought it couldn't happen without my signature, but apparently it can. I have no choice in the matter.'

Alice had the look of a bar brawler who wanted to take him outside to the parking lot and pummel him. He should have told her this, he supposed, but she'd been working most all afternoon.

'Your grandparents must be happy,' Judy said. She was tactless sometimes, especially if one of her many agendas was involved.

'Do you not want it?' Alice asked.

'I'd take it,' Riley offered.

'I'd rather have yours,' Paul said without thinking.

'Yours is worth ten times more than this one,' Alice pointed out practically.

'No. It isn't,' Paul said. He'd spent some time thinking about the way money worked and the way it didn't. He knew what it couldn't buy.

'What will you do?' Judy asked.

'I don't know,' he said. 'I just found out today.' But in truth, he knew he'd sell it. One conviction, not entirely deflated, was that he was not the sort of person who owned a multimillion-dollar beach house, however much he was managing to enjoy staying in one.

⋆ ⋆ ⋆

'So you did open the letter after all,' Alice said to him when she walked him home.

149

'After you left. I'm not sure why.'

'Swell house you got.' She looked up at it, looming its three grand stories.

'Thanks.'

'I've got to go back and finish the dishes,' she said.

He grabbed her and pulled her off the walk, into the shadows. He kissed her.

'We'll get ticks,' she protested feebly.

'I'll check you for them later.'

'Ooh.'

'Please come tonight.'

'I don't know. My mother has bionic ears.'

'Come anyway.' In his life he'd developed the habit of refusing people things because of how badly they wanted them. Mercifully, Alice wasn't like that.

'Okay.'

★   ★   ★

And, true to her okay, Alice appeared in his bedroom before midnight.

'Is Judy on your tail?' he asked, looking up from his computer.

'No, I think I got away clean.'

'Good girl.'

Alice sat on his bed. 'Anyway, I think she might be happy if she knew that I was going out to meet someone.'

'You think?'

'She hates it when we are independent of her, but she also hates it when we aren't.'

'She thinks you aren't?'

'She worries, I think. She worries about Riley the most.'

This was tricky territory. Paul knew what Judy worried about and why, but he didn't like to acknowledge it to himself, and certainly not with Alice. Riley was enough like a sibling to him that it made her sexuality unpleasant to contemplate. Was Riley gay? Was she sexual at all? Was she lonely? The smaller minds speculated about that, he knew, and it had always seemed a betrayal to join them. Another betrayal.

'What about you? What does she worry about with you?'

'That I don't go out with boys.'

He smiled. 'Do you?'

'Just one.'

They made love in his bed, and later they made hot chocolate, naked, in the kitchen. He suspected the mix had been there since the nineteen-eighties. Alice found an apple in her bag and they fought over it, both of them starving. At last they agreed to share, passing it back and forth.

What would he do with all the stuff in this house when he sold it? How would he confront his father's things? What was he supposed to do with them? Maybe it was time somebody thought of it.

He watched Alice sitting on the counter, drinking her hot chocolate, her beautiful body in the slanting light from the pantry. He felt a stirring that came from wanting her, of course, but also something more. How could he sell this house? This kitchen counter on which Alice's ass had sat? The sink where she'd tossed the apple core? The nineteen-eighties hot chocolate mix?

Later, he watched her sleeping in his bed and he felt it again. A feeling about the future. It was beckoning him to look. *Look at what you could have.*

As a matter of principle, he'd resisted the future. He'd tried to resist most things he wanted or that made him feel good. He sensed the trick of them. The bribe he would not fall for.

And now? Now he wanted Alice in his bed. It made him feel good. He wanted Alice in this bed in this house with him forever. He felt as though he'd leapt off his trapeze, spun in midair, and caught on to a different one flying just as fast in the opposite direction.

What if he kept the house? It was unthinkable, but what if he did? What if it were Alice's house? What if he kept it for her? What if they lived in it together and named the beaches when they were old? What if they got two of those old-man beach chairs and read detective novels all day long? What if they had babies who grew into children who swam in the ocean and massacred clams, fish, and crabs?

What if he learned to love what he had? What if he loved himself? What if he stuck around to enjoy it? These were dangerous thoughts to have, but he couldn't help them. What if he lived here with Alice?

12

A Fitting Curse

Alice heard the emergency signal blasting about five in the morning. Several long and a few short. She was too sleepy to count, and she'd never learned the meaning of the different patterns anyway. Riley knew them.

She blearily looked out the window for signs of a hurricane or tsunami, and when she didn't see any, she acknowledged that another geezer probably suffered a real or imagined stroke. Both happened here with a certain frequency. Listening for the *whoop-whoop* of the medevac chopper, she wriggled in closer to Paul's warm body and fell back into a deep sleep.

When she crept home to get in bed before her parents or sister noticed her absence, she perceived a strange disorder in the kitchen. The message light on the phone was blinking double time. Riley's bed was empty as expected, but so was her parents' bed. How had they gotten out before her? Her first order of worry was that they had discovered her absence, but when she saw the state of her mother's closet, the robe in a pile on the floor, her worry kicked up to a second order, that there was something wrong.

'Hello?' she called down the stairs. 'Hello?' she shouted to all parts of the small house. No one was in the bathroom. No one answered.

With a hectic feeling in her chest, she ran back into the kitchen and flipped on the light. This time, her eyes went straight to the note on the counter, the tipped scrawl.

Alice — At Good Samaritan with Riley.
Tried to find you. Call my cell.

She grabbed the kitchen phone. Her fingers were clumsy on the numbers. She thought of dreams she'd had where she had to make an urgent call and dialed the number wrong again and again and again.

Good Samaritan. Good Sam, people called it. A nickname for a hospital. It was Riley. Was it Riley? Was it her dad? The phone buzzed in her ear.

'Alice?' her mother's voice came on.

'Mom? What is going on?' The background noise was loud and the connection was fuzzy.

'Alice?'

'Yes!' she practically screamed into the phone. 'It's me! What happened?'

'Riley, honey. She's — ' Her mother broke off in the middle of an intercom announcement and a lot of noise.

'She's what? What?'

'She was having trouble breathing last night. We thought it could be pneumonia or asthma, but now they seem to think it is something with her heart.'

Alice suddenly thought of the siren in the middle of the night. She thought of her own

154

placidity, her nakedness, the indulgence of Paul's body. She felt a chill, the haunting feel of a punishment bubbling up from darkest pitch. The kind you deserved, and even taunted fate to get.

Her mother's voice was ragged and poor. 'The doctors have picked up some kind of valve damage. They are trying to figure out what caused it.'

'How can you have heart damage that young?' Alice demanded.

'I don't know. That is what we're trying to figure out.'

'What's she doing? Is she awake? Does she feel bad?'

'She's awake. She says she feels all right now.'

Alice couldn't imagine Riley being conscious and saying anything else.

'Can they fix it?'

'We don't know. We'll find out soon.'

Her mother used the off-putting 'we.' Ordinarily, Judy was quick to divide from Ethan, and though Alice usually resented it, she would have found it comforting right now. It would have meant that her mother could play at misfortune, that marital discord was the worst of her troubles.

'I'll come, then,' Alice said.

She wanted her mother to say, *Don't come, Alice, we'll all be home soon. There's no reason for you to come.* But she didn't. She said, 'It's room six ninety-four.'

Alice thought of telling Paul before she went to the ferry. He would get dressed hurriedly and come with her. He wouldn't consider anything

155

else. He would be worried about Riley.

But for some reason she didn't. The drizzle soaked her bare arms and the bay smashed against the breakfront and doused her. She kept her head down for the long walk to the ferry.

She sat on the bench and waited. She didn't even know the time or which boat she was waiting for. There was nothing else but to sit here until the next one came.

It was her penance. She remembered the long and short blasts in the middle of the night. Or rather, she hopped over the memory like a scalding surface too painful to land on. She'd dismissed the tragedy as belonging to someone else. She'd practically celebrated it for its distance from her happiness. How could she have been so brazen?

She waited. It was the only punishment she could think of at that moment for having been happy with Paul when Riley was lying in a helicopter on the way to the hospital.

★　★　★

Alice sat on the bed of the plucky patient and tried to figure out what had gotten her parents so spooked.

'I had this dream where I was underwater and running out of breath, and finally I took in this big breath of water. Have you ever had that kind of dream? And then I woke up, but the feeling stayed. I still felt like I was trying to breathe underwater, like the water was flooding into my lungs.'

'God.'

Riley shrugged. 'Mom heard me in the hallway, and when I tried to explain, she started freaking out and calling the security office.'

Alice nodded. She moved her legs around so they made a bridge over Riley's knees. Riley allowed Alice to warm her cold fingers.

'Kind of an overreaction with the helicopter and everything, but here we are.'

Was it an overreaction? Alice wanted to know.

'You can breathe all right now?' Alice asked.

'Mostly. Yes.' She sat up more in the bed. 'So, what did you tell Jim?'

'I left a note at the lifeguard house saying you were sick today. Is that okay?' Alice didn't want to act too solicitous. It would make it seem like something grave was going on.

'You didn't talk to him?'

'No. He wasn't there yet. Should I have?'

'That's all right. I'll call him later.' Riley pushed back her hair. Her face wasn't exactly the right color. 'If you talk to him . . . don't say anything, okay?'

'About you being here?' Alice asked.

'Right. It'll sound so dire if you tell him.'

Maybe it is dire, Alice worried. *Maybe that's how it ought to sound.* 'When is the doctor going to be back?' Alice asked.

'Which one?' Riley shrugged. 'There are a bunch of them.'

'I don't know. The heart doctor.'

Riley concentrated on her feet. 'I hope I can get out of here for the one-fifty-five. I'm supposed to teach my last swimming class this afternoon at four.'

'Do you want me to call?' Alice asked.

'No. Maybe I'll get there. Anyway, I'll take care of it.' She pointed to a canvas bag on the chair in the corner. 'Will you see if my phone is in there?'

Alice picked it up. 'What happened to your regular bag?' When Riley didn't answer, Alice turned to look at her.

'I lost it.'

Alice was surprised by the guarded look on her sister's face. She hadn't meant the question as a challenge.

'I don't see your phone. I'll go ask Mom, okay?' She was eager to get out of the room and fill in a few of the holes.

Her mother was in a hallway waiting area with her head in her arm. 'Is Riley going to get out of here by this afternoon?' she asked.

Her mother glared at her as though she'd spit on her shoe. 'Riley's had a medical emergency, Alice.'

Alice struggled to swallow past her worry. She wanted to return to Riley's side of the story. 'What does that mean?'

'It means she's not getting out of here this afternoon.'

Her mother usually got wound up by drama, even hideous drama. Now she looked sour and tired. 'The doctors are trying to figure out what happened. They've lined up a bunch of tests today.'

'Where's Dad?'

'He's trying to get the insurance company on the phone.'

How quickly and completely Riley became their child again. How quickly her parents assumed total responsibility for their lives. Riley was twenty-four, but they weren't even letting her into the front seat of her own emergency. Whose fault was that?

'Is she going to be okay?'

Judy rarely tolerated a question asked for reassurance. 'That's what we're trying to figure out.'

★   ★   ★

'I'll be back tomorrow morning,' Alice said to Riley.

Over the course of the day and evening, nurses had taken vial after vial of Riley's blood, performed an EKG and some kind of scan. Mostly Alice and Riley stared up at the TV, watching a woman build a deck on an endless home-improvement show.

Alice kept looking to the faces of the nurses the way you studied the flight attendant when your plane ride got bumpy. Did they know more about your fate than you did?

Now it was dark outside. Alice would be lucky to catch the last boat. Her father was snoring in the chair in the corner.

'Okay.' Riley had a wistful look, and Alice knew it was because Alice was going back to the beach. Sometimes when you weren't there, Fire Island felt like an idea. It was hard to imagine it existing alongside a place like this, where real things had to get done.

Riley looked like a child, propped up on the pillows. Right as Alice was leaving, she sat up straight in her bed.

'Hey, Al. Can I ask you a favor?' she asked.

Alice turned, struck. 'Of course.' Her spirit lifted at the thought of being able to do something. 'Anything.'

'When you see Paul. Don't tell him about . . . this. Okay?'

Alice glanced at the flecked linoleum, spirit downwardly plunging. 'But, Riley — '

'I mean it, Alice. Please. I don't want everybody blabbing about it until I know what's going on.'

'Paul wouldn't blab. You know him better than that.'

Riley's face turned uncharacteristically flat and impenetrable. 'I know, but just don't, okay? Promise me you won't?'

Alice felt a strange desperation accompanied by punishing guilt. The single thing Riley asked she resisted. 'Riley,' she began. Riley wasn't thinking straight. She'd thought she was going to spend her afternoon teaching swimming.

But then Riley's face opened a crack to let Alice see in, and for a moment Riley looked neither numb nor delusional. It was as though Riley had guessed Alice's primary reservation, Alice's one possible excuse to override her.

'If it's something serious, I want to be the one to tell him myself. I think that's a fair thing to ask,' Riley said.

Alice nodded. Riley was covering an earnest appeal with paper reasons, but how could Alice deny her? 'So what should I say? What do you want me to tell people?'

'Monday is Labor Day. I'll call Jim to reassign my last few shifts if I have to. After that, everyone is shipping out anyway. If somebody asks, just say I had to go back to the city a couple of days early.'

Alice nodded again.

'You promise?' Riley said. She licked her lips.

'I promise,' Alice said. What else could she say?

★ ★ ★

'Alice.'

Paul was waiting for her in her kitchen. So unfamiliar was his expression, she hardly recognized him.

'Where have you been?'

She had thought about this. She had tried to prepare. She'd had to walk all the way in from Field Five because of missing the last ferry, so she'd had lots of time. Maybe too much time. Whatever hope she had of lying with élan was lost in the miles of sandy overthinking.

She considered her knuckles. 'Went off-island this morning,' she said to the ground. She didn't go to him as she would have. If not for all this, she'd be on his lap by now. They'd be mostly undressed. Her body felt like it had a lot of parts, all stuck out and unaccompanied. That's the way his looked, too.

She went closer. She felt tears gathering in her eyes. She needed to collapse, but she couldn't do it on him.

There was that moment the night before, when the signal was blasting and she was in his arms. The feeling of it flashed in her mind again and again. There was no moment that couldn't be rewritten and reversed in the future, no degree of joy that couldn't become your undoing a few hours later.

'All of you? You all went off-island? Where's everybody else?'

Alice realized it was easier to lie when her fingers were covering big sections of her face. She blew her nose into a paper towel. 'They went back to the city a few days early,' she said rotely.

'Riley went back early? Why?'

'Uh. A, uh, interview, I think. The NOLS people are in town, I think.' What was she even talking about?

He cocked his head skeptically. 'And you?'

What should he think? She wanted to protect him, to neutralize his questions. What sensible world could she create for him that did not include the truth? She was worn-down and confused. She was a horrible liar and possessed none of the discipline or follow-through required for large-scale deception.

She had betrayed Riley already. They both had. She couldn't do it anymore.

She couldn't tell him anything. She could tell the first lie, but she could not offer it any

162

support. She didn't dare. Paul was dogged and he was thorough. Which of them was suited to a career in the law?

His face was hardening. 'Alice, just tell me.'

This was becoming an inquisition. Sides were forming. A line was appearing down the middle of them. It was because he didn't trust her. He didn't trust her because she was lying.

For all the things she and Paul had done to each other and felt about each other over the years, honesty was unquestioned. Even brutal honesty. Especially brutal honesty.

She wanted to tell him the truth so badly. But the more she needed and wanted him, the guiltier she felt, the more deserving of punishment. This punishment. In her mind's ear, she heard the emergency signal again. This was a fitting curse, a near-genius design.

She just needed to get in her room and shut the door. 'Did some shopping and whatever,' she mumbled into her paper towel.

'Is something wrong? What is going on?' He looked at her impatiently. 'Why are you all the way over there?'

She wrapped her arms around herself. 'Because I'm tired, I guess. I'm going to go to bed.'

His distress showed itself differently on each of his features. She watched them closing up.

How could she push him away like this? She knew the danger of it. But how could she be with him after what had happened?

'See you tomorrow.' Her voice came out so high and strange, she had to clear her throat and try again. She turned away so she wouldn't have to see the way he looked at her.

The one thing Alice knew was that she deserved neither pleasure nor comfort. She would mess up her heart, too.

⋆　⋆　⋆

Paul walked the empty bay front. The lamps overhead gave the cold, blue light of purgatory. The wind blew eerily in circles, deranging the dune grass and the silver leaves above. He couldn't go to sleep. He couldn't go to Alice. The living universe had come down to those two things.

He wanted to pretend to himself that there was some sort of explanation, some easy fix, but he knew.

Of course he knew. Why had he held back from her all that time? The reasons were returning to him, a bit late to be helpful. He wanted too much from her. She saw what he needed, how big it was. She saw how little else he had. Who could love that? He should not have let her see it.

He walked onto the bay beach, roped and netted, just on the other side of the ferry dock. The Baby beach, they'd called it, as soon as they were any bigger than babies. The blanket of green muck swayed on the surface. He thought of all the swimming classes and races here. You could smell the ferry fumes, see the iridescent patches of gasoline adhered to the chop, floating alongside you. He remembered standing forever under the shower after swim class, the counselors rotating the kids under the freezing spray so they wouldn't bring sea lice home.

He looked back at the empty lifeguard's chair, a black silhouette. Riley had spent little time in that seat. She'd been impatient to get past the bay-sitting stage, burning to prove her mettle and move to the ocean, the big time. He remembered the day of her promotion, when they vowed never to swim in the bay again. Most kids rejected the bay because they were in a hurry to grow up. Riley yearned for the ocean because it was wild.

Paul stepped up onto the dock, so empty you could hear the creak of the wood and the pull of the water. He looked for the stupid crabs under the lamp. He thought of Alice's heartlessness toward them, desperate as they were for light.

13

Leaving Badly

After three days, Alice hated Good Samaritan Hospital, and Riley hated it more.

'I feel fine,' Riley announced as Alice arrived in the early morning. In spite of the nurse's orders, Riley sat rebelliously on the bed in her regular clothes — a gray tank top and a pair of khaki shorts. Alice could see the goose bumps on Riley's arms.

'Where are Mom and Dad?'

'I sent them away. I told them to go back to New York.'

Alice nodded, doubting that they'd complied. 'So, what's the news?'

'What?' Riley looked up at her irritably.

'Have you talked to the doctor again?'

'More tests. Another scan today. More of that disgusting thing they make you drink.'

'No news, though?'

Riley aggressively flipped the channels. She spent less time with each channel as the hours passed. 'There's something wrong with my heart.' She kept her eyes on the TV.

'We knew that already.'

'Well, that's the basic idea. God, I hate all these dancing shows.'

Alice went down to the cafeteria to get Riley a

hot chocolate. She was not stunned to see her parents there.

'No news?' she said to them, stopping at their small table.

Her parents looked as humorless as a pair of losing coaches.

'Is that what Riley said?' Judy was violently picking the side of her thumbnail.

'She was vague.'

Ethan put his coffee cup down. 'Dr. Teirney believes she has rheumatic heart disease.'

'What is that?'

'It's an infection that starts with strep throat. If it goes untreated,' Judy said.

Alice felt the hot chocolate burning the tips of her fingers through the paper cup. 'Riley had strep throat, but she treated it. I picked up the medicine for her from the ferry.'

'Apparently, she didn't treat it enough,' Judy said.

'What do you mean?' Alice asked.

'You have to take the full course of medicine. You can't just stop when you start to feel better.'

'Is that what Riley did?' Alice asked.

'I think so. We hope Riley's giving clearer answers to the doctor than she's giving to us,' Judy said flatly.

Ethan sat back in his chair. 'The doctor's almost certain there was some underlying problem that made this recent infection more serious. We think Riley probably also had rheumatic fever when she was a toddler, but it was misdiagnosed. If it happens a second time, it can be much worse.'

The words were hard and indigestible. They knocked around in her head like marbles. 'Can they fix it?'

'Dr. Teirney is talking about surgery to repair her mitral valve.'

'It doesn't *fix* it,' Judy said. 'But he says if you're careful, it's a condition you can manage.'

'Does Riley know all this?' Alice asked.

Judy gave her a look instead of an answer.

'Because she says she feels fine.'

'Riley's had congestive heart failure, Alice. She's not fine.'

★ ★ ★

Alice was avoiding him. She was disappearing in the morning, impossible to find all day long. He needed to see her.

Paul walked to the yacht club. He'd fish in a barrel if he had to. He found a seat at the bar that gave him a view of Alice. She had her sailor hat stuffed into the back of her waistband.

She met his eyes as she went by. She went so far as to touch his arm, but she didn't stop to talk. It was pity in her eyes, wasn't it? She didn't want to hurt him, but she didn't want to be near him, either.

He longed to make her laugh, to change the mood, but the wary look in her face kept him silent. She looked pained, hollowed out. Two pink splotches appeared on her pale face.

In two days, the summer would be over. When the universe was bigger, he'd been pressed to get his paper done and to start school. That's what he was supposed to be thinking about. He had a meeting with his future adviser in a week. He'd planned to leave for New York on Monday afternoon. He'd imagined he'd leave with Alice.

All those seasons of leaving empty-handed, enviously watching Riley and Alice drive from the ferry parking lot in their gasping, overpacked AMC Gremlin with Ethan at the wheel and Judy arguing with him about whether to take the Southern, the Northern, or 495. Paul had thrilled at the thought that this year, year of years, he wouldn't leave alone. He'd leave with Alice.

He'd made the mistake of drawing out his wishes with some specificity. He'd stay in the 72nd Street apartment for a minimal number of nights while casually getting a place near school. The Village was absurdly expensive, he knew, and he felt shamed by how he'd rely on his money for this plan — though apparently not shamed enough. He'd lure Alice there every evening after her classes. They'd make love day and night. Before long, her toothbrush would live on the edge of his bathroom sink. Her lacy bra would hang over the side of the tub. Together, they'd repaint the place in colors they'd (she'd) chosen. How happily he'd deprive the infernal Jonathan Dwyer, the entire borough of Brooklyn, of Alice.

Now, he feared, he'd reached for too much. He was back to empty hands.

The wine tasted sour in his mouth. He could barely discern the pretty face of the girl behind

169

the bar who liked to ply him with bowls of goldfish crackers.

Alice would have to talk to him sometime. At least she'd have to say goodbye.

She was only twenty-one. A virgin until two weeks ago, and he wanted to attach himself to her physically, mentally, emotionally every minute of every day, for now and ever. Of course it was too much. He was right to be suspicious of himself. He'd known that when he finally opened up to her, he would blast out like a fire hose, destroying everything in his path: every spark, every tender thing.

He looked at Alice taking an order from a young couple he didn't recognize. Her hand shook over her pad. Did she know he was looking?

Alice was rejecting him, and he missed her so much. He wanted to throw himself at her mercy. Part of him was so reckless, he would have done anything to be close to her. But that was the trouble, wasn't it? It was her mercy he'd come to rely on.

As he stood at the door to leave, she turned a sweet, almost wistful face to him, like she had something she wanted to say. Was she sorry he was leaving? It sent his thoughts spinning in yet another direction as he walked home.

Maybe she would come to him tonight. Maybe she missed him, too. Maybe her bed felt as intolerably empty as his. Maybe she'd be willing to give him another chance.

And maybe he could take it easy for once.

Maybe he could just be with her and stop hoping for so much.

So he lay in his bed, where he'd made love to her in a dazzling variety of ways. The hours passed and she did not show up, and by morning he knew how devious, how hopeless was his penchant for hope.

★　★　★

Alice packed one canvas bag with the important things. She left the house quietly. Her head was down. She was leaving badly.

She was going to meet Riley at the hospital. She let her mind travel forward exactly to that distance. She could picture Riley waiting for her in the parking lot, desperate to make her escape. They would ride in the cab to the train station and go back to the city. Riley was being released into the care of a team of cardiologists at Columbia Presbyterian as an outpatient, thank God. Their parents were going to Bay Shore to retrieve the car, and Riley refused to wait and ride home with them. She wanted to go home with Alice.

Alice walked briskly toward the day's first ferry, followed by the wind and rain and Paul, she realized with a start. He had gotten up uncharacteristically early.

She didn't stop for him just yet. She didn't acknowledge that she'd seen him. She didn't know what to say. It was so hard for her to lie to him. He'd want to know where she was going, and what would she say? She just wanted to get on the ferry and pull away from this island. If she could just keep ducking for a few more minutes, not seeing and not being, then that would finish off this disastrous end of summer. After that, she would be able to think.

She knew the wreck she was leaving behind. Further damage was being done right now by her inability, her unwillingness to look back at him. This was the demise of her greatest hope, happening in slow motion. But she felt her misery remotely. She was sitting on a hilltop, watching her city burn.

Her legs felt shaky. She hadn't eaten last night. She couldn't remember the last time she'd sat down and eaten something.

The previous afternoon, she and Riley had changed the shape of their lives. With one reluctant call, Riley had withdrawn her leadership of a National Outdoor Leadership School semester course in the Rockies. With another, more determined, Alice had deferred her entry to law school. A lifetime of planning could be canceled in less than five minutes, it turned out. Really, it was Riley's heart that changed the plans, but it was the nature of things to imagine you did it yourself.

How slow and painstaking it had been to coax Paul into loving her. She'd done more than coax. She'd practically demanded it of him. Maybe it was wrong to have to work that hard. And yet how quick and easy it would be, she knew, to scare him off. He didn't trust her enough to stand for a doubt, and she was giving him a pile of them.

She wanted to collapse into his arms. She wanted the comfort of his body. But she couldn't allow it. Again and again, she heard the alarm sounding from where she'd lain, curled up in Paul's bed, wrapped in his arms.

The worst thing was not telling Riley about her and Paul. She didn't tell Riley because she was guilty. Because she knew it was wrong. If she couldn't say it to Riley, then she shouldn't have done it.

Could Riley possibly know? God, what if she knew? What would she think? Alice and Paul were the two people she trusted most.

The clouds were so thick and low, Alice could sense them right over her head. The bay beaches were deserted, and she saw no sign of the ferry.

The sun could find a dazzling variety of colors: the navy blue of the bay, the pale green of the dune grass, the saturated red of the wagons, the rainbow of boat hulls resting on the sand. But when the sun disappeared, the color disappeared and so did the people. It was remarkable how quickly and completely. The landscape turned so desolate, it was hard to imagine there had ever been families here. Water, sky, plants, houses, boardwalks all weathered to relentless, close-valued gray.

When she felt joy, Alice stayed small and to the edges. In her guilt she grew all-powerful, as though she was the one who'd chased the sun away. Or maybe she and Paul had cast themselves outside of its graces, into relentless monochrome. They had left what comfort they'd known, and they'd done it on purpose. They'd thought they could have everything good at once.

Alice could stagger forward a little bit. She could tell herself something hopeful. If she could just avoid his questions and his demands for a little longer, then once they were off this island it would look different. In a week or two, she would call him in the city. Maybe it would be too late to save what they had. Maybe she didn't even want to. But at least by then Riley would have told him what had happened and he would understand.

★ ★ ★

She was not leaving. She couldn't be. It was unthinkable that she would leave without saying anything to him.

She had shoes on. She was leaving.

He should have let her be, let her go if that's what she wanted, but he was furious. What was the matter with her? Did she honestly not see him? Or was she running away from him? What did she think he would do?

Did she really plan to disappear from this island and from his life? Is that what she wanted?

He walked faster to catch up to her. She would see him. He saw the anxiety in her steps and in the artificial set of her neck.

When she turned onto the bay front, he caught up and walked alongside her.

'Alice, where are you going?' he demanded. She turned briefly, but she didn't stop. Her face was a misery.

'To the ferry.'

'I figured that. Are you leaving for good?' His T-shirt was already soaked through. He hadn't shaved in days, and he felt self-conscious about it.

'Not for good.'

'For the summer, though?' He didn't feel like hiding his anger. 'You weren't going to say goodbye to me?'

'I didn't — well. I was going to — but — '

'You were going to? God, Alice, what is your problem?'

Her face was not sorry exactly, but it was pleading. 'Paul. I just — I feel like — you don't understand, and I can't explain it right now. But I was going to call you in the city and — '

'You were going to call me?' He knew this coldness in his voice. He hated her right now in a way he never had before. He hated her stammering, stupid attempt to break his fall.

'I think for now,' she said, 'we — we can't keep doing what — we can't do what we were doing.'

'What can't we do?' He caught her gaze and held on to it. 'We can't fuck five times a day?'

She stumbled and stopped. She looked as though he had slapped her. She started walking again. He saw her brush her eyes with her fingers. She kept her head down.

'Is that what we're talking about?'

She pulled her bag up onto her shoulder. She wanted to get away from him, and it made him want to follow her all the way to New York City.

'Where are you going, Alice?'

She refused to look at him.

He followed her all the way to the end of the dock, where the weather was at its full power. He crossed his arms against the cold. She was shaking.

'You're a coward, you know,' he said to her. 'I didn't realize it before.'

★ ★ ★

Alice saw the ferry over his shoulder. She couldn't stop shaking. She didn't want to cry. What if he followed her onto the boat? What if he tried to follow her all the way to the hospital? It would be a tremendous relief, in a way, for Paul to know.

But what would Riley think? A further betrayal of her sister scared Alice more than anything.

She wrapped her arms tight around her body to make the shaking stop. As soon as the boat docked, she strode on board. She shot up to the top deck and stood stiffly. She silently commanded the boat to pull away and end this torment. She'd rather end her life than stay here.

When you were late and running for the boat, the departure was pure efficiency. Today it was jerky and ponderous, as though they'd hired a whole new crew. At last the crewman threw the rope. She heard the engines notch up and at last the boat pulled out.

She saw him standing on the dock, watching the boat creep away. She expected relief and it came, but it was a paltry emotion and ran its course quickly.

He was shouting at her, and though she would

rather not have heard him, the words made their way to her ears anyway.

'You should have left me alone!' he shouted to her.

She cried as the boat picked up speed, wishing she had. She watched in bewilderment as he strode to the edge of the dock, lifted his arms over his head, and dove into the gray water.

14

Closing Up

The sun was out, and though it was a vivid autumn sun, it picked out surprisingly little in the way of life or color. Again, Alice thought to blame herself. She blamed her eyes, which had grown dim these last weeks, not so much to sharpness but to color.

'Look at the Jeffreys' place. They've lifted up the entire house.'

It had been seven weeks since she'd left the island. The building time was well under way. Another bunch of the knock-downs and fix-ups of the kind that Riley hated and her father followed with a certain fascination.

Alice nodded blandly at her dad, not caring very much. All the changes happened off-season. You left the island one way, and you came back in June and it was different. It was like your school friends over the summer. You accepted that they came back different without bothering too much about how or why.

He strung his arm around her shoulder. It was mildly constraining as they walked, but she didn't shrug it off. She knew that he knew that she was feeling sorry for not being Riley today.

Usually, Riley helped their dad close up the house at the end of the season. Riley was the one who had learned how to drain the pipes. She took a gritty pleasure in putting on waders over an old bathing suit and climbing under the house, even in October when the wind mocked you for being a one-seasoner. Riley kept her pilly, faded lifeguard suits around for that very purpose. She didn't like to throw them away.

They didn't discuss it with Riley that morning in the apartment, because they'd already had the fight in several parts. The cold water was not acceptable in Riley's condition. Her legs were still swollen, which meant that any exertion could be dangerous. That morning, Alice and her dad just ate their cereal and banged out of the house. Judy was staying home for company and distraction, though Alice doubted the success of either.

At one time, years before, Alice and Riley had made a big hole in the ceiling of their family's life and climbed out of it. Riley had enrolled in NOLS. She had spent an entire month of January in a hole in the snow. Alice had gone to college. Both of them had lived different places and met people. They'd cooked their food and washed their clothes — Riley mostly washing them in puddles in the backcountry, and Alice never separating dark from light.

And now they were both back home. How quickly the hole in the ceiling grew back over their heads without even a scar to let you know it had once been open there.

Healing wasn't always the best thing. Sometimes a hole was better left open. Sometimes it healed too thick and too well and left separate

179

pieces fused and incompetent. And it was harder to reopen after that.

While her father muttered and cursed under the house, Alice did nonexpert things, like sweeping out the house and cleaning the moldering things out of the refrigerator.

When you stood at the open refrigerator, it was difficult not to contemplate the future. If she froze the orange juice, would it last until Memorial Day? What about the sandwich bread?

What about them — her family? Would they last longer in their cryogenic state? Would it mean they could come back as they had been before? With Riley swimming and running as she had always done?

If only she could stash Paul away along with them. But he was warm and lively, she knew. He was going forward into the world, and he'd left her behind.

She packed the deep freezer, the single appliance that would stay on through the cold months. It seemed strange in a way to devote electricity to keeping their stuff frozen, when the air outside would mostly be frozen anyway.

Whenever she thought of deep winter in the house, she felt uneasy. She thought of the cold invading the rooms, the house living at an unlivable temperature. For some reason it made her think of a sinking ship, the cabin slowly filling with seawater.

She heard her father banging and scraping his wrench under the floor. She thought of Riley's small and precise way of doing things. It seemed a shame to have a grow up to get big, clumsy, and easily frustrated.

Alice folded the summer clothes that had been left in the dryer and arranged them in appropriate piles for the time when they would come back and wear them again, though she only half-believed that they would. It was hard to believe in summer in the winter, to remember health in sickness.

Would they really be back here? Would the world keep them in its rotation? It was hard to think of next summer beyond frozen orange juice.

She came upon a skirt she had last worn with Paul. She'd worn it sitting on his lap, feeling the fabric of it bunched up around her middle. She heard the pitiable whimper in her chest as her body disloyally recollected things her mind would not allow. Had that really been her body doing those things with Paul? This very one, right down there? It was hard to imagine. She felt like someone had cut her off at the neck and had sewed her back together badly, without reconnecting the stringy parts that ran back and forth.

Her hands felt cold and damp as she wheeled the bikes into the shed. She was supposed to cover the furniture with old demoted sheets, but she balked. This was normally her mother's job, and she didn't feel like doing it. She didn't like leaving the house looking so spectral.

She sat on the rail of the deck and glanced up at Paul's house. Had he closed it up, now that it was his house? It was hard to picture. Had he come back this autumn? She sort of doubted it.

He was good at putting her behind him. She and her family were always behind him, weren't they?

She picked up a pebble from a planter and chucked it at his house. No matter how good or bad your aim, it was a thing you couldn't miss.

'You done?' her father asked, emerging from under the house. He looked as though he had rolled over three times in the mud. He reminded her of a wallowing sow, but she didn't say so. Her father had his pride, his clinging, middle-aged vanities. She waited patiently while he took a shower and dressed.

'Do you want to go to the beach for a minute?' he asked, locking up the house behind them. It was part of the ritual to say goodbye to the ocean after they said goodbye to the house, but the rituals were tentative this time, partly on ice.

'I'm cold,' she said. 'Let's just go home.'

While they waited for the ferry, hands shoved in their front pockets, she heard two ladies she vaguely recognized talking about real estate. She knew it to be a riveting subject to all who owned a place here or hoped to.

She didn't really mean to listen, but she didn't take pains to walk away, either. In truth, she tuned her ears to a particular name, and for better and worse, she heard it right away.

'You must have heard the Moore house is for sale,' the dark-haired one said. 'Bobby told me there is already a buyer.'

'Really?'

'So he says.'

'You didn't hear the price, did you?'

At the clam bar in the parking lot, Alice's dad

182

bought her two powdered-sugar donuts and a pint of chowder. He took over the eating of the chowder when she left it to get cold.

They stopped the car at the train tracks, and he reached over and held her hand for a minute. He was sorry for her, she knew. He didn't even know what all to be sorry for, but there was some comfort in his care.

★　★　★

She knew about Paul from Riley. There was nothing new in that, but it seemed ironic nonetheless. Paul and Riley had always been the pen pals. It enabled their friendship to circle the calendar in a way that Alice's relationship with him never did. And now Alice had to pretend that her hunger for news about him had no different a cast than before.

'So, where's his new place?' She sat across from Riley at the tiny kitchen table where in the old days the two of them had eaten breakfast every morning until Riley left for NOLS. The strangeness of being back here all together dawned on Alice slowly, some part fantasy and some part nightmare.

'West Eleventh Street. He said he got a garret.'

'I guess he didn't like Brooklyn.' Alice engrossed herself in the clipping of her toenails.

'I guess not.' Riley went back to the hole she was mending in an old pair of her shorts. 'I'm going to go crazy if I can't swim. Dad said the water at the West Side Y is too cold. Do you buy

183

that? He took a candy thermometer with him to check it.'

Alice wasn't sure if the right answer was yes or no. She was genuinely invested in Riley's dilemma, but she couldn't leave the subject of Paul yet. 'Did Paul say how school was going?' It was late, and Alice knew she should be going to bed. If she stayed up talking on this subject, she would not be able to fall asleep for hours.

'He said he's started the graduate program, so I guess he finished that paper.'

Alice chewed on her cheek. She finished with her toenails and started on her fingernails. Had Riley written anything to him about Alice? Had he asked about her? Did he know she hadn't begun law school? If so, did he care anymore? These were awkward questions to ask and all cast in shadow by the bigger question.

Alice pushed the clippings into a white circle on the table, a tiny thatched moon. 'Did you tell him about what's going on with you?'

'What?'

'I mean, did you tell him about your heart?' Alice felt the nervous thud of hers.

Riley looked back down at her shorts. 'Not yet.'

Riley had begun to tell their few extended family members and old family friends about her condition. Still, she tended to understate the seriousness of it, to control the flow of information, and to get annoyed by any noisy or outsized demonstration of concern. Their remaining grandmother in Boca Raton had called with her own doctor's pager number and sent four giant boxes of Florida oranges.

Alice tried to make her voice not sound strangled or psychotic. 'Why not?'

'Because I didn't feel like writing it in a letter or an e-mail.'

'Are you going to tell him in person?'

'Yeah. At some point.'

'Why are you waiting? He is your best friend. Doesn't he need to know?' Alice's frustration came out more than she intended.

Riley gave her a look that sent Alice back on her heels. It was Alice who wanted and needed him to know. How quickly her anger was undermined by her guilt.

'He is my best friend. That's why I get to decide how and when I tell him, Alice.'

Later, lying in bed and not falling asleep, she thought about Paul. Some nights it was impossible not to think about him.

Some nights she felt like she had Riley's heart with all its troubles, beating arrhythmically and inefficiently in her own chest. She felt her blood pooling and catching in places where it shouldn't have been. She wondered whether it was medically possible that she could have suffered the same affliction. Maybe it was contagious. Or perhaps she had a version of it that you brought on yourself.

*　*　*

Alice put on her park-issued coveralls on Saturday morning. She zipped them all the way up in the front, over wool pants, two layers of sweaters, and a parka. She looked like a sausage. She braided her hair high up on her head so it wouldn't get caught in the zipper while she worked. She looked like a sausage trailing its casing from one end. She glanced in the mirror to see if her hair had turned dark yet.

If every mirror gave you a particular version of yourself, the mirror over her old scuffed Victorian dresser provided Alice with her oldest and most familiar one. The glass seemed to contain all of her selves from when she was first tall enough to see herself in it. It used to contain Riley sometimes, too, until Riley was fifteen and volunteered to move out of their shared room and into the tiny room off the kitchen.

Riley's room thereafter was the size of a large closet, supposedly intended for a maid, built at a time when even people who rented cramped, dark apartments had maids. Riley could barely fit her twin bed in it, but she claimed to like it. She couldn't fit her shelves of trophies, so she'd thrown them into a box and left them for the garbage pickup. Alice remembered being horri-fied by that, but Riley didn't seem to care.

Riley seemed to think she was doing Alice a favor by giving her her own room, and there were things Alice had enjoyed about it. At first she'd encrusted the place with terrible rainbow stickers and boy-band posters, later replaced by photo collages, Fire Island memorabilia, and old-fashioned movie posters. But Alice missed sharing with Riley. She looked back longingly on the time when she and Riley had twin beds with matching wildlife bedspreads and talked in the dark before falling asleep.

'You're working today?' her mother asked her as Alice trudged into the kitchen and poured herself a bowl of Rice Krispies. 'I thought you didn't usually mow on weekends.' Her mother uttered the verb 'mow' with a degree of distaste suited to smoking crack or mugging children.

'We're raking. We're in a state of raking emergency.'

Her mother nodded. Alice stared at the cereal box, making a close study of Snap, Crackle, and Pop, hoping to avoid the juncture where her mother wondered aloud in what way Alice's extraordinarily expensive BA in history from a fine college prepared her for a job mowing the Great Lawn in Central Park.

'Will you be back for dinner tonight?'

In principle, Alice did not want to answer. You permitted the first round of incursions and the second soon followed. She didn't want to set intolerable precedents for this new stage of living at home. At the same time, when you were living with your parents and not paying rent, you had to accept these things.

'I don't know yet.'

'Well, I'd like for you to decide, because I'm going to Fairway this morning.'

'Okay, then. No.'

Her mother gave her a sharp look, and Alice knew she had to be careful or the wondering aloud about the BA would start. It was a delicate calibration, being subversive and obnoxious without your mother quite noticing. It was a forgotten art to Alice through most of college,

187

but now that she was living at home again, it all came back.

She'd planned on spending part of her law-school loans on housing, but she'd deferred the loans along with everything else. She wished she was making enough money to pay for a room with her friends, but she wasn't even close. It was a well-documented curse of growing up in New York City: In order to return to your old hometown, you almost invariably had to live in your old home. What you saved in rent you lost in self-respect and personal growth.

November in New York could bring almost any kind of weather, and today it brought clean, cold air. Alice put on her gloves and turned into the park at 96th Street. She walked south along the road. It wasn't the prettiest way, but it was the most direct, and the traffic on the weekend was closed off for the benefit of walkers, runners, and bikers.

She was sorry, in a way, to be called up in uniform on a Saturday. She'd forgotten how packed the park would be on a sunny weekend with people she would potentially know, and how stupid she would feel among them in her coveralls.

She kept her eyes out for Riley. On days when her sister felt well and her ankles and feet weren't watery, the doctors allowed her to walk, and Riley walked for miles, even if it left her exhausted.

Alice looked up at the towers of the fancy buildings along Central Park West. In most parts

of the world, human-made things were surrounded by tall trees. In the case of Central Park
it was reversed, God-made things were surrounded by tall buildings.

Her eyes fell on the back of a man wearing a
green down vest and a brown wool hat.
Alongside him walked a blond woman wearing
pointy shoes. Her arm was tucked in his, and it
made Alice feel mournful. She began to walk
faster. After the reservoir, she could duck into
the interior of the park and mind her loneliness
less.

As she came closer to the couple she felt
agitated, and it dawned on her, slowly and
discordantly, that this man walked like Paul. And
though she rarely saw Paul wearing layers and
walking in winter light, she began to suspect that
the similarity between this man and Paul did not
stop with his walk. She looked at the man's
hand, the one that wasn't involved with the
blond woman's arm, and she knew the hand. She
knew the fingers. Her body, badly attached as it
was, would have whimpered if she hadn't caught
it in time. Her breath shuddered. Her heart
mismanaged its work of beating.

Should she stop or should she try to scoot
around? She couldn't disappear completely
unless she climbed up a small cliff, and that
would be conspicuous. Not only did she not
want the possible Paul and his pointy-toed friend
to see her as a sausage, she did not want to know
for sure that it was him. She wanted to preserve
enough doubt to be able to convince herself,
over days and weeks if necessary, that he was not

Paul and that Paul did not have a girlfriend. There were easily non-Paul people in New York City who had Paul's walk and his hands. A case could be made.

She slowed almost to a stop, cursing them for not getting ahead of her faster. Walking slowly seemed the province of people who were enjoying each other too much. She never walked anywhere slowly with Paul. Either he was yanking her along or she was racing to catch up. So it probably wasn't Paul.

She was feeling good about that until he turned around and he was Paul. She was still trying to think of a way out of it when he stared directly at her face.

Some people who had been your closest friends since you were a baby might have made some pretense of being pleased to see you, but Paul was not. He stopped walking and looked at her as though she had called him by an unpleasant name.

'Alice?'

It was tempting to turn and run in the other direction. 'Hi,' she said.

He walked toward her, unlooping his hand from the woman's arm. 'Why are you wearing that?' he asked.

'Because I'm working here.'

'You're working in the park.'

'Mowing and raking usually,' she said. *Why lie?*

'What about school?'

'I'm not going.'

He looked genuinely surprised by this, but he

190

didn't have the gall to ask why not. He looked discomfited and itchy to her, like his skin didn't fit. In these many weeks his anger had cooled apparently, and now he was cold. His lips were pressed in, the same color as his face. It was hard to believe that it was the same mouth that had kissed her.

'Your family's all right?'

She paused, then nodded. How could he not know the truth? How could she not tell him? She felt angry at him for not knowing, angry at Riley for not telling him. Alice was going to come apart in a minute, and it seemed best to get away before she did.

Paul suddenly remembered his slow-walking companion. 'This is Monique,' he said, somewhat brusquely. He didn't even bother with the second half of the introduction.

'I'm Alice,' Alice said.

'Hey,' said Monique. Her lips were perfectly shiny. Too shiny for kissing, Alice thought. She didn't seem like the kind of person who hung out with park employees very much.

'Tell your folks hi,' Paul said, and turned around again. He was done with her. He was back to his walk, though he kept his arms to himself this time.

She could practically hear Monique commenting on her jumpsuit. She could practically hear Paul's laugh in reply. She could practically see them walking off together to a café, holding hands and celebrating the fact that they never had or would wear a park-issued coverall.

* * *

'Who was that?' Monique asked.

Paul was no longer in a talking mood. He felt stormy and uncomfortable. 'She's an old friend. Well, her sister's really my friend.'

'Quite an outfit,' Monique said lightly.

'Meaning what?' His face was hard, and he didn't have the will to soften it.

'Nothing.' She retreated quickly.

'You meant something,' Paul persisted, knowing he should let it go. He was furious at Alice, why should he still protect her?

'I meant nothing. Seriously. Just drop it,' she said. It had been made clear to her that there would be no scoring points off Alice.

What was it with Alice and her jobs requiring costumes? he wondered. It seemed to him a sign of her perpetual underemployment. And yet it made him ache for the eagerness and completeness with which she approached her life. She had her dignity, but in a broad way. It didn't confine her as it did other people.

He looked at Monique in her dignified and attractive clothes. Angry as he was at Alice, Paul suddenly felt he could only ever want a woman in a dark green zippered jumpsuit.

15

Blame Here and There

'I think this would look good on you,' Alice suggested somewhat hopelessly.

'I think it would look good on Aunt Mildred.'

'Oh, come on,' Alice said, though she put it back quickly.

Riley pulled out a dress of greenish Lycra. 'What about this? It would sort of go with your eyes.'

'Too shiny.' Alice checked the price tag. 'Also, it costs two hundred dollars.'

'All right, then. This is the one.'

Alice couldn't help laughing. It was bright red oversized plaid and about ten inches long from waist to hem. 'That would cover half of my ass.'

'Megan would wear it.'

Alice considered. She would. Megan had been close to them as children, and her parents were some of her parents' best friends. But Megan had hit puberty with a vengeance, and by fourteen she was regarded as the village slut. By the time she was seventeen, Paul was the only boy she hadn't slept with, and Alice and Riley were the only girls she hadn't pissed off. They remained her only friends.

'I wonder what her wedding dress will look like.'

'I wonder, too,' Alice said thoughtfully. 'When you think of it, it's hard to believe Megan's only going to give blow jobs to one man for the rest of her life.'

Riley nodded. 'That's true.'

'I wonder if it will last,' Alice said.

'The marriage?'

'Yeah.'

'It might. People change. Okay, how about this?' Riley pulled out a striking dress made of crinkly wine-colored silk that went in a column from shoulder to foot.

'Nice. But I think it will be too short for me.'

Riley looked almost shy for a moment. 'I was thinking for me.'

Alice tried to be measured. 'Really?'

'Do you like it?'

Alice held it up under her sister's chin. 'I do. I love it. I think you should try it on right now.'

In a state of amazement, Alice followed her sister to the fitting rooms.

When Judy had sent them to Bloomingdale's to get dresses for Megan Cooley's black-tie wedding, Alice hadn't really expected that they would come home with two. Riley had a long history of eschewing dresses. She'd preferred keeping her hair short and dressing like a boy, even wearing boys' bathing suits until she was eight or nine. And ever since, she'd mostly found ways to avoid them. When her friend David from NOLS got married the year before, she'd worn a tux and stood with his groomsmen. Alice laughed when she saw the pictures, but she remembered the look of strain on her mother's face. Her mother was always looking for confirmation that Riley was gay and also for proof that she wasn't.

'You can come in if you want,' Riley said on her way into a fitting room.

Alice felt warmed by that. Riley never let Judy come into the fitting room. She hadn't let Judy dress her since she was old enough to say the word 'no.'

Alice had always been more tractable about being mothered, but then Alice always had the idea that she wanted, someday, to be a mother herself.

Alice perched on the bench. She didn't want to notice the changes in Riley, the shallow way she breathed. She looked away and her own heart began its routine of copying.

Riley wrestled with the dress a little and pulled it over her head. It fell neatly and straight to her feet, leaving only the ends of her toes sticking out.

'Wow,' said Alice. It was rather shocking to see Riley like that, but she didn't want to make a big deal of it.

Riley snuck a few quick glances at herself.

'You look beautiful, you know.'

'Do you think?'

'Yes.'

Riley turned to see herself from behind just like any other girl, and Alice smiled. Riley had the kind of body that girls yearned for and boys didn't notice. She was straight-down and lithe. She had no unsightly parts that stuck out. No dimples, swags, or cottage-cheesy bits. Her hips were narrow like a boy's, and her breasts were small.

When Alice was in the full trauma of middle puberty, growing breasts and hips in every direction, she wished like anything she was Riley. While she got teased and tortured and bra-strap snapped, she wished it even more. Sometimes even now she wished it.

'Let's just buy it,' Alice said.

Riley looked pleased. 'How much is it?'

'Don't even look. You can have the share for my dress, too, and I'll wear one of Mom's.'

'Alice, no.'

'I mean it. Come on.' She took the dress and marched toward the sales counter. 'We'll take it,' she said grandly to the saleslady, and threw down her debit card.

As they walked home, slowly, because she could tell Riley was tired, Alice found herself not dreading the wedding for the first time. Because even though most of her clothes were in storage and she would be wearing a hideous dress of her mother's, she had the idea that unexpected things were not always bad.

⋆　⋆　⋆

'Would you like your receipt?' Alice had developed a special persona for her night job at the Duane Reade on Eleventh Avenue. She wore the blue smock and the name tag that said hi, she was Alice, but she brought only a fraction of herself to work.

'Just toss it,' the large customer said, who

196

probably didn't want a record of his two king-sized Snickers bars and his cherry fruit pie.

It was a shitty job, maybe, but they'd hired her on the spot. She didn't feel like working in an office, nor was she in the mood to wait around for one of the restaurants where she'd left an application to call. This place was out of the way, and it was the kind of job you could quit any minute and not feel too bad about it.

She wore nicer shoes than were comfortable for this much standing. She'd have to remember to pack sneakers in her bag along with her smock. She told Riley and her parents that she was going out with her friends the nights she worked here, so when she left the house, she tried to look like it. She wanted the money more than the social life, but she didn't tell them that. She was their proxy, in a way. They were counting on her to live a life in the world they could pretend was normal.

She had gone out with her friends a few times. 'Why did you defer law school? What are you doing over break? What are you doing next year? Are you going out with anybody? You should meet so-and-so. What's Riley up to?'

When you were her age, just out of college, the future was like oxygen. Without it, there was nothing. She didn't like telling the truth: She was stalled. She was waiting.

She saw a couple of girls in the shampoo aisle she recognized by sight from Fire Island. Not from her town but maybe Saltaire or Fair Harbor.

They wouldn't recognize her, she knew, even

as one of them dumped an armload of hair products at her register. The blue Duane Reade smock had the supernatural power of making you invisible, especially to the kind of girls who majored in art history and got internships at Christie's or *Elle Decor* magazine after college. Alice had grown up with such girls, but she could not mistake herself for one of them.

A big part of Alice had wanted to go to law school so she could go on trying to blend in with girls like these. If you ran out of ways to please and you had no family money, you went to law school. It was a sad version of ambition, to want not to stand out but to fit in. Over time, she could bury the evidence, she thought. Who would know by the time she was in her fifth year at an upstanding law firm that she didn't belong?

She felt like her family clung very thinly to the white-collar, vacation-home world, and that if they messed up at all, they would be cast out for generations to come. She needed to do her part.

So why was she here? Why wasn't she there? Why wasn't she at least in a training program at a bank or a big corporation? She'd earned her degree with distinction, her history department prize. She couldn't held on to her honor. She could have gotten one of those jobs. Why hadn't she?

Because they required commitment. Because she'd have to give herself to them, and she couldn't do that right now. She couldn't look ahead. She needed to stay close to Riley. She just needed the hearts to keep beating and the days to pass.

As much of a pleaser as Alice was, she had her strange bouts of self-negation. She'd learned rebellion from two masters, but the kind she practiced occurred without romance or principle. Mostly, she just undermined herself. It was usually connected to guilt.

She didn't feel mad at Paul for giving her a hard time about law school. She didn't give him credit for her decision not to go, even if he deserved it.

But she did feel mad at him for not knowing how miserable and worried she was, for going about his life and walking with pointy-toed women while Riley was sick. Alice was mad at him for that, even though she hadn't told him and he couldn't know. She could manage only to blame him for the things he didn't deserve.

She got off at 10:30 and walked over to Columbus Avenue and up to a posh gym on 68th Street that stayed open late. She approached the guy at the membership desk.

'Do you think I could take a look at your pool?' she asked.

★ ★ ★

Paul knew why his mother signed the house over to him. He swiveled in his father's old swivel chair and he saw it clearly among the twelve hundred vinyl LPs, the curled and decaying piles of magazines, papers, photographs, and posters.

The sale happened faster than he'd expected. He'd left it to the broker, Barbara Weinstein, a former acquaintance of his mother's, whose kids he'd grown up with on the island.

Barbara had gotten her price for the house right away and presented Paul with a contract of sale within two weeks. Now the buyers, married hedge-fund managers with three little kids, wanted to close by Thanksgiving.

He'd done it in anger. He'd done it with the idea that he never wanted to see the place again. But anger had a way of bending around and biting its owner. Now he found himself further into this house than he had ever been before.

He swiveled around, blurring past the pyramid of empty cardboard boxes he had constructed at one end of the room. He hated how his mother spent her way into and out of commitments, but he would have stooped to almost any hypocrisy to get someone else to do this job.

The more times you had put off a job, the harder it was to do. That could be scientifically proven. He had not only to surmount the number of times he had not done this job, but the much larger number of times his mother had not done it. It was another dubious inheritance.

Maybe he could see if the hedge-fund couple would be willing to take the house furnished. 'Eclectically furnished,' he could say. Including the complete works of Jefferson Airplane and Starship. Enough paraphernalia to start your own head shop.

Maybe he could just start putting things in boxes. Not sorting, just putting. Just put it all away, seal it up, ship it to a storage facility, and the job would be done.

That was the idea that stopped him swiveling

and got him out of his chair. He got the first box.

He glanced at the photograph at the top of a disorderly pile. It was of his father, not long before he died, sitting on the kitchen counter of the old Brooklyn Heights house. Paul looked away. He couldn't start with the pictures.

He picked up the first stack of LPs and laid it down in the box. On the second stack, he couldn't help reading the title of the album: *Their Satanic Majesties Request*. He turned it over to the back, seeing the pale brown dust on the cuffs of his dark shirt. 1967.

Without thinking, he walked to the old turntable and plugged it in. He lifted the plastic top to inspect the condition of the arm and the needle. He blew on the needle. Gingerly, he tipped the album out of its cover. It came out in its paper sleeve, perfectly preserved. His father had always respected his music.

He laid the album on the player and moved the needle over to start it turning. He remembered these UFO lights, but back then he saw them from underneath. He remembered imagining them as a three-dimensional place that you could climb into. He didn't even know he remembered them until now.

He remembered trying to set the needle on the lip of the record when he was young and having the needle slide off again and again, making a terrible noise as it dragged in the gutter. But he really didn't like to put the needle into the safe grooves where the song was already playing. You had to hear it start. You had to place it just right.

He carefully set the needle down, the muscles

in his hands setting off another sizzle of memory. He could see his hand as his father's hand. He could picture his father's hand.

He sat on the floor and listened. He listened all the way to 'She's a Rainbow.' Then he put his head in his arms and lay down in the carpet. He let the misery overtake him. For this house and all the things that had happened here. For the single minute that he'd let himself want to keep it for Alice.

He wished he hadn't let himself have that thought. He knew it was a trick. He knew it at the time, but he'd done it anyway. He'd spent his life girding himself against that very trick, and he'd gone right ahead and fallen for it.

She was cruel, but he was stupid. He blamed her for pulling away, but he blamed himself more. He loved her. He loved her too much. That was the trouble.

A part of him wanted her to call on the phone just so he could tell her off properly. He imagined she would try that emasculating strategy of wanting to be friends again. She'd already ripped him apart; he wasn't going to let her pick through the bits to see which ones she still wanted. He wouldn't give her the opportunity to assuage her guilt by being friends with him. But anyway, he didn't get to tell her off because she didn't call.

When he woke up the next morning, he had an inscribed pattern of shag pile on his face. He saw stuff all around him and the pyramid of boxes minus the one on top.

This project was going to take more than he

had. He knew as he walked to the ferry that he'd just put one more layer of not doing it between him and getting it done.

★ ★ ★

'Okay, so here it is.' Alice opened the door of the health club and ushered Riley inside.

'Here is what?'

'Here is what I wanted to show you.'

'In this health club?'

'Yes.' Alice said. She took out a card and slid it along the sensor so the turnstile let them through.

'You belong to this place?' Riley followed her into the elevator, and Alice pushed the button for the top floor.

'Well. Not exactly. Follow me.' Out of the elevator, Alice led her through a humid locker room and out into a giant glassed-in pavilion. All around were sea-blue tiles and plants growing and climbing from pots. But most extraordinary were the views of the Hudson River in one direction and Central Park in the other. If you walked to the wall and flattened yourself, you could see south all the way to New York Harbor.

'Oh my God.'

'Beautiful, isn't it?'

'I never even knew this was here.'

Alice got down on her knees and dipped her hand into the water. 'Warmest in New York City.'

'Really?'

'Try it. Rich people don't like it cold.'

'It really is warm.' The beginning of a question

203

was forming in Riley's eyes.

Alice pulled out the card and presented in to Riley. 'Ta-da. Your swimming membership.'

'You aren't serious.'

'I couldn't afford the full membership.'

'How did you afford this?'

'My rent is cheap.'

Riley laughed. 'I can't believe you, Al.'

'You need to swim. So here's a way.'

'I can't believe I can swim here.'

'Anytime you like.'

Alice was suddenly worried that Riley looked teary, and it was so uncharacteristic that it scared Alice. But then Riley was fumbling with her shoes, and without ceremony she pointed her hands in the air and dove into the warm water, clothes and all.

Then Alice was the teary one and Riley was bobbing happily in the water and the world spun straight again.

They walked home, thirty blocks up Amsterdam Avenue, with Riley stumbling in Alice's sweater and coat and too-long pants and Alice striding next to her in a double layer of terry robes, swinging a plastic bag of wet clothes beside her.

16

Somebody's Wedding

There was no good reason for Paul to go to Megan Cooley's black-tie wedding. He wore a top and bottom from two different tuxedos and brown shoes. His tie was aquamarine.

There would be easier ways to see Alice. He could have buzzed at her apartment building, for instance, or called her on the phone. But he couldn't have made his point in either of those ways.

'This is Diana,' he said to Mrs. Cooley, presenting his date at the front of the church after giving his congratulations. How particularly happy this particular mother looked to be settling this particular daughter.

He saw and greeted a few other Fire Island families. The Greenblatts and the McDermotts and the Rosenheims. There was something with each of them. A bike he'd stolen, a house he'd snuck into, a toilet he'd clogged, a speaker he'd blown. They forgave him because he was rich and his father was dead.

He casually scanned the assembly, pushing hair out of his eyes. His hair was outgrown and shaggy, and he hadn't gotten it cut since Alice's amateurish job. Grown-out hair put the test to the quality of a cut, and hers was crap. But he didn't move on, did he? As many nights as he had stayed up hating her, he still clung to her. Always hated her, always clung to her, always for the same reason.

Except for the brief interlude when he'd loved her out loud. Did she even remember it? Did she think of it one time for every million times that he did? Alice accused him of amnesia, but she was the one who had it last and best.

They were seated toward the back on the Cooley side of the church. He looked toward the front. Ethan and Judy were their close friends. They would be up near the front. He looked for Alice's hair.

What if she didn't come? If she didn't come, he would have wasted a lot of wasted energy.

He didn't think about his own appearance, but he checked Diana's, who was more beautiful than Monique and less challenging. He completely forgot about there being any bride until everyone was standing up and she was sashaying down the aisle.

Now was the time. Everyone was standing and turning to the back of the church. He craned. He might have been the only person looking in the wrong direction. And there she was. She had Riley on one side and her dad on the other. Or so he assumed. He could see only pieces of them. Judy was sticking halfway into the aisle with her little silver camera. Paul felt Alice's mother mortification on her behalf. And as soon as he recognized this impulse toward sympathy, he snatched it back.

He wanted to think that Diana was more

beautiful than Alice. He really did try. And it was quite possible that she was, to some objective eye. But he couldn't make himself think so, and that annoyed him. How could you will yourself to like one thing more than another? How could you change your tastes? He remembered Judy once saying that when she was a teenager, she discovered that chocolate made her skin break out, so she learned not to like it. It was one of those random things he thought of strangely often.

Riley spotted him and waved. Her smile was enough to change his mood. For a moment, he was a human being again. He waved and smiled a real smile back. He wanted to be her friend Paul, his best self. Not this maggoty, bitter version.

What would Riley think of Diana? She would think he was a faker and a half. If it were five or even three years ago, she would tell him that to his face, but now she wouldn't. That was kind of sad.

Riley had on a dress. The realization hit him slowly. She looked small and boyish but also pretty in her dress. Had he ever seen her in one? Was Riley finally entering the low-down world where the rest of them lived and blundered? He couldn't really picture her there.

Riley poked Alice. Paul saw it happen and held his breath. Riley pointed to Paul. What did Riley know? That meant Alice had to turn around. That meant she had to wave at him. Paul wanted to glower at Alice, but he found himself waving back, flattened, neutralized and disappointed in himself. The point of this was to have some control. He put his arm around Diana. Alice looked at Diana. He didn't care about Immanuel Kant at that moment, or the distinction between appearances and things in themselves. He was glad he had Diana.

★　★　★

Riley stood on the patio outside the reception with the smokers. Through the windows and glass doors you could see the blur of the party. Framed and behind glass, it made more sense to her. The colors and shapes made larger patterns on her eyes. Most of the people were indistinguishable, and their words and gestures blended into a single conversation, a particle-board of interaction.

Mainly, the person who stood out was Paul. It seemed all right not to have told him about her heart until she saw him. And then, suddenly, it didn't. She hadn't imagined she would see him here. It took her by surprise. And now it distressed her. Why hadn't she told him?

What if somebody else told him? She hated that idea. It would make her feel victimized in the way she most despised. The Cooleys knew, and so did a lot of other people. Her parents would assume Paul knew. She was unaccustomed to deception and the husbanding it required. The first lie led to others. Is that how she had gotten here?

Riley had been her best self with Paul. She had spent her happiest times with him. If she could stay the same in Paul's mind, then her real self was preserved, it existed in one place at least. When she was with him, even now, she could feel like the person she'd been before.

And then there was the question of Alice. In the beginning, Riley hadn't meant to push a secret between Alice and Paul, but that's what she had done. Maybe she had meant to. Maybe it was what she'd hoped for. Otherwise, why hadn't she set it right?

Now she and Alice were together, living back home again. Time was moving backward, it seemed, and the future was mostly forgotten. Was that what she had wanted?

She thought of the way Paul had looked at Alice in the church. She had never looked at anyone like that. Or been looked at like that, she suspected. She'd been pursued before, but her few romantic entanglements had been brief and shallow, mostly entered out of curiosity or getting it over with. She had never loved anyone the way Paul loved her sister. Was she jealous? Jealous of Paul? Jealous of her sister? The thought made her cringe. She couldn't really think of Paul like that.

'It's the kibbutz effect,' Catie Mintz, her friend from NOLS, told her once when she'd described her friendship with Paul.

'What does that mean?'

'Kids who grow up on a kibbutz together act like siblings. They almost never fall in love.'

It wasn't the only reason, Riley knew, but maybe it helped explain why Paul always kept Alice at a distance, judged her harshly, ignored her when she most wanted his attention. Because he knew someday he'd want to love her.

Riley could not stand the thought of Alice and Paul commiserating over her. She felt the danger, in her dreams, all around her, of being sealed into the past. She was scared they were on the cusp of a life that wouldn't include her, and, like last summer, they would willfully keep her in ignorance. They were the ones who'd started the secrets.

She saw the turquoise green of Paul's tie through the faceted glass, and then Paul was standing with her.

'Did you take up smoking?' he asked.

'I don't love being inside with that many people. Now it's just as bad out here. I wish the smokers would get lost.'

'I never saw you in a dress.'

'I never saw you with a girlfriend.'

'Well.'

'Well.'

Riley looked at the ground. She had to tell him. She needed to think of the right way to tell him.

'Hey, it's supposed to snow all day tomorrow. If it does, do you want to rent cross-country skis from Paragon in the afternoon? Remember when we skied up Fifth Avenue?'

She laughed. It was the last winter of high school. Paul was home from boarding school for Christmas break. She'd tried to ski off the back of a bus, and she'd almost gotten flattened.

'What do you think?' His face was so much the same, so dear to her.

Her parents would die. Her heart would explode. Alice would kill her if she wasn't already dead. She couldn't tell him.

'I'll come,' she said.

★ ★ ★

Alice sat stiffly in the company of her mixed greens as the commodities trader to her left drank his third vodka and tonic and kicked her shin. It seemed an effort to make small talk, even with her father sitting across the table. She was so plagued by self-consciousness that she couldn't get up and talk to the people she knew.

How could Paul have come here with a woman who looked like that? It was so unkind. It was so distressing that he was here with a beautiful, fashionable woman, and she'd worn her mother's dress with the gold belt and the shoulder pads. She would have looked better in her grass-mowing outfit. Why had she done it? It was that perversity of hers, that self-negating guilt. She deserved everything bad. She deserved to look bad while being so.

'Did you meet Paul's girlfriend?' Rosie Newell asked her, coming around to her side of the table. Alice told herself that Rosie didn't mean to be cruel. Rosie had nursed her own crush on Paul for many years.

'Not yet,' Alice said.

'She's gorgeous, isn't she?'

'Yeah,' Alice agreed sourly. She was happy when Rosie went off to dance with the commodities trader. Let him kick her for a while.

211

Paul danced with his gorgeous girlfriend to a Latin tune. Alice wished he were a bad dancer, but he wasn't. Every person at her table got up to dance, including her parents.

Alice spent some alone time with her salad, chewing greens and wondering which dark bit of leaf would lodge itself between her two front teeth.

Paul danced like a dream. He made loving eyes at Diana. He had moved on. He'd forgotten all of them. He'd left them behind. He was good at that. He could do it for years at a time.

And immediately, as though to negate her, Paul took a break from his gorgeous girlfriend and asked Riley to dance. Alice could see by his face that Paul had no idea anything was wrong. Riley looked happy and well, and Alice felt relieved to participate in the idea, for a few minutes at least, that nothing was wrong.

For the next song, Paul cut in on her dad to dance with Judy. It was sort of corny but the kind of thing Judy adored. Paul dipped her in the middle of the song, and her mother screamed in joyous protest. Okay, so he hadn't forgotten all of them. He'd just forgotten Alice.

Alice saw her father coming toward her. Out of pity, he was going to try to get her to dance with him. But then she'd have to stand up and show her dress in all its 1991 glory. No. She grimaced at him before he could even ask. 'Don't try to make me,' she muttered out of the side of her mouth like she was Clint Eastwood.

Alice felt hungry, but she couldn't make herself eat. She felt poor.

She'd had one thing all her life, and though it had been a burden at times, it had also been her greatest gift. Paul had loved her. It made her special. It was bound up in her identity from the very beginning. Now she'd lost it.

Love was a rose, according to the song, and you weren't supposed to pick it. Well, she'd picked it, and now she had the handful of thorns. Diana had the rose. Rosie had the drunken trader. Alice had the shoulder pads and a gold belt.

★ ★ ★

Paul knew as he went for that sixth (seventh?) glass of wine that he would do something stupid. He drank it down eagerly and proceeded, right on schedule, to abandon the lovely presence of his lovely date. He walked over to the table where Alice sat. 'Want to dance?' he asked her.

She didn't want to. He could see that. 'Nice dress,' he said, almost as a challenge.

She stood up. He knew how she hated to back down. She followed him onto the dance floor.

He touched her remotely, directing her through a swing number with minimal swing. Her cheeks flushed awkwardly and prettily. 'How's it going?' she asked.

'I sold the house,' he told her a little too eagerly. To what extent had he done it just so he could say that to her?

There's no future, Alice. There are no hopes. Our lives overlap no more. It's all the past now, officially. He watched her so intensely for a reaction that it was hard to give these words of his much credibility.

She nodded. 'That's what I heard.'

Arg. She'd heard. What could he do for a fresh wound? 'It's a good feeling to be done with the place finally.'

She nodded.

What could he say? *I'm going to get married. I never loved you. What was your name again?* He was reckless and ashamed of himself at the same time.

How good it would be if she lost her composure. If only she would act like a baby, so maybe he didn't have to. If she would just yell at him or accuse him of something, what a relief that would be! But she didn't, of course. She never did. If she had, he wouldn't be in quite this tangle, would he?

He wanted to take his love back from her so badly. The old techniques didn't work anymore. In fact, they'd never worked. How did you stop loving someone? It was one of the world's more brutal mysteries. The more you tried, the less it worked.

If that dress she was wearing didn't help, then what would?

The song changed to a slow one. He should have let her go, but he drew her close instead. He smelled her and clung to her and hated her and hated himself. Now he had the added curse of knowing her under the dress. He put his hand on her lower back and held her tighter than he should have. He was wretchedly, pitifully hungry for her. Why? What did she have that he needed?

He saw her eyes, shiny and round. She looked over his shoulder, straight past his head, but still he caught the dot in her eye.

He let her go and trod back to his table, aroused, frustrated, and miserable. He wondered about this night, this whole enterprise. Why had he come to this stupid thing? Who, exactly, had he intended to torture?

17

Cryogenics

For a while they thought Riley would have to have surgery to fix the fused leaflets of her mitral valve. That went from being the bad news in the middle of November to a distant hope in the end. The aortic valve was almost equally damaged. They thought they could fix her arrhythmia with a pacer. But even that hope receded as the doctors found more damage, both residual and progressive.

Each time Riley came back from the doctor, she said, 'Seems all right,' and disappeared for a few hours. And each time, late at night, her mom would give Alice the full story, including her fears. She'd line up the new bottles of medicine: beta-blockers, anticoagulants, antibiotics. All for a girl who loathed to swallow a pill.

Sometimes Alice felt that Judy's patient and her sister, Riley, were two separate people. 'Every time they look, they see more damage,' Judy said at the end of the year. 'Surgery on one valve or another isn't going to fix the problem.'

★ ★ ★

They stayed frozen through January but alert and waiting. Riley was going regularly to the transplant center, and because of her age and the progress of her disease, she was near the top of the list. As the doctor explained, when her name came up and a suitable heart became available, it would all transpire in a matter of hours.

Riley was fitted with a beeper clipped to her pants at all times. It could take days or it could take months, her doctor said. And so they waited. While Riley went to and fro, Alice and her parents kept their eyes fixed on the beeper.

Once, in the morning, when Riley left it on the kitchen counter, the three of them stood staring at it as though it would jump off into their hands. 'It's not a heart,' Riley told them jokingly.

Later, after Riley left, Alice sat in the kitchen alone and noticed things she hardly saw anymore, like the spice rack Riley had made in wood shop in middle school. She noticed the terrible pot she'd formed out of clay snakes, glazed, fired, and brought home in third grade, in which Judy still kept the salt. There were the two trailing ivy plants that sat companionably in the window, collecting what little light came in from the square of sky at the top of the air shaft. Alice and Riley had brought the plants home from a spring fair years ago, and Judy had watered and kept them alive all this time. There was love expressed in the places you usually forgot to look.

The following days and weeks crumbled into units of waiting. Her father came home during his breaks at school. Her mother worked more in the apartment and less at the library. She did errands one at a time. Old plans evaporated and future ones were not made. When her parents went out in the evening, they found dumb excuses to call home.

Alice was afraid to think even a day ahead. Like a toddler, she lived in the present and she didn't follow her thoughts around the corner. She went from activity to activity with little thought about the mechanics of forward motion.

We are all going backward, Alice thought.

By late January, Alice recognized that it was not going to be mere days of waiting, and that you couldn't maintain a state of high alert for months. It was not in the human wiring.

'I don't think I want a different heart,' Riley said one time when they were walking in the park. Whenever the temperature broke forty degrees, they walked.

'It'll be your heart once it's in there,' Alice said.

They watched her too carefully. Alice compulsively pictured Riley's laboring heart, imagining the dreaded blood clots and annihilating them. They all asked too many questions about medications and salt intake and fluid retention. Riley was eager to get away from them.

'Where've you been?' Alice asked her casually when Riley came home on a blustery evening in February. Alice didn't like to admit that she'd checked the temperature ten times since lunch.

'I went downtown to see Paul.'

Alice tried not to choke on her saliva. 'I hope you stayed inside.'

Riley gave her a look.

'So, how's he? Did you tell him?' Her voice

came out a little too loudly.

Riley took off her layers. 'He's all right. We had fun,' she said, a little too loudly in return. 'And no, I didn't tell him. I feel fine right now. It's a lot more fun spending time with people who don't know I'm sick.'

'Thanks a lot.'

'Seriously, Al. I know how much you care about me, but you're a pain in the ass.'

★ ★ ★

People left a lot of things behind when they went in the water. Their clothes, their stuff, their makeup, their fixed-up hair, their voices, their hearing, their sight — at least as they normally experienced them. 'People look pretty much the same underwater,' a scuba-diving instructor told Riley once. Some people lost their individuality in the water, but Riley always felt most herself. Water was supposed to symbolize renewal, she knew, but when Riley swam — pared down, alone, and unreachable — she felt a deeper sense of who she already was.

The ocean was the best place, of course. That was what she loved most. It was a feeling of freedom like no other, and yet a feeling of communion with all the other places and creatures the water touched. The ocean was best, but an overheated swimming pool atop a building on West 68th Street would do.

Riley pushed off the wall and made a long underwater slide into a breaststroke. She built the slow rhythm between pull and kick. She'd

219

alternate freestyle and breaststroke for the first half-mile and free and backstroke for the second. She'd promised herself at the outset that she'd stop after a mile. That was what she allowed herself.

The repetitive motion of her limbs was a meditation, the stretch of her muscles a narcotic. She heard her breath and even her heart. She gradually lost the awareness of the few other people in the pool, the activity on the deck, the buzz of the city beyond the glass.

The regular things couldn't follow you here. You could escape the demands of the world. Even the demands you imposed on yourself seemed to recede and reorient underwater. You couldn't hear and you couldn't talk. Your ears were full, but it was quiet.

Lap by lap, Riley slowly increased her pace, and toward the end, fell off again. She resisted the sixty-fourth lap, the end.

The trouble with swimming was that eventually you had to come out. You had to dry off and put all your stuff back on. You had to become more yourself again, or, in her case, less so. The demands were still there, waiting.

★   ★   ★

The message light was blinking madly in the kitchen, and it gave Alice a bad feeling when she came in from the park. Her fingers were frozen crooked when she pushed the button.

'This is Dr. Braden's office at the transplant center. We're trying to reach Riley,' the message began. It went on to give specific and urgent callback instructions. The next message was from the same anxious receptionist, and the third was from Dr. Braden herself. All had come within the last forty minutes.

Alice felt a conditioned panic. She'd planned this panic, even launched it several times before this. With her hag fingers, she dialed Riley's beeper and then her cell phone and got no response. Riley was dead or she was negligent.

Alice waited and worried. These were the two occupations into which she had poured her energy these last several months, but she hadn't gotten any better at them. Practice offered no advantage.

She called again and again and again. The sixth time, Riley answered. 'What is your problem?'

'Did you talk to Dr. Braden?'

'No. Why?' Alice could hear Riley's breathing. 'Check your beeper.'

There was a pause. 'I'll call you back,' Riley said.

They met up later at the apartment. Judy and Ethan were there as well.

Riley had her sock feet on the kitchen table and was pushing herself back in her chair.

'You are sure it's too late,' Judy said. The tendons in her neck stuck out.

'I am sure. Dr. Braden is sure.'

'Someone else got it?' Judy persevered.

'Yes,' Riley said. 'There is a happy heart recipient tonight.'

'But not us,' her mother said.

221

'Not me,' Riley said.

'Honey, why didn't you get the call?' Ethan asked. He clutched the back of an empty chair. 'I don't understand what happened.'

Alice worried that Riley would push herself so far onto the back legs of her chair that she would tip it over and crash to the floor. How ironic it would be for Riley to break her neck after all of this.

'Just explain it to us, please,' Judy said tightly. 'We have these systems in place for a reason.'

Riley banged her chair down onto four legs. 'I was swimming,' she said, her voice uncompromising. 'That's what I was doing.'

⋆ ⋆ ⋆

Riley was emboldened. In the days that followed, she forbade them from talking about the list anymore. They were not to talk about the temperature outside or salt intake or pills or the scale, either. 'I swear to God I'll move out if you do,' Riley threatened. She stopped apprising anybody of her appointments and outlawed her mother from going with her. She gave no updates after she went.

'Stop staring at the beeper,' she snapped at Judy one morning when it lay unclaimed on the coffee table.

Late at night that same week, Alice overheard Riley talking to her father. 'I don't want to become this disease,' she heard her sister saying. 'I feel like it will take me over and there will be nothing left of me.'

* * *

Under the queasy fluorescent lights of the drugstore, Riley didn't recognize her sister for a minute. The context was strange and unpleasant, but it was more Alice's expression. Riley was thrown by the blank inwardness in Alice's face, the absence of warmth and animation that Alice always wore for her. It was a trick to see someone you loved without being seen, particularly rare with Alice.

Riley stood concealed by a tower of antiperspirants, casually perusing a wall of toothbrushes. Alice manned a register. The other three in the row were empty. With nobody to ring up, Alice stared vaguely down the shampoo aisle. A stooped woman appeared, trying to buy a lottery ticket. A man shuffled over, pointing at something hanging behind the counter — batteries maybe.

This place bore no relationship to the outside. It was Riley's nightmare, in a way. No window to look out of. Layers of doors to keep out the air. Not that the air was so fresh on Eleventh Avenue. The light was sticky yellow; the music endlessly recirculated. Nobody looked pretty in a Duane Reade, but she'd never seen her sister look so plain. It was sometimes a hardship having a beautiful sister, but there was no joy in having her look bad.

Riley didn't want to stay, but she couldn't quite leave, either. She could understand Alice working in the park for minimum wage, but she could not understand working here for anything.

Was this where her swimming membership money was coming from?

What are you doing, Alice?

Alice went out in the evenings and told them she was seeing friends. Her parents took an almost perverse comfort from that. Somebody in the family needed to be living a life. What would they think if they saw where Alice really went?

Alice was supposed to be in law school, not selling lottery tickets. They all had roles to play inside their family. Alice was the ivy-leaguer, the white-collar hope. She was falling down on the job.

Riley remembered the day Alice had gotten her letters from the colleges she'd applied to. Riley had lived in Jackson Hole, Wyoming, through that winter. She'd come home for a few weeks in the spring before heading out to Fire Island to open up the house. Her parents had watched Alice open the envelopes with nervous fanfare, cheering to find out she'd gotten accepted to six out of eight places, including Dartmouth, where she'd ended up going. That night, their parents arranged a celebratory dinner at Moon Palace on Broadway. Riley had been happy for Alice. Mostly, anyway. That was her intention. But at the last minute, Riley had skipped out on the dinner, claiming she'd had something else to do. She'd run around the reservoir in Central Park, mile after mile, in the deep dark. She was sorry for that, when she thought of it. She hadn't meant to begrudge Alice her big night.

You couldn't get very mad at Alice. 'I'd be

happy to get into one school,' she'd said. She would have shared her wealth if she could have.

Riley remembered the day three years earlier, also in April, when the letters had come for her. She'd opened the envelopes secretly in her room, just as secretly as she had filled out the applications. When the letters were all thin and the answers were all no, she wanted to be able to say, *I want to go to an instructor's program at NOLS. It's what I wanted all along.* Maybe it was.

'I chose this,' she wanted to be able to say. 'I always chose.'

⋆ ⋆ ⋆

With numb fingers in thick gardening gloves, Alice cleared the beds along the bridle path. It was a new assignment and new scenery, which Alice was grateful for. The old scenery had absorbed her worries over time. In time, this probably would, too.

There wasn't much to do, but there were few people to do it. Everybody loved to work in the park in the spring and summer. By February, the volunteers were mostly gone and the paid force was small. Alice spent a lot of time alone in February, and the air was so cold, her thoughts slowed almost to a standstill. It suited her.

Alice saw a horse clomp by. She had never ridden a horse. She saw people and their dogs. The people looked cold, and the dogs looked happy. She saw a tiny dog carrying a large and ragged teddy bear, and though she did not like tiny dogs, she thought how they looked cute when they carried objects larger than their bodies.

She saw a runner pass with lithe and graceful strides that reminded her of Riley. It was such a familiar stride, but one she hadn't seen in a long time. She pictured Riley running on the beach and running along the boardwalks and running up 97th Street. It was harder to picture her walking. Riley used to run two miles in the time it took Alice to run one.

Suddenly, Alice stood. She shook off the big chunks of cold dirt and walked into the path, her chaotic heart knocking around in her chest. She saw the runner moving ahead quickly on legs made to run, nearing the bend. Alice was still close enough to shout and be heard, and she opened her mouth to shout but she stopped herself. She just watched, a mysterious feeling soaking through her.

If Riley wanted to run, Alice couldn't stop her. All she could do was watch. So she did. She watched and remembered, and it made for a strangely beautiful vision.

★   ★   ★

Riley wasn't feeling well that night. She didn't say so, but all of them could tell, and Alice knew the reason why. Judy wanted to call her doctor, but Riley said no. 'I am not a minor,' Riley said, and finished off the argument that way.

Later Alice went and sat on the bed in Riley's little room. She considered the few things left there from before they first left home: a picture of Alice and Riley holding each other at the top of a hill in Central Park laden with snow, an old photo of Riley and Paul and a giant sagging blue fish on a fishing boat in the Great South Bay. 'I switched to working over by the bridle path today,' Alice said. She looked at Riley, and Riley looked at her, and they both knew what it meant.

Riley's face pinched together, and Alice tried to think of the best way to confront the subject. She wanted to think of a good way to express her distress and also her love. And then she realized there was no good way, because the two things didn't fit together. Her comfort and Riley's comfort were not necessarily the same thing. She began to sense that her aims and Riley's were possibly quite different. Sometimes you had to recognize the split in order to be close.

'I love it over there,' Alice said finally. 'With all the dogs and horses.'

It took a few minutes for Riley to realize that Alice wasn't going to say anything more.

Over the passage of the evening, Riley's face relaxed into an old kind of sweetness. While Alice paged through *The New Yorker* on Riley's twin bed, Riley fell asleep with her ankle crossed over Alice's.

★　★　★

It took Paul a minute to recognize Ethan's face in the lobby of the philosophy building on Mercer Street. His first unchecked impulse was pleasure, and his second was suspicion. 'What are you doing here?' he asked.

'I was hoping to run into you,' Ethan said. He looked much older to Paul. Maybe it was seeing him in the winter. Ethan was a summer man.

'Is this like a stakeout? How long have you been here?'

Ethan looked at his watch. 'Twenty minutes. Riley told me you had a seminar in this building.'

'You could have just called my cell phone,' Paul pointed out, feeling somewhat hypocritical.

'I could have.'

Paul walked out the doors, gathering his coat around him, and Ethan followed.

'What are you studying?' Ethan asked.

'Philosophy.'

Ethan remained patient. He had put up with a lot of rejection, and he was fairly good at it. 'I recognize that. What kind of philosophy?'

Paul turned to look at him while they walked. 'Moral philosophy.'

Ethan nodded.

'And political,' he added in a mumble.

He remembered how Ethan tried to take a role in his education. Ethan was the one who taught him to read in the summer between second and third grade, when his school was threatening to kick him out. Ethan read the entire *Lord of the Rings* trilogy to him and Riley during the very rainy summer after fourth grade. Paul wouldn't say it, but he'd loved that: lying on the couch with his legs pointing one way and Riley's the other, Ethan sitting in the big, brown upholstered chair, making up all the different voices. Ethan could

228

have been an actor, Paul sometimes thought.

They would hear the rain and the wind mixing into the sound of the ocean. Sometimes Alice would curl up with them. Paul could almost feel the way her elbows dug into him when she tucked herself between his body and the back of the couch. He always complained, but he'd loved that, too. Alice would vanish for the scary parts, and Paul would tease her about it.

At the time Paul had thought Ethan loved him, but later he revised that view. It wasn't him Ethan was interested in. That summer after fourth grade was the very happiest one, and yet it ended so badly.

'Are you enjoying it?' Ethan asked.

'Sure.'

'Going for the Ph.D.?'

'That's the plan,' Paul said. Ethan had given up on his American history Ph.D. somewhere in the middle of his dissertation. He once heard Ethan, at the annual bayfront picnic, describing his academic career as ABD, which he later learned meant All but Dissertation. That seemed to fit Ethan: full of intention but useless.

They walked through Washington Square Park, under the triumphal arch. Paul wondered how long Ethan would stay with him. He didn't give much credit to Ethan's resolve.

'Have you seen the girls recently?'

Now Paul began walking more quickly. Did Ethan know something? The thought had not occurred to him, but now that it had, he felt a surge of agitation. 'I saw Riley a week or so ago,' he said casually.

He did not want Ethan to know about him and Alice.

'How did she seem to you?'

Paul hardly heard him. He made a sharp turn onto 8th Street. 'Listen, I've got to be somewhere, and I'm already late. Call me if you need something, okay?'

Paul left Ethan standing on Fifth Avenue and strode hurriedly toward the West Side for no reason at all. He was relieved that Ethan didn't try to follow him.

Only later Paul realized, in his petulance and his narcissism, he'd forgotten to ask Ethan why he had come.

18

The Tear in the Net

In early March, Alice moved to her new assignment: cleaning the Ancient Playground. It was on the East Side at 84th Street just north of the Metropolitan Museum. It was one of the great New York City playgrounds, and Alice remembered it well. When her parents took them to the museum, Riley would get antsy, and her reward was always a visit to this playground at the end.

Alice's job involved scrubbing the bathrooms, which she did not mention to her mother. She knew if she did, the wondering about expensive BAs would arise immediately and deafeningly. She was glad that she had this job in March instead of August. In August it would really start to stink. The whole city stunk in August, which was why the people who could afford it, even barely, went to the beach.

Alice was happy on her third day at the playground, when Riley appeared. Even though it was cold, she felt happy to see her.

'What are you doing here?' Alice asked, but not in a worried way. Riley's face was too animated for bad news.

'I pictured you here and I couldn't resist,' Riley said.

While Alice swept away dead leaves, Riley swung on the pirate rope, shouting things every so often.

The place was nearly empty. Because of the cold, Alice reasoned, and because school was in session.

After Riley tired of the rope swing and climbing to the top of the ziggurat, she came over and sat in the sand while Alice raked it.

'I like all the sand at this playground,' Riley remarked. There wasn't just a sandbox but also big lakes of sand underlying most of the playing structures. Alice remembered that her mother made them take off their shoes and dump them out before they got on the bus to go home.

After a while, Riley started raking, too. Not with an implement but with her fingers. 'Hey, look,' she said, holding up a piece of broken glass.

Alice took it from her and put it in the garbage bag. 'Good thing you found it.'

Riley worked diligently and with deepening satisfaction for each potentially hazardous thing she found and removed.

Around lunchtime, Mrs. Boxer, Alice's superior, showed up. She saw Riley helping with the sand and looked on it with a suspicious face. 'I'm not paying the two of you,' she said.

'That's fine,' Riley said pleasantly.

'We know,' said Alice.

★ ★ ★

The following week, the weather turned. Alice knew it was probably an empty promise, or at least a premature one. But still, her skin seemed to grow a million extra pores, and all of them opened to take in the warmth and tenderness of the air. The sun on her face made her want to cry. She was glad the playground was empty and that Riley didn't show up that day.

She lay back on the sand and felt the thaw in her bones. Her muscles, held so tight these months, turned to water. She wasn't sure she could resume her raking or even get herself home.

Into all those millions of open pores came the sunshine, and other feelings as well. In and out. She was porous.

The air smelled like beach air. The sun smelled like the sun. The bathrooms, a few dozen yards away, smelled like bathrooms. She heard the cars and the buses roaring just beyond her feet, discordant with the sky over her head and the sand under it.

She thought of Paul, and how his back felt sandy when she put her arms around it the first time. She thought of Riley and curling linoleum and egg sandwiches and the foot wash that worked and the shower that didn't. She thought of her losses. She let them out and in and out. She felt languorous.

She felt stupid when Mrs. Boxer cast a shadow over her and asked her what she was doing. She sat up quickly.

'Just lying here for a minute,' Alice said,

wiping her eyes with the front of her hand and her nose on the back of her hand.

★ ★ ★

When she got back to the apartment, she saw Riley reading a book on the couch. 'What are you reading?'

Riley turned the cover to Alice, showing a crimson-haired woman, her bodice full of cleavage, embraced by a long-haired swashbuckler. It made her laugh. '*Anna and the Pirate*,' she read. 'Is it good?'

'Pretty silly,' Riley said. 'Good, though.'

Alice couldn't remember another instance of Riley reading a book of her own accord.

Alice sat at the foot of the couch. She realized she still wore the sunshine on the surface of her skin. 'It's beautiful today. You can feel a little bit of summer.'

Riley nodded. She looked tired. 'I went for a walk earlier.'

Alice sat there cross-legged while Riley put her feet on Alice's lap and read. It was nice. The apartment was quiet for once, no ambulance sirens or noisy trucks on Amsterdam Avenue.

After a while, Riley put her book down and moved over to make more room for Alice. Alice spread out so they pointed opposite directions on the couch, with Riley's sock feet resting on Alice's stomach and Alice's toes up near Riley's chin. It gave her a familiar feeling.

'Can I tell you something?'

'Okay.'

'It's about Dad.'

Alice nodded.

'Remember when he cheated on Mom years ago, and you asked me if I knew who the person was?'

Alice nodded again. Her heart began ticking noticeably.

'I did.'

'Really?'

'Yes.'

'So, who was it?'

'It was Lia.'

Alice heard the word. It went into her ear but not quite into her brain. 'Paul's mom?'

'Yes.'

'Dad had an affair with Lia?' The concept still hovered outside of her brain. She couldn't seem to take it in. 'Paul's mom?'

'Yes.'

'But it couldn't have been her. Dad used to say she was a pain in the ass.'

Riley breathed out slowly. 'You can take my word for it, Al.'

'How do you know?'

Riley tipped her head, thinking. 'Because I saw them.'

Alice perceived Riley's fragility. She didn't want to push her. 'You saw them . . . together?'

'Together as two people can be,' Riley said. She looked solemn, but she held up her book as a demonstration.

'Oh, no.' The name Lia did make it into her brain, but it just sat there, unwilling to dissolve or be absorbed.

'Paul and I both did.' Riley pulled the collar of her shirt up over her chin. 'We were in the bay, trying to catch bait fish with a net. Remember the old mesh net with the green handle?'

Alice nodded. She could picture it perfectly.

'Remember it got a tear in it? Paul had the idea that we could use nail polish to fix it. He said his mom had nail polish, so we went running into their house and upstairs to get it from her bathroom.'

Alice nodded again, slowly. 'You didn't knock, I bet.'

'No.'

'Oh, no.' A part of Alice wanted to know just how lurid. But by the look on Riley's face, she knew not to ask. 'What did Paul do?' She wouldn't ask what her dad or Lia did.

'He grabbed my arm and we ran out of there. I felt sick and dizzy, I remember. We stood in the middle of Main Walk. We didn't know what to do.'

'So what did you do?'

'I walked home. He went somewhere else. I don't know where he went, but he couldn't really go home, could he? We didn't see or talk to each other for three days.'

'I think I remember those days.'

'And on the fourth day, he came over for cereal as usual, and that was the end of it.'

'What do you mean that was the end of it?'

'For us, I mean. We never talked about it again.'

'You never talked about it?'

236

'No.' Riley shrugged. 'Not straight out. We couldn't.'

'God.'

'Dad tried to talk to me about it, but I refused.'

Alice nodded.

'He made me see the school psychologist in the beginning of fifth grade.'

'I remember that.'

'I didn't want to talk to Mom, either. Believe it or not, I never really talked to anybody about it.'

Alice felt stunned and a bit queasy. She wished she didn't have a million pores but only one or perhaps none. She thought to ask why Riley chose to talk about it today, whether you needed a half-working heart in order to do so, but she wasn't sure she wanted to know the answer.

She looked at Riley warily. 'Do you have anything else you need to tell me?'

Riley thought about it and shook her head. 'Do you have anything you need to tell me?'

* * *

Alice had been happy to see Riley at the playground, but visitation had its limits. She was not happy to see her under the fluorescent lights at Duane Reade.

'What is it with you and my places of work?' Alice asked. She was festering and preoccupied, thinking of Lia and her father and all the related things that made the past a less comfortable place to hang around.

'I'm checking up,' Riley said flatly.

'Seriously, what are you doing here?'

'I followed you. I found your uniform, and I knew it wasn't Dad's or Mom's.'

'You're such a sleuth.'

Riley looked around. 'You are making me sad, Al.'

Alice pressed some buttons on her register.

'Why are you here?' Riley demanded. 'What are you doing working here?'

'You sound like Mom.'

'Do you think you are doing this for me?'

Alice shook her head.

'Because if you are, you should stop it.'

Alice looked at her thumbnail.

'You should have a good job. A real job. You can do a lot better than this. You're supposed to be the smart one.'

Alice started crying into the sleeves of her smock. The material was too oily and fake to absorb any of her tears. She couldn't say anything.

Alice thought she'd known what she was doing here, but now she realized she hadn't. She thought she knew the kind of guilt that dogged her, but there were more kinds than that.

She would have given whatever gifts she had to Riley if she could've. And if she couldn't, she would pretend for both of their sakes that she didn't have them.

A woman in her seventies wearing a green Fair Isle sweater approached the counter with a multipack of toothbrushes. 'Are you open?'

'Yes,' said Riley. She went behind the counter and moved crying Alice to the side. She took the package of toothbrushes.

'That's eight ninety-nine,' she said.

'Do you work here?' the woman asked.

'Not usually,' Riley answered. She had a general sense of how to work a register.

The woman handed her a ten and Riley gave her change from the drawer. 'Thank you,' Riley said, giving her a receipt. 'Have a good night.'

Alice was watching her now. She was still crying but also amused.

'I'll get a good job sometime,' Alice said, wiping her nose.

'What are you waiting for?' Riley asked.

Alice shrugged.

★   ★   ★

The subway ride was familiar and long. Riley's excitement had carried her the other times. Her mind hadn't known worry. She'd trusted her heart. Her feet hadn't felt like this then.

Since she'd banned her parents from speaking their worries, it left more time and quiet for her own. She put a hand to her chest, as she'd taken to doing sometimes.

At the entrance to the aquarium, she paid her money and walked through the turnstile. The cashier offered her a map, but she politely refused. Here was a place where she knew her way around. She first passed down into the wide, dark hallway, to the underwater viewing place for the dolphins.

At first she saw no dolphins, and then one. It

was Marny, she thought, though her once thick, shiny skin looked scarred and thin. She was getting older, too. The look of her gave Riley an ache.

For some reason, Riley couldn't conjure the pretense of the habitat. She saw the drain, the mechanics, the pits and stains in the plaster. The water had a dingy, yellowish cast. She couldn't see past all that and believe it was a pocket of the sea.

She walked slowly around the tanks and pavilions. It was a Tuesday morning, and the place was nearly empty except for one unhappy-looking group of schoolkids. They looked like seventh-or eighth-graders, Riley thought. She watched the gulls wheeling, screeching, and bad-tempered, eating popcorn kernels from the asphalt. Besides Riley, they were the only ones who chose to be here.

Riley used to spend her attention on the big creatures with the big faces and big fins, but today the virtuous otters and the swollen-eyed walrus looked tragically pent-up and out of place. Did it make a difference to them if no one wanted to see them? She spent a long time studying the smaller tanks with the multitude of crawling, swimming things, where you could get the feeling of a whole ecosystem. These little creatures kept to themselves; they didn't notice you one way or the other, and they seemed better off for it.

She used to scorn the displays of local marine life. They were always brown. But today she looked more carefully and saw more things. She read the placards.

Her legs felt tired and her head spun a little as she climbed up the steps to the old dolphin stadium. The deck of the pool was still roped off from when they used to do the shows.

A lone worker was scrubbing the sides of the tank with a long-handled sponge mop. She breathed in the salty smells of old herring and dead water, so damp they stuck in your nose. She watched for Marny's familiar gray back, but Marny preferred to stay under.

'What happened to Turk?' Riley called across the pool to the man with the mop.

The man looked up. 'He died last year. We're supposed to be getting a new pair.'

Riley nodded. She shuffled around the deck, wondering what that meant for Marny. She wished Marny would surface for a minute or two, whiz along on her back as she used to do. It would have been such a comfort.

Riley wandered out of the aquarium and onto the incomparable Coney Island beach. She kept her running shoes on but surrendered them to sand. The spring wind crept into her inside her jacket and under her hat. The sand, sea, and sky were three horizontal bands of clear, wide, flat color.

She watched the water with her practiced eyes. She felt a mixture of things for Turk, sad for the loss of him, glad for his release. For Marny, she just felt sad.

★ ★ ★

Paul was surprised that Riley wanted to meet him for coffee. She didn't like coffee, and she never wanted to do anything inside. When she showed up, she looked tired and small.

'What's going on?' he asked.

'Hold on,' she said. She went to the counter and came back with two hot chocolates. She handed one to him, even though he already had a cup of coffee.

It was strange to see her in this environment, walking among strangers, counting out money. It was as though she had been cut-and-pasted into the scene, and sort of jerkily, not using the newest or best technology.

'Is everything all right?' he asked.

'Well. That's what I wanted to talk to you about.'

He felt a growing unease, creeping up from the bottom of his stomach. He put both hands on his thighs, feet on the ground, square to the earth.

'I should have told you months ago, but I didn't feel like it.' She tried to stir the whipped cream into her hot chocolate. 'Alice wanted to tell you, but I wouldn't let her.'

He nodded. 'Okay.' This had the quality of being forced to look at something you knew you did not want to see.

'I don't feel like telling you the whole thing, and I don't feel like answering questions about it.'

He nodded again. The unease was general now, spread all around.

'I've had rheumatic heart disease, probably twice. The first time, I was really young. The second time was last summer, and it was more serious.'

He sipped coffee. Then he sipped hot chocolate.

'There might have been some other underlying problem with my heart. Anyway, it's gotten a lot worse.'

He nodded. Usual expressions of sorrow were not worth much to Riley. She had an impatient look about her.

'So it made a real mess of my heart. That's the thing. I probably need a new one.'

He couldn't hide his surprise anymore. 'A new one.'

'A new heart.'

'What?'

'That's the idea.'

'*What?*'

'Listen, Paul. My family is a wreck. Alice is a wreck. I like you when you're not a wreck, so do me that favor. It would really be helpful.'

He nodded. He was suddenly anxious to hide somewhere where he could be a wreck. But he couldn't do it now.

'Thanks.' He noticed that her face was blotchy and her eyes shone. 'You were always my best friend,' she said. 'You always understood me best.'

He put his hands over his mouth, because he couldn't let her see his expression. 'You're mine, too,' he finally mumbled.

She talked for another minute, something about Coney Island, but he couldn't listen. He looked instead at the little scar that cut through

243

her eyebrow and gulped for a thought that might offer some relief. He would suffocate for the lack of it. He felt like he would die.

The first glimpse of her fragility had always haunted him. Among the most punishing images he had logged in his memory was of ten-year-old Riley, blinking at him in surprise, blood running down her eye and cheek. He had tried to hurt her, yes, but he had never believed he could. She was not a regular human being to him. She could not be hurt. He felt like shouting that at her, like it was her fault. He felt mad at her for it. He couldn't feel sorry for her.

They got up to leave. She said she had somewhere to go. He followed her, dazed and unwilling to go off into the world with this knowledge seeding in his head. He didn't want to let her go and leave him with the opportunity to wreck.

'Are you going to be able to get a new one?' he asked in a voice so tight he hardly recognized it.

'I'm not sure if I want a new one.'

What? What does that mean? What will happen if you don't? He followed her down the street, stinging with questions he knew she didn't want him to ask. She descended a few steps into the subway. 'See you,' she said. She wanted to see his fragility about as much as he wanted to see hers.

'When did it happen?' he asked. His voice was breaking, and he felt ashamed of himself. Then he thought for a minute.

'What?'

'Never mind,' he said to her disappearing back. He realized he already knew.

★ ★ ★

Paul called the apartment later that night. He was relieved when Ethan answered.

'It's Paul,' he said. He was sitting at his desk, picking a piece of red wax that had melted there a long time ago. As many times as he'd moved, he'd managed to hold on to his desk.

'Hi, Paul,' Ethan said, laying a bright tone over the deep weariness of his voice. 'Who'd you like to speak to?'

'You, please.'

Ethan was silent for a few moments. 'That's fine.'

'I wanted to tell you I'm sorry.'

Ethan waited some more. There were many possible things to be sorry for on both sides.

'When you came to see me a couple of weeks ago, I didn't hear you out.'

'You were in a hurry. That's all right,' Ethan said. 'As you said, I should have called.'

'No. I should have given you a chance to talk.'

Ethan let out a breath. 'Well. Consider yourself forgiven.'

Ethan was always too easy on him. He thought if he kept it nice, if he forgave Paul his ills, that Paul would feel too guilty to go on hating him. He thought if he forgave and forgave, he might put Paul in the mood of forgiving himself.

'That is more than I deserve,' Paul said. 'You see, when I saw you, I thought you were coming

245

to offer me something. A Mets game or a concert ticket or something like you used to. I realize now you might have come to ask me for something. If you were, I wish I had given it.'

Ethan seemed to put the phone down for a moment. When he came back, his voice was slightly muffled. 'Thanks, Paul. I appreciate it.'

19

A Stove and a Fire

When the air finally thawed on the first of May, Paul went back to the house on Fire Island. He listened to more than one hundred of the albums over four days. He swiveled in the swivel chair. He sat on the carpet. He thought a lot about Riley.

He carefully packed forty-two of the albums in a box for himself — mostly the ones that stirred his memory like Joni Mitchell, Ian and Sylvia, *Godspell*. He saw the cover of a Joni Mitchell album that showed her naked from the back, and he remembered staring at it as a child. He found an album of dolphin and whale songs that he set aside for Riley. He put the rest away in boxes. He'd sell them on eBay maybe, or find somebody to give them to. He didn't want to keep on going with the things in the Robbie museum.

He threw away seven garbage bags of junk. That was as satisfying as anything. The longer he spent with his father's things, the less remote and the less precious they became. He got better at throwing them away. It seemed analogous to the moment in a relationship when you got comfortable enough in another person's presence that you could waste time together. It seemed a shame to get to this point with his father's things and not with his actual father, but so it was. He had lost his father. He'd already derived all possible bitterness from that.

That was the thing that kept surprising him. He imagined that any proximity, any light or air shed on this central tragedy, would nourish it. Instead, the bitterness was like botulism. It required a dark and anaerobic environment to grow.

He put the *Hair* soundtrack on the turntable. He remembered his mother belting along to 'Let the Sunshine In.' It was so happy and depressing at the same time, he had to sit down to laugh. *Let ze sunshine een.*

How could a person have changed so much? This house had once been chaotic and dirty, with music blasting and various friends coming and going. A lot of drugs, no doubt. They had a Ping-Pong table instead of a dining room table. Sometimes they ate at the Ping-Pong table. Now there was slip-varnished mahogany, three tiers of china, built-in drawers full of linen and real silver. When he pictured his mother's old hair, he couldn't quite picture it on her present head. It was sort of disembodied. It stood for lost time.

His father belonged to that time and got lost with it. Some people, like Lia, were good at changing. Other people, like his father, were not.

Paul had a feeling for the old days, even though he was born too late. Part of it came from Ethan telling him stories, back when he used to listen to Ethan.

Paul looked through and saved nearly all of

the photographs. The early ones were campus rallies and antiwar protests. His father always seemed to have his shirt off, his hair to his belly button, and to be hanging from a signpost or roaring into the camera. There were two newspaper clippings from when he went to jail, and a mug shot to underscore the point. He was as proud as a graduate in that picture. There were no actual graduation pictures. He'd gotten kicked out of school well before then.

Robbie had lived in D.C. for a while. He'd worked on George McGovern's presidential campaign, the first of many spectacular losses. He'd lived in his car for three cold months, according to legend, and had gotten arrested while lounging on his hood doing bong hits. There was a picture of him wearing a sandwich board in front of the White House.

Like a Beatle, Robbie had gone to India to learn about more drugs to take and brought home a few trippy, experimental pictures to remember it by. His actual memory was probably blown sky-high at that point.

He'd met Lia at a music festival in Georgia in the late seventies. He'd bought the famous sandals from a craftsperson in Virginia on the way home. They'd lived together in the East Village for a while. Lia was unabashedly pregnant and wild-haired in their one wedding picture. The officiator was barefoot, and Paul's grandparents were not in evidence.

The seventies were over by that point. Even the hangover was ending. There were a few pictures of a small Paul after 1982, but the exuberance of Robbie's drawings, drug-addled poetry, and song lyrics had stopped. There were no more political pamphlets or clippings from lefty newspapers. From what Paul could tell, his father had bought almost no music after that. Maybe a jazz album or two.

Paul wasn't sure of the timing, but he knew his father turned to God for a time. He'd rediscovered his *Godspell* album during Paul's early childhood. Paul didn't realize how many of the songs he knew until he put it on. It made him sad, especially the sweet-voiced Jesus actor begging God to save the people. Sad, in part, because it didn't seem like God had helped Robbie so much.

He couldn't say why exactly, but Paul had the sense that Lia had been impatient with that phase.

His father's hair was short in the few pictures that remained. He looked thin and confused, sort of squinting in most of them. There was one nice one with Paul on his shoulders at the Central Park Zoo. Posed, Paul guessed, but it was still nice.

They'd gotten this house at the beach around then. Robbie had known a couple of *Village Voice* commie types who'd gotten a place near the bay, and Lia picked the big house with the views. Paul found a picture of himself and Riley with Robbie, and even one with the three of them proudly holding the tiny, squealing Alice. Sometimes he forgot that his father's life had overlapped with Alice's, but of course it had.

His parents had gotten the house in Brooklyn

Heights a couple of years after. Lia had picked that one for the views, too. She'd had all the furniture specially upholstered in coordinated fabrics and made a big deal about getting a gourmet stove. Paul had thought that had happened after his father's death, but he studied the picture of his father in the kitchen and there was the stove.

Ethan said his dad had mostly kicked the drug habit before he died. He said it often happened like that.

'Robbie really loved the counterculture,' Ethan had told him and Riley one night after a few too many beers. 'It's hard for you kids to understand because it's all different now. People used to talk about the war, and music and politics. Now they talk about stocks and real estate.'

When Paul thought of that, when he looked around even as far as this house and this town, he felt for people like his dad and like Riley, who weren't good at changing. Was it admiration he felt for them for staying true, or was it pity for getting left behind?

He was glad in a way that his dad hadn't stuck around to see what had become of his wife, this place, the world.

★   ★   ★

Though it was still early in May, the weather was warm and good. Riley wanted to go — in fact, she insisted on going — and the majority of Alice wanted to go, too. The minority of Alice was afraid of the reason Riley wanted to go. The minority did not want Riley to get the chance to say goodbye to anything.

On the ferry, they sat on the upper deck. Alice found herself making prints in her memory.

'Spring comes so much later here,' Riley observed as they came into the dock. The tree branches were fuzzy with yellow-green buds, not yet paper leaves. As soon as they disembarked, Alice went for the wagon. She put the bags onto it, and was relieved when Riley didn't try to do it, too. 'I'm saving my strength,' Riley mentioned primly. Alice laughed, but she didn't ask Riley what she was saving it for.

Alice figured they'd make do without water for the day. They could pee in the bushes or in the Village Hall if it was open. But an hour after they had arrived, she found herself under the house in Riley's waders with a wrench in her hand, staring up at a web of pipes. Riley shouted instructions, and Alice tried to follow them. She didn't want to learn this skill. She felt superstitious about it, but Riley gave her no choice. *Don't think you are off the hook*, she felt like saying to Riley.

After, when Alice flushed the toilet and it worked, she felt quite proud. She flushed it again.

They walked on the beach. Riley gave the finger to each of the SUVs that passed. 'It's not a highway,' she shouted after them and cursed. It was one of the troubles of the off-season.

By Fair Harbor, Alice heard Riley's breaths getting shallow. There was a moist sound in her lungs, and that made Alice nervous. 'I'm hungry,' Alice declared. 'I'm starving. We have to go back.'

At home, Alice opened the freezer to begin the annual defrosting. She realized the electricity must have gone off at some point. She pulled out the orange juice. It was already melted.

'So, guess what?' Riley said, appearing in the kitchen when Alice was cooking sauce for spaghetti. 'There's a light on in Paul's house.'

'Really? Did the new family move in already?'

'I don't think it could be them. Paul told me he still hadn't closed on the house. He keeps putting it off. He said he had to finish cleaning it out.'

'Do you think it could be Paul?' Alice felt nervous and slightly sick to her stomach when she pictured him. *We ruined everything*, she felt like saying to Riley. *You were right all along.*

'Either that or he left a light on whenever he was out last.'

'He probably left a light on.'

'We'll know in a minute,' Riley said.

'We will?'

'Yeah. Because you are cooking.'

Sure enough, a knock came on the kitchen door and it swung open just as they were sitting down with a lit candle and a large bowl of spaghetti between them. It was so familiar a sight, and also so strange. 'I didn't know you would be here,' Paul said.

He looked calm in some way, Alice thought. He looked different than he had the last two times she had seen him.

Riley slapped another place setting on the

table before Paul made it to the chair. 'Are you sure you have enough?' he asked.

'Don't be polite, Paul. You'll confuse us.'

He laughed. He did look polite. Polite and tentative and careful and rather grown up, Alice observed.

Alice felt herself shutting down. She couldn't think all the things there were to think. She'd spent the last months overprocessing a very small number of things. Worrying, fretting, considering, wishing, dreading on the basis of little stimuli. She'd gotten accustomed to a low volume. Now it was all in front of her, and her circuits immediately sizzled and failed.

She couldn't open her mouth, because if she did, she would somehow give everything away. She would give away that Riley was sick. She would give away that she'd made love to Paul repeatedly and wantonly, and that their old friendship was ruined. She couldn't look at him. She couldn't look at Riley. She couldn't even look at her own hands. She looked at her fork. She could barely keep track of all the things she shouldn't say. She hated secrets. Hers and everyone's.

Yet, when she looked up from her fork and her misery, she noticed that Riley and Paul were laughing about something. They were both wolfing down noodles, while she couldn't touch hers. Why was she the only miserable one? It was not fair now, and it never was. She could never keep up with them. She was always left out. As soon as she caught on to the game, they moved to the next one.

'Let's play poker,' Riley suggested after dinner. When they were teenagers, they'd played poker almost every summer night. The other kids were taking Ecstasy, getting drunk, and having sex with each other, and they were playing Red Dog, Night Baseball, and Five-Card Stud. Riley was an ace at poker, and Alice stunk. Alice suspected they had taught her imperfectly so she would lose her money to them.

'I'll do the dishes,' Alice offered.

'You have to play,' Paul said.

Alice looked at him. She tilted her head. As far as she knew, these were the first words he had addressed directly to her all evening. 'Why?' she said. Her voice was airy and strange, she knew.

'Because you have to,' he said.

'Because you want to take my money,' she guessed.

'Because two is not enough to play.'

'Maybe it is,' she said.

She ended up going along with them, of course. Paul and Riley made a fire in the fireplace, and Alice finished cleaning up. Afterward, Paul laid out the cards. Alice sat cross-legged on the couch and burned two times in Red Dog. Riley took the pot, quite pleased with herself as usual.

As terrible as it all was, as ruined, sick, tortured, betrayed, and hopeless, Alice looked at the faces of her sister and Paul. The wind blew outside the windows, the ocean sucked and crashed, and Alice handed over her money. She couldn't help thinking how strangely comfortable it felt to be with them, how in spite of the

255

ravages under the skin, so little on the surface had changed.

★ ★ ★

Riley went up to bed and Alice walked Paul to the door, a formality they had never bothered with before. They could barely look at each other as they said goodbye, their bodies remained yards apart. He had a thousand things he wanted to tell her, but they were so jammed up that not one of them came out. What could he say to Alice? Which words could express the things he felt? He ached for her. He was sorry for her. He understood her finally. His anger was gone, his feeling of shame its only residue.

Over the years, he had undermined her so relentlessly. He had purposely hammered away at her security, her identity, her faith. And all this, perversely, in the name of love. He'd undermined her ambitions, her love life, all of her possibilities. He'd acknowledged this before but conceptually. Now he felt crushed by it. How could he have done that to her?

He was so accustomed to resenting her security, her family, how much and easily she was loved, how difficult those same things were for him. And God knew he made it harder. She had everything he didn't have, including his love. He thought her so effortlessly powerful in relation to him that nothing he could do or say would ever take her down. But what was she left with now? In a sick way, he'd gotten what he tried for. So often you wanted to want things but you did not want to get them. You wanted the deficiency but not the cure.

At the end of last summer, he had not been able to come up with a reason for her to vanish like she did. In large part, that was because he was an asshole. He was forever focused on his own troubles, which made him unable to see anyone else's. It disgusted him about himself, but it was better to know. He thought of his petty attempts to make Alice jealous and felt like an idiot. He had easily imagined all manner of cruelty, coldness, and betrayal, but never that her withdrawal had nothing to do with him.

He had no faith. That was a magnificent failure, bigger perhaps than all his others. The author, perhaps, of all the others. He was luxurious in doubt and incapable of faith. Alice had faith.

I understand now, he wanted to say to Alice. *I love her, too. I feel the way you do. I would have done the same thing.*

What he and Alice had done together constituted a betrayal of Riley. Right or wrong, that was true. He'd tried to ignore that at the time, but he saw it clearly now. They had tried to elude her, to slip away from her with no explanation. It might have been justifiable in the regular world, according to the regular rules, but the three of them had agreed to live by different rules. You had to acknowledge them at least. You couldn't just forget them. No kind of love or amount of love warranted it.

But what were he and Alice supposed to do? What was the alternative? Could they have stayed how they were for the rest of their lives? It seemed impossible.

He could have remained in California. That was an option. He could have lived in California forever and built a different kind of life. When he went back to Fire Island last summer, he told himself he could just swing through, say hi, and be gone. But on a deeper level, he knew that by coming back he had chosen Riley and Alice, past and future. The trouble was that the two did not coexist.

Oh, Riley. He thought of her eagerly looking over her cards earlier that night, winning hand after hand. Her singleness of mind, her peculiar innocence was unchanged, even in spite of everything. *We can't take you with us, and we can't leave you.* He realized this was true before they knew there was anything wrong with her heart.

★ ★ ★

Alice was trying to turn down her noisy, irritating brain and get some sleep when Riley appeared in her doorway. 'I'm freezing,' she said. She looked a little bluish, and that made Alice worry.

Alice pulled her covers to the side. 'Climb in,' she said.

Riley and Paul were such a pair. They were always pushing her around and taking her stuff and then trying to find warmth in her bed.

'We shouldn't have stayed tonight,' Alice said in a regrettably motherish tone.

'Yes, we should've.'

'It's cold, I mean.'

'Not in here.'

'Oh, fine.' Alice let Riley stick her ice-cube toes against Alice's warm calves. She balled up Riley's cold fingers and put them in the crook of her arm. She tried to be mad, but she cherished the closeness. She couldn't help it. She printed some more pictures.

'Hey, Al.'

'Yes.'

'I told Paul.'

'You told Paul what?' Alice wriggled closer to the wall to give Riley more room.

'About my heart.'

'You did?' Alice's circuits fizzled once again and shut down entirely.

'Yes.'

'Tonight?'

'No. Almost a month ago.'

★　★　★

Alice figured she would never fall asleep. She was too angry, confused, and tired to fall asleep. Paul knew about Riley. He'd known for a month. Why hadn't Riley told Alice that right away?

Why is it your business? Alice had to ask herself. *What right have you to know?*

Alice would never sleep again. But when she opened her eyes the next morning, the sun was blasting so fully into her window that she found herself sweating in her bed. She pulled on a pair of jeans and checked the clock. It was almost eleven and Riley was gone.

She was dull-headed and hungry. She wished she could get an egg sandwich, but the store wouldn't open until Memorial Day. She made stale oatmeal and spooned it in, staring at nothing. She wondered how long she could go without focusing her eyes.

She took a book and a towel to the beach. The sun was powerful, and though she'd been longing for it for months, it was almost too much.

The surf was spirited, and the water a crisp and pretty blue. It wasn't a wimpy beach, and yet the effect of it was pleasingly calm.

She saw a dark head a long way out. She realized there was a second head not far behind. They bobbed like seals, stopping to look around before they continued on toward the lighthouse. Alice watched them for a long time with a sense of longing but also a sense of relief. She didn't want to be all the way out there.

It occurred to her that she hadn't seen Riley since she'd gotten out of bed, nor had she seen Paul. They were probably together, she thought. They were probably fishing or finding a boat to take out. Alice wondered, how honest had Riley been about her heart?

Paul knew something, at least. Riley had told him, but what had she said? Alice wondered if she could look Paul in the eye and talk to him now. Could they repair any of their friendship? Would he understand? Or was it too late?

The swimming faces came closer to shore, and Alice kept watching them. She had an uneasy feeling that blossomed into a suspicion and then a worry. She stood and began to walk. She picked up her pace, almost jogging. The lighthouse was half a mile away, but the atmosphere was so clean, it looked as if it was right in front of her. There was the thud of her querulous heart.

What are you doing? she thought. *Why?*

She couldn't see the swimmers' faces, but as she hurried along, she felt certain she knew whose they were.

Alice walked slowly back to her towel and sat down on it. What could Alice do? What could she say? It wasn't her heart. Not officially, anyway.

★ ★ ★

Paul appeared in Alice's kitchen door late that afternoon, laden with bags and boxes. He was clearing out, he said. It was finally goodbye to the big house.

Riley had come home exhilarated from her swim two hours before but so tired she could barely move. She'd dragged herself up the stairs and immediately fallen asleep. Alice faced Paul alone and with extreme awkwardness.

'I've got to catch the ferry,' he said into their clumsy silence.

'Okay,' she said. The wound-up and reckless look he'd worn at Megan Cooley's wedding was gone. His dark eyes were uncertain. He looked either older or younger, but she wasn't sure which.

'All right.'

'Well. Bye.'

He put his things down, and to her astonishment, he came toward her, stiff as a zombie, and put his two arms around her. Together they shared the most excruciatingly inept hug that ever was hugged. Alice thought, fleetingly, of the graceful way their bodies had fit together once.

'I'm sorry, Alice.'

Everything was different now, but his body still communicated with hers. He meant to say, she knew, that he did understand.

20

I Loved You First

The day before the start of the Memorial Day weekend, Paul received a check for exactly three million dollars, representing the sale price of the beach house. On the same day, he received a check for two hundred and seventy-one dollars, representing the sale price of his father's record collection. His father had prized the second thing so much more than the first.

Without quite deciding what he was doing, Paul stuck both checks in his wallet and put his wallet in his back pocket. He put on his shoes and walked north. When he got to 27th Street, he walked east, nearly to the river. He walked into Bellevue Hospital through the front doors. In the course of twenty-odd blocks, he had stopped being angry at the money in his pocket and started to like it.

'Can I talk to somebody in the business office?' he asked. In the business office, he explained his intentions to a fairly patient woman behind a desk. She, in turn, sent him to a woman in the administrative office in the Substance Abuse Division. When he presented her with the two checks and tried to sign them over, she got nervous.

'Are you serious?' she asked when she saw the

amount, breaking her professional demeanor for a moment. She was a middle-aged woman with an open face and a lovely West Indian accent.

'Yes. My father died here. Can you accept it for me?'

She considered. She looked at him, from his scuffed shoes to his poorly groomed hair. She was trying to make sense of him. 'Well. I can't see why not. You leave me your telephone number in case we have a problem, will you?'

'Of course,' he said. He gratefully accepted her business card when she gave it to him.

She squinted, studying the checks for another moment. 'You are sure this is what you want to do?'

'I am sure . . . ' He checked the name on her card. 'Jasmine.' *I've thought about it a lot*, he was going to say, but that would be a lie. His shoes brought him here, and they tended to be more trustworthy than the rest of him.

'These are not going to bounce?' she asked. She waited a few beats to smile at him, and when she did, he was quick to smile back.

'I hope not.'

She was not overimpressed by his money, he perceived. She remained somewhat suspicious of him, and he liked her better for it. 'Do you want to talk to the divisional director?' she asked. 'I think you might qualify for an audience.'

'No, thanks. I am happy to meet with you.' He felt himself in the presence of a real mother. He always had his sensors out for them.

'You're a good man, Mr . . . '

'Paul. I'm Paul.'

She reached out and shook his hand. 'You're a good man, Paul.'

'Will you see it goes to the people who need it? You'll know better than I do who they are.'

'I will certainly do that.' She smiled again. 'If your checks clear.'

When he left, he walked along the East River and saw the exultant sun sending its red and orange beams down the perpendicular streets. He suddenly had an idea that made him feel happier than he had in a long time.

He had lots more money, and his grand-parents had more than that. He would find out about heart transplants. He would figure out who was doing the best research. He would start working on it tonight. He couldn't buy Riley a new heart, but he would give everything he had if it would help her.

He walked fast, bouncing along, the way Riley used to walk. Maybe he was finally getting somewhere.

* * *

In early June, Alice lay on the couch across from Riley in the living room of their apartment on West 98th Street. She noticed that Riley hadn't gone out at all that day. She'd read one of her novels and slept and eaten little. Alice shared a worried glance with her mother in the kitchen, but they didn't say anything.

'I had an idea today,' Alice told her.

Riley rested her book on her chest. 'What's that?'

'I think I might have an idea for what I want to do.'

Riley propped herself up a little better. 'So tell me.'

Alice had talked Riley into letting her paint Riley's toenails a pretty shell color, and now Alice could see it through the hole in Riley's sock.

'I walk by this building downtown sometimes. Do you know the NYU School of Social Work on Washington Square? A few weeks ago I went in and walked around. This morning I passed it again, and I decided to go in and get an application. I started filling it out this afternoon.'

'Really?'

'Yes. I'm meeting with somebody in the admissions office next week. I was thinking I should look into it at least. Maybe I could work with kids and teenagers. I could do counseling. As you've pointed out, I seem to be good at worrying about people.'

Riley looked at her thoughtfully. 'You are good at taking care of people, Al. You always were.'

'Half the time I think I'm trying to give people things they don't want,' Alice said.

'They do want it, Al. We all do. You are generous enough to let us act like we don't.'

Alice was struck by Riley's perception, one she'd never even thought of. *That is what children want*, Alice thought, *from their mothers*.

'Anyway, the money's a lot worse than being a lawyer, but I think I'd like it better.'

Riley nodded. She hugged Alice's feet. 'I think you would, too.'

'Even if I could get in, I probably couldn't start until January at the earliest, but I guess it's worth trying.'

'I know you'll get in,' Riley said.

'The trouble, though,' Alice said, 'is that I'm afraid I'd have to give up my job at Duane Reade.'

Riley laughed, and Alice had the feeling it took an effort. 'Everything good requires sacrifices.'

★ ★ ★

Riley wanted to walk on the second Saturday in June, and though she looked fragile, Alice didn't want to say no. It was an extraordinary morning in the park, and Alice was grateful to be there in ordinary civilian clothes. It was a day, in fact, for the beach. Alice and her parents kept thinking Riley would want to go to Fire Island, but she didn't say anything about it.

They strayed through Strawberry Fields and spent a moment standing together in the circle of tiles on top of the black and white fragments that spelled 'Imagine.'

From a cart by the road, Riley bought them bomb pops that turned their lips purple.

'Alice, how come you don't have a boyfriend?' Riley asked as they walked downhill toward the road.

'What?' They stopped at the terrace overlooking Bethesda Fountain and the lake just beyond it.

'You are beautiful. You could easily get one if you wanted.'

Alice tried not to look as astonished as she felt. She smiled with her purple teeth. 'Riley, what are you talking about? Why don't *you* have a boyfriend?'

Alice was trying to be light, but Riley looked at her a little more seriously than she liked. 'I don't think I have the heart for it,' she said.

Riley could usually be counted on to participate in any version of joking around, but today her mood was different. This answer made Alice sad. 'So then maybe I don't, either.'

'I think you do,' Riley said. She leaned her weight on the railing.

'Oh, do you.'

'Is it because of Paul?'

Alice kept her thoughts ahead of her, not letting them stray to the sides or behind. It took a while to get some words out, even obvious ones. 'What do you mean?'

'I saw you together last summer.'

For one frantic moment, Alice thought to try to play innocent or at least stupid, but it seemed wrong. She thought to try to figure out what Riley saw, to know the extent of the damage before she confessed to the whole thing, but the mood between them was too honest for those kinds of tricks. That was for people on opposite sides of the truth, and Alice knew they were not. 'I'm sorry for that,' Alice finally said.

'Why sorry?' Riley asked.

'I am sorry that it happened. I'm sorry for everything. I wish I had told you instead of you finding out in that way.'

Riley tossed her Popsicle stick into the

garbage. 'You don't have to tell me everything,' she said.

'But I should have told you that.' A brown muttish dog stopped to sniff Alice's ankle. Alice absently patted it around its ears and Riley did, too.

'You thought I'd be hurt,' Riley said.

Alice turned and looked at her sister's face. There was so much willingness there, it was hopeless to try to stay away. 'Were you?'

Riley set her elbows on the ledge and rested her chin in her hand. She didn't have an answer ready. Alice respected the fact that Riley trusted her enough to think it through in her presence. Riley trusted her, even after what she'd done.

'I was, maybe, but it was more that I was scared.'

Alice nodded. She wondered if she'd ever heard Riley say she was scared of anything before. 'What were you scared of?'

Riley chewed the inside of her cheek. She put her chin in her other hand. 'I was scared that I'd lose the two of you. That you'd move on together without me.'

Alice nodded again. She touched a piece of Riley's dark hair, grown all the way down to her shoulder. 'That's what I was scared of too. That's what I am sorry for.'

★ ★ ★

Honesty was a tough customer. That's what Alice decided as she sat down on her bed that night with her knitting needles and her bag of

269

yarn. She had started a new scarf for Riley, but she couldn't say so, because Riley would think Alice was fussing over her and get mad. Once you started allowing yourself some honesty, it couldn't easily be contained or limited to one part of your life. It was like poison ivy or a bossy houseguest. Once it was there, you couldn't tell it what to do. You had to really fight it to keep it from taking over.

Honesty was requiring Alice to love Riley in a way that felt perilous, considering how tentative Riley's place on the earth was.

'Sometimes, I try to feel mad at her,' her mother had confessed to Alice a few weeks before. 'I think of the things she does that drive me crazy. But I know that's just to make it easier on me.'

Alice had thought about that so many times since. It was tempting to maintain the wall with Riley. Alice thought of reasons not to love her. Because the sweeter their closeness, the deeper the misery waiting for her just beyond the light.

There was another spot where the honesty had settled in and begun making its demands. When she was being honest with herself, she couldn't maintain the feeling of distance from Paul. Though she didn't see or speak to him in the weeks after Fire Island, his presence had made its way back. He was sharing her thoughts again. She was missing him.

You could feel things or you could find a way to shut down. But once you were feeling things, you couldn't decide exactly what to feel. That was the trouble with letting them in at all. They made such a mess of the place.

★ ★ ★

'Is this yours?' Alice asked, holding up the old hardbacked copy of *Huckleberry Finn*. She'd come home from working in the conservatory gardens and found Riley on the living room sofa under a blanket, even though the apartment felt warm.

'It's Paul's. He's been reading it to me. He came over and read a few chapters today.'

As Alice sat down with her knitting, she felt the itch again, the missing. 'I love this book,' she said. She sat where she imagined he'd sat. She imagined she could feel the warmth he'd left on the couch. She took her shoes and socks off and lay back on the couch across from Riley in their usual way.

'It was nice. We talked about his father. He had all these old pictures he wanted to show me.'

'Did he really?'

'Yes.'

'He doesn't usually talk about his father.'

'He never did before this. He wanted me to tell him everything I could remember.'

Alice could imagine the warmth Paul left on the couch, but she could not imagine this. 'And you did?'

'I was happy to try,' Riley said. She poked her finger through a gap in the blanket weave. 'Also, he wanted to know how you were.'

'He did? What did you say?' Alice was past

271

pretending it didn't matter.

'I said you were fine but that I thought you should have a boyfriend.'

Tense as she was, Alice heard herself let out a laugh. 'You did not.'

'I did so.'

'And what did he say?'

'He was pretty honest. He said he would rather you didn't.'

Alice felt her eyebrows shoot up so high that they might have disappeared into her hair. 'He said that?'

Riley was quiet for a minute. She gathered her blanket all around her. 'Paul always loved you, Alice. He knows I know that. I know he loves me, too. But it's different.'

Alice opened her mouth, but nothing came out at first. 'He loved me once. But I think that part is over,' she said slowly.

'No, it's not. It hasn't even begun.' Riley took Alice's bare foot in her hand and squeezed it. 'I told him, though, that he better be good to you. When you came along, I said I'd share you, but I told him to remember that you're my sister. I loved you first.'

21

Things Taken and Returned

When Alice came home from her late shift at Duane Reade, she reached into her bag for her key to open the door and saw that the door was already open. She dropped her key and closed her eyes. She didn't need to push into the apartment to know what had happened.

★　★　★

Alice arrived at Columbia Presbyterian hospital just before midnight of the last day. She had her hopes, she let them hang around, but she knew.

Her parents were waiting for her in the lobby. Her hopes began to float off, seeking better odds elsewhere. Both of her parents held her.

'It was too late by the time they got her here,' her mother said.

Alice nodded into her father's shoulder.

'It was a blood clot, they think,' her mother said. 'They'll know more soon.'

What did it matter? It was a blood clot, an aneurysm, a stroke, a heart attack. They had come to be prepared for any and all of these. It didn't matter which one.

'There wasn't anything they could do.'

Alice smelled her parents' old smells. Her

father's dandruff shampoo, the waxy rose smell remaining from her mother's lipstick, and the rare and particular smell of the two of them combined. People seemed to smell most like themselves in their neck, she mused discordantly. She could imagine the smell of Riley's neck if she tried.

People passed them and just by looking they knew, Alice knew, that somebody of theirs had died. Like in highway accidents, people did a bad job of hiding their curiosity sometimes. *Hey, who died?* the faces seemed to ask.

My sister, their daughter. She just turned twenty-five, Alice thought of telling them. She wondered what was wrong with her that she was thinking about other people in the middle of her tragedy.

'It happened quickly,' her mother said.

Alice wondered whether her mother was trying to get her to ask the gritty questions of exactly how it had unfolded. Alice didn't want to ask those questions or hear those answers, and she felt irritated at her mother for trying to make her. And then she wondered what was wrong with her that she could be irritated at her mother at a moment like this.

Grief was transforming, Alice knew, but it was surprising how it also left you to your petty devices.

'Did you see her?' Alice asked.

'We were there,' her father said.

'I wish I was there,' Alice said, and a maverick sob escaped her throat.

'You were there,' her father said.

★ ★ ★

In his tears, Ethan shook like a child, and Paul felt old and grown. He stood in the living room of the apartment on 98th Street, knowing he could give comfort here. Though he hadn't let Ethan so much as touch his shoulder since he was ten, Paul now put his arms around him. He could feel Ethan's agony. He had his own agony, but he knew it was separate. He wouldn't try to share.

'We knew this could happen. We tried to be ready,' Ethan said.

'You can't be ready,' Paul said.

Paul looked around the apartment with a sense of wonder. He felt numbly disconnected from what was inside of him and vividly attuned to what was outside. He considered the family's true home to be Fire Island, because it included him, but this was where they lived. He'd been in this apartment very few times, considering how powerfully his life connected to theirs. He realized he could see better here than on Fire Island, where his eyes were worn in. He could see, for instance, that it was small and mostly bereft of natural light. He'd always romanticized their economies, as though they were a style and a choice. But in the condition of the furniture, the water damage along the ceiling, the sagging bookshelves he saw their privations, too.

'There are things I wish I could change,' Ethan said after a while. As uncomfortable as it was to see him cry, Paul acknowledged that

275

Ethan did it gracefully. He was an authentic crier.

Paul nodded.

'There are parts of my life I wish I could do differently.'

Paul nodded. He felt he knew a part Ethan was alluding to.

'For Riley's sake. For your sake, too,' Ethan said.

Paul thought of the words Ethan used. 'Consider yourself forgiven.' He realized he was playing God, but he sensed that Ethan needed it.

'None of that matters anymore.'

Ethan looked too miserable to accept this outright but also eager for the moment when he could.

'It really doesn't,' Paul said, and for the first time he felt the truth of his words.

★　★　★

Alice couldn't stay in the apartment with her parents. She couldn't stay indoors. She could barely stay in her skin. She didn't have a choice about that, but she walked alone through the Ramble in Central Park just in case.

Here she was walking around like any other person, like it was any other day. *Do you have any idea what happened?* she felt like demanding of the sky and the trees and the mud puddles and every creature, even dogs and babies, whom she passed. On this day they had no troubles of their own. *You have no idea!* she wanted to shout. She had not imagined that grief would feel smug.

By noon she couldn't stay in the park anymore and she couldn't stay outside anymore and she couldn't stay among strangers anymore, so she went back home, where she could barely make herself stay, either. She wished she could fall asleep. Was it too early to call it a day? To call it the next day or the one after? She would have liked to sleep through the next several days and perhaps even the summer. But did time lose its healing properties if you slept through it?

She fell onto her bed fully clothed. Ordinary transitions, like getting undressed, seemed to open the way for pain to leap on you unprepared.

Her father walked by her room and saw her lying in her bed. 'Paul was here,' her father said when he saw her. 'He was hoping to see you.'

★   ★   ★

Paul couldn't cry for himself yet, but he found himself crying for Alice as he walked down Columbus Avenue, away from their apartment. Instead of thinking his own thoughts, he found himself thinking hers. His grief was hard to feel, but hers was easy. Imagining her face and her sorrow had the near-instantaneous magic of translating concepts into feelings.

Riley was Alice's valiant defender, her buffer. Sometimes he wondered if having Riley out in front, taking the punches, was what allowed Alice to grow up so sweet. Hardship made you stronger, maybe, but it didn't appear to make you any happier.

And him, too. He thought of his house out there on the dune, belted by wind, rain, salt, and sand, offering shelter to their little house behind it. It seemed so lucky, everyone thought, him having the big house right there on the water with views to eternity. And maybe it was. But nothing stood between you and the pitiless sky. For those views, you took a beating sometimes.

Riley was gone. The house was gone. He had pushed Alice and distressed her, denied her what little comfort he might have offered. He thought of her the last time he'd seen her, her colors faded, her motions slow, her voice slow.

He wished he could do something to make it better. He would do whatever he could to restore what he had taken from her, even if it meant getting out of her way. All the other attempts he'd made to love her had only hurt her. That was maybe the best he could do for her.

When he got home to his apartment, he saw the piles of articles he'd collected on heart research, transplants, and artificial hearts. His desk was covered with them. He'd pushed all of his schoolwork aside to further the project. He'd already done most of the paperwork to make a gift in Riley's name to the center at Columbia Presbyterian hospital.

But now, sitting down at his desk, he didn't want to look at them anymore. He sat with his chin in his hand, staring at the wall in front of him, letting in little glimpses of Riley. And as he did, he knew she would not want to be associated with her heart disease forever. If he tried, he could think of what she would like: wildlife preservation on Fire Island, a new lifeguard chair to protect the long stretch of beach beyond Cutter Walk, funds to help save the white dolphin.

He put his head in his arms and he let Riley in.

★   ★   ★

Freeport, Merrick, Bellmore, Wantagh, Seaford, Amityville, Copiague, Lindenhurst, Babylon.

It made for a strange poetry in Paul's ears. He had never stopped in any of these places, only gone through them, but the names had a legendary feel to him, especially since he'd thought he'd made the trip for the last time.

He got off the Long Island Rail Road at Bay Shore. He waited for less than a minute for the taxi company before he got impatient and set off walking. The sun was long set, and it was a Tuesday night. He wondered how many ferries were left. He ran to the dock in time to miss the last ferry, so he took the Saltaire boat and walked.

In a strange dream, he walked along Lighthouse as it turned into Main Walk, the thoroughfare he knew so well he could barely see it. He saw it instead through Riley's eyes tonight. And Alice's.

He walked directly to his house, counseling himself not to think of it as his house anymore. It was another strange trick of money, that in transferring a large amount of it from one person to another you could lose all official connection to a place that held the most significant experiences of your life. It would be easier in a way if the new owners tore it down. That way, his life in it could be laid to rest in the ground rather than overlaid by another set of lives and memories. You had to think of it like a body with a soul gone out of it, he thought.

He tried to prepare his explanation as he walked the final block. But when he got to the door and knocked and nobody answered, he had no need for it. He tried the back door, too, but doubtfully, as no lights were on. He tried turning the knob, but the door was locked. He tried all the doors, even the sliding ones. All were locked.

When had they ever locked this house? Who ever locked their house around here? He remembered going out in the off-season at fifteen and sixteen, and helping himself to food and drinks at every house on Dune Walk. But that was before they cost three million dollars.

Now what could he do? He was singularly focused. He felt the need to stay focused. He couldn't look around too much, and he certainly couldn't give up. If he could fix this one thing, maybe the rest would be fixable, too.

He strode to the Weinsteins' house two walks over and knocked. He felt a little bad when Mr. Weinstein appeared in his bathrobe. 'Sorry to bother you. Is Barbara here?'

'Hold on.'

Barbara, thankfully, was not in her pajamas.

'I need to ask you a favor,' Paul asked. 'Can I

get a key for my old place? I just need to get in there for a couple of minutes.'

Barbara looked at him strangely. 'Paul.' She looked at her watch. 'It's eleven o'clock at night and you are asking me for a key to a house you no longer own.'

'I'm sorry. I realize it's an inconvenience. I won't stay long, I promise.'

'Paul. You don't understand. I can't do that.'

'Why not?' He realized that he looked particularly unkempt. He hadn't combed his hair or shaved in days. His shirt was dirty and his eyes, he suspected, were wild.

'It's not yours anymore. You have no more right to it than any other house on this island. I can't give you that key more than I can give you any other.'

He didn't want to get angry. He didn't want to point out that she'd been cut a check for more then two hundred thousand dollars. 'We lived there for twenty-three years,' he said. 'I owned it three weeks ago.' *Riley is gone. Can you understand that?*

'I'm sorry,' she said. 'I'd help you if I could.'

He wouldn't give up. He walked back to his house. He didn't want to look at the beach. It was overwhelming. All the things that happened here were crowding in, and he couldn't keep them back. It was a dangerous idea to come here now.

Sometimes sheer vastness was terrifying. The volume of the universe hanging above them. The mystery of the ocean connecting you to places cold and deep. The infinite nature of time before

281

this beach and the restless eternity that stretched on after.

There was one thing to do. He climbed up the planters to the first set of eaves. The wind was starting to blow, and he half expected it to peel him right off the side of the house and fling him into blackness. Would Riley be in the blackness? He clutched the second-floor windowsill with his hands while his left foot skidded down the shingled surface, looking for traction. A shingle popped off, and he watched it circle once and hit the ground. His hands were shaking with the strain. At last his foot found purchase, digging the toe of his sneaker into a narrow ledge where the shingle had been. He hauled himself onto the sill, balancing his weight on his knees, and pressed his fingertips under the mullions to push up the sash. It was locked, of course. What was with these people? What did they have worth protecting?

He would break the window if he had to, but he didn't yet. He climbed sideways across the face of the house from windowsill to windowsill. He heard the ocean crashing at his back. And then, far worse, he heard voices. There were people passing on the beach while he was stuck to the side of the house like an incompetent spider. He kept still. His fingers were shaking from the effort of gripping the exterior. The sound of conversation got closer, and after a seeming hour or two, got farther away. He thanked God they hadn't looked up.

The trick was the corner of the house. Adrenaline, thankfully, had begun to flow, protecting him from the suffering of his muscles. There was the drainpipe. In his memory it was substantial, but now it looked flimsy, particularly in relation to his body weight in rapid motion. He looked at the deck below. He pictured himself sprawled on it. He grabbed the drainpipe with one hand and swung onto it. *Shit.* It wailed and creaked and pulled away from the wall, but he managed to ride it long enough to get a hand on the window frame around the corner before they both went down.

Riley would love this, he couldn't help thinking. *Riley would love to be doing this right now.* He felt her with him, even though he didn't believe in that kind of thing.

When he got himself settled on the window, he assessed the state of the drainpipe, now bent and dislodged. He wondered if he ought to pay the buyers back some of their money.

He climbed from the window to the narrow balcony at the side of the house. He stood on it. He'd probably stood on it two other times in his life, both times wondering why nobody ever stood on it. People didn't stand on balconies, did they? But the thing he remembered from those times was that this door didn't really lock. It had one of those wimpy doorknob latches that you could turn right through if you turned it hard enough. Indeed, the door opened in a welcoming way and he walked into his house. Which no longer belonged to him.

I guess I'm robbing them, he thought. Could you be prosecuted for breaking into a house that you'd owned for twenty-three years and taking something out of it that was yours?

He walked quietly to his room, hearing the same old creaks. He did not turn on the light, but the moon showed him that there was no longer his desk or the bed where he had slept rarely and made love to Alice repeatedly. He felt a pang, a physical ache, in the bottom of his abdomen. There was a crib and a changing table and a glider and a rug with a pattern of dragonflies.

He went into his closet and pulled open a small built-in drawer, old and sticky with layers of paint. He put his hand in and felt all the way to the back. There it was, just as he'd stuck it there fifteen years ago.

He wasn't actually taking something out of the house that was his, he recognized as he bunched it up in his hand and walked down the stairs and out the back door. He was taking something that he'd stolen. Two wrongs supposedly couldn't make a right, but he felt in his heart that sometimes they could.

★   ★   ★

On the train ride home, Paul held Alice's pink-beaded rosary in his sweating hand.

He considered God, whom he hadn't much believed in up to this point. Neither the father nor the son. But the rosary felt warm, and he felt guilty for being such a heathen and carrying it around like this, having no idea what you were supposed to do with it. It reminded him of the time he went to church with Alice and Riley and took Communion by mistake.

He didn't want to be at odds with God, if only for the reason that Alice believed. Paul wondered if he apologized and if there was God, if God would hear it. *Sorry*, he thought, just in case. Now that Riley was out there, he was kind of hoping so. He thought of his father and felt guilty again. *It wasn't your fault*, he told God, just in case.

*   *   *

The Church of the Blessed Sacrament on West 71st Street was filled with tragic faces, none more than theirs. For all the events and masses they had ever been to here, always anonymous, late, insufficiently dressed, it was off-putting to get the VIP treatment on account of being the most bereaved.

It felt like a funeral mass for a child, in a way, Alice thought. The mourners were the village that had raised them: family friends, but mostly by way of their parents; school friends, but many through her father; childhood Fire Island friends. There were three people from Riley's years at NOLS, a leader and two former students. There was one guy she'd worked with at a restaurant in Jackson Hole the winter she'd spent skiing there. Riley hadn't studied or worked inside any institutions. It was harder, perhaps, to create your own circle of acquaintance when you didn't like to be inside at all.

And then, when nearly everyone was seated, the lifeguards arrived. *There*, thought Alice.

285

There was Riley's institution. You didn't need to be inside, did you? Another surge of tears brewed behind her eyes. The lifeguards came in force: at least twenty-five of them, including Chuck, Jim, and a couple of old-timers. They were tall and regal to a person. They understood the grandness of Riley.

Alice looked for Paul. She'd hoped he'd come and sit with them, but that wasn't his style. He was Riley's true lifelong friend, her partner in a thousand adventures. He was the only one, so far as Alice knew, to whom Riley ever wrote a letter. He was such a friend, Alice suspected, that all subsequent friends seemed counterfeit by comparison.

It seemed sad to give Riley her send-off in church. She had found it almost painful to sit inside in the dark on a Sunday morning, whereas Alice had secretly enjoyed it.

Paul was possibly the last to arrive. He did approach her family but not to sit. He had something for her, he said. Into her hand, he put a chain of some kind. She couldn't figure out what it was until she held it up and looked closely, and then suddenly memory flooded in.

He had taken it from her. He had given it back. She looked at him questioningly. His face was tight, and his eyes were swollen. 'I'm sorry,' he mouthed to her. Then he disappeared to find a seat at the back of the church.

She held her old rosary in two hands. Back then she'd thought it was so exceptionally pretty. 'Are these real stones, do you think?' she'd asked her mother long ago. She'd hoped they were.

'I think they're glass,' her mother had answered.

She remembered the nights she'd said her Hail Marys and Our Fathers again and again and again, feeling transported, wondering if she was transported.

So he'd taken it. She'd suspected him at the time, but she'd given him the benefit of doubt, as she often did.

What a shame, in a way. What a stupid thing to do. It was him she used to pray for.

★   ★   ★

Paul called his mother to tell her that Riley was dead. He couldn't remember the last time he had tracked Lia down and dialed her number. He felt he needed to do it, and he wasn't sure why.

As he told her, he cried silently into the phone. Then he just listened as Lia asked some questions and made some appropriate comments. 'What a shame. What a tragedy for the family,' she said, and with too little a pause, she launched into a tirade about an old friend who had stolen money from her.

Paul held the phone away, wondering. Why had he called her?

Maybe because Lia knew Riley a long time ago, when everything had been different. Maybe because it harkened back to a different Lia, with different hair and a different way of being. Maybe some part of him thought that he could access that lost version of Lia and, in the scald of tragedy, restore her for a minute.

When he hung up the phone, he understood his mistake.

Lia was lucky, in a way, that Robbie got out when he did. Lia considered Robbie's death her life's misfortune, but Paul now understood that it was her saving grace.

When Paul had looked at the old pictures, he saw something he'd already known. His parents were headed in steeply different directions well before his father died. He could guess what would have happened if Robbie had stayed on, how it would have ended up.

But as it was, Lia could imagine they had been happy. She could imagine that she had the capability for happiness, that she was a righteous person at heart, that indeed she could be happy again.

And Paul, in his way, had indulged the same fantasy, hadn't he? He would remain passive and faithless as long he could tell himself that he would have and could have been loved if only his father had stuck around. But could he have? He'd had Ethan's love and he'd seized a reason to reject it. The idea of love was always easier than the practice of it.

It took his father's death to make the idea possible. They had him to thank. He was their martyr, leaving them with one, shining, untarnished thing. It wasn't much, maybe, but it was more than some people had.

22

No Person Is Ashes

Alice and her parents went together out to the beach the last week in July. They had avoided it until then. They walked together toward the lighthouse. They'd stripped down to their suits and waded into the ocean. The surf was rough and multilayered, and Alice could see a look of near-panic on her mother's face. Judy hardly ever swam in the ocean anymore. Alice suddenly felt like more of an expert than she really was, more confident than she really was. She paddled to her mother, regained her footing on the bottom, and held her mother's hand. Her father walked steadily and ceremonially, holding the jar over his head.

You couldn't be too ceremonial in your bathing suit, spluttering and dodging waves. That's what was good about this idea. You could almost laugh.

Alice wished Paul were there. He belonged with them for this. But he was gone. He had no house here anymore. He could have stayed with them, she thought aimlessly. But where would he have stayed? In Riley's bed? In Alice's?

Ethan made sure he had a fix on the wind before he did anything. It always swirled around the ocean, but today it prevailed from the northwest, Alice calculated. They set their backs against the wind. Ethan unscrewed the top and then he paused. Already the ashes began to rise into the air. Alice thought he was going to say something, and she girded herself for a duty of meaningfulness. It was hard to feel the right emotions at the right time. They didn't come at all when you set a place for them, and they sacked you when you weren't ready, when you were just innocently flossing your teeth, for example, or eating a bowl of cereal. But Ethan didn't say anything. He handed the jar to her mother.

Alice had to give her mother's hand back, and she did it regretfully. Her mother's face was hard to look at, the sorrow so plain. She was less complicated than Alice had ever seen her, here with her agony and nothing else. But she accepted her job bravely. She had brought Riley into this world, and it was right for her to send Riley to the next. She hadn't been able to do much mothering of Riley in between.

The ashes seemed both heavy and light. Some sparkled, some fell. That seemed right, too. The ocean received them without much notice, but that was the ocean's job. It didn't meddle.

The ashes swirled on the surface for a while, and then they sank, folded into the body of the sea. Alice wondered if those ashes were really supposed to be Riley. They weren't, really. No person was ashes. It was one of those things you knew but did not believe in.

Her mother's hands were unflinching, and her face determined and raw. For a moment Alice did see a flash of Riley, but not in the ashes. She saw her in the set of her mother's hands.

★ ★ ★

Alice had volunteered to stay and take care of the house business. That included putting the house on the market, finding a seller, conducting the sale, and cleaning out their stuff. She didn't mind. She had nowhere to be, no thoughts to think, no one to love.

There were all the subtle hierarchies, little ticks up and down, the story lines on which you spent the hours and minutes of your life, and then a tragedy blew a hole right in the middle of them. It felt useless to try to reconnect those bits and refocus on them, but what else did you have?

The second morning, Alice woke up alone. She brought her cereal out to the deck and ate it in the sunshine. You needed to think of new rituals when you'd lost someone you loved.

She looked up at Paul's old house with a certain feeling of dread. She was scared to see new people there, covering up the life that was there before. She felt violated by the thought of them, as though they had the power to take a part of her life away. Now that Riley was gone, you couldn't make more of it. You had to hold on to what you had. The price went right through the roof.

She meant to be purposeful throughout the day, but in the afternoon she found herself reading a detective novel on the beach. Her mission was large and ominous, but you couldn't spend much of the day on it. She'd visited both real-estate offices and entered the listing for the house by ten in the morning. Life-altering events fit into a disproportionately small amount of time. Like death, for instance. Or changing a friend into a lover.

'Hi, Alice.'

She looked up to see Gabriel Cohen. He sat on her towel with her. In less than a minute, it was bunched up and sandy.

'How's it going?' she asked. His dark blond hair fell in perfect silk strings over his forehead. He was bigger. His limbs were longer and leaner. You could see knees, elbows, and knuckles emerging from his cloud of babyness. Sometimes she wished adults continued to grow and change physically at the rate that children did, just to remind you how dramatic the effect of time. When you couldn't see it, you could fool yourself into thinking it wasn't happening.

'I made a swimming pool.'

'Oh?'

'Down there.' He pointed to a clawed-up patch of sand near the water.

'Helen helped me.'

'Who's Helen?'

'Some kid,' he said. 'Did you bring any snacks?'

Alice laughed. Once his babysitter, always his babysitter. 'No. I have snacks at my house, though. Do you want me to get you something?'

'Okay.' She got up, and he followed her.

'Do you want to come?' she asked.

'Okay.'

'Where's your mother? Go tell her.'

He ran down the beach to his mother, who was sitting under an umbrella. Mrs. Cohen looked up and waved, and Alice saw the look she saw everywhere. Mrs. Cohen was mindful of their tragedy. She knew, just as everyone here knew. She wanted not to confront the fact, as she knew it without having been told directly. She wanted to look and seem the right way in respect to Alice's status. Alice turned her eyes, with some relief, to Gabriel, who just wanted her snacks.

Gabriel raced back with a smaller blond girl on his tail. 'Can Helen come?' he asked.

'Sure,' she said, figuring Mrs. Cohen's blessing was good enough for the two of them. Helen had small, fat thighs that brushed together when she walked. She had a severely bobbed haircut, a yellow one-piece bathing suit, and a tiny cupid's mouth.

The two of them were coated in sand like two sugar donuts, and Alice had the fleeting thought that she should wash them off before she brought them into the kitchen, but she didn't bother with it. She thought of the joke her mother used to make when they'd cooked up a feast in the kitchen, dirtying every pot and pan. 'Let's just sell the place,' her mother would say, as though she were Marie Antoinette.

'Crackers or apples or . . . cheese?' Alice asked, looking through the cabinets and into the refrigerator. Kind neighbors had left trays of sweet things, but Alice figured she would give

293

them something healthy if she could get away with it.

Helen looked to Gabriel. 'Crackers,' he answered.

'Crackers,' Helen answered, too. Alice could see that Helen didn't want to make a wrong move. She was younger, and thus had to earn her way. Gabriel would as easily banish her as keep her on.

'How's your brother?' Alice asked.

'He went to corkball,' Gabriel said, shooting most of the cracker out with his answer.

'Gosh. Is he old enough for that already?'

'He is seven,' Gabriel said, almost reverently. He looked to Helen to see if she'd absorbed the fact that he had a seven-year-old brother.

'How old are you?' Alice asked Helen.

'Four.'

'Well, I'm five and a quarter,' Gabriel countered, as if to add perspective.

'I know that, because you were four last summer,' Alice said, and Gabriel looked slightly defeated to have to be reminded of that.

'I'm four,' Helen mentioned again with a little more pride.

They went out to the deck to finish the pile of crackers.

'Do you live here?' Helen asked. Alice could hear the sand granules crunching in her small molars. She saw how sandy Helen's hands were. She should have washed them.

'I do. Where do you live?'

Helen turned around and pointed with a sandy finger to Paul's house. 'Right there.'

1

★   ★   ★

Breakfast was no longer a solitary affair. Now that Helen had seen the proximity of Alice's house and the number of snacks therein, she not only came herself but brought her sister, Bonnie, who was only two. They might have brought Henry, their brother, they explained, but he was only seven months old and couldn't walk yet. Toward the end of breakfast, their mother arrived and introduced herself as Emily.

'I hope they are not disturbing you,' Emily said. She had the little brother under one arm and a pleasantly harried look in her khaki shorts and bathing-suit top.

'No. Not at all,' Alice replied. She, Helen, and Bonnie had each eaten a bowl of Cheerios while sitting on the deck, though Bonnie had spilled hers halfway through. 'I'm happy for the company.'

'Are you here alone?' Emily asked.

Alice was surprisingly happy for a direct and uncomplicated question. Everyone she knew here avoided questions altogether. 'Yes. For now. My parents usually come on weekends, but I'm not sure they are going to be out this summer.'

'That's too bad,' Emily said. 'Well, I'm happy to meet you. I look forward to being neighbors.'

Alice looked at her wistfully. Emily had her falling-down mom ponytail and the look of a purposeful life. Alice tried to remember her predisposition toward hostility. Why didn't she like this person? She couldn't even remember.

'Come on, girls,' Emily said.

'We're staying with Alice,' Helen said.

'Honey. Alice has her own things to do,' Emily said.

No, she didn't. Alice suddenly didn't want Helen or Bonnie to go. Bonnie could spill every single thing in the house if she liked. Alice would help her. 'They can stay,' she said to Emily. 'Really, I like having them. I'll bring them home before lunch.'

Emily cast her a grateful look as she went back out to the board-walk.

Alice cut up a watermelon and taught them how to spit the seeds off the side of the deck. 'We'll have a forest of watermelons!' Helen proclaimed.

Alice got out her old crayons and drew an underseascape with them. They purposefully made all the creatures very friendly, even the ones with fangs. Alice drew a dolphin.

She found her old collection of picture books and read them her favorite William Steig and Dr. Seuss books. They watched the hummingbirds float around the orange trumpet flowers. She held Bonnie up so she could see, enjoying the feel of her little pellet body.

'Okay, thing one and thing two,' she said to them. 'It's time to go home.'

When they complained, she thought of an enticement. 'Follow me and I'll show you something important,' she said.

She showed them out the back way, and crept with them along the phragmite path right to their back door. 'This is a secret shortcut,' she said to them in a voice just above a whisper. 'This is the way my best friend used to come to see me and my sister.'

The following morning, she was just getting out her bowl and cereal box, perching on the deck, enjoying the morning sun, when the two little blond heads appeared through the reeds of the secret path. *Life goes on,* she thought.

★   ★   ★

For a month, Alice read and entertained her tiny flock. Not only Helen and Bonnie came but Gabriel and others, too. She liked to teach them things, she realized. She taught them how to catch crabs, how to dig for sand fleas, how to boogie board. You couldn't let these traditions be lost. She taught them how to kill a silverfish and how to improve hand speed for slapping a mosquito dead.

She taught Helen, Gabriel, and another five-year-old named Bo how to ride two-wheelers. She taught Bonnie how to ride a tricycle. After that, she taught them all how to do it no-handed. *Those who can't do teach,* she thought.

She started to see beauty in this place again. Not beauty in the beautiful things, necessarily, but beauty in the ordinary things, like the rows of telephone poles along Main Walk and the way the sun glinted off the draping cables. She appreciated the ways the trees arched over the walks that ran perpendicular from the ocean to the bay, and how when you stood with the ocean at your back, you looked straight through a green tunnel to a circle of blue bay at the other end. She noticed how quickly the reeds grew through the cracks between the boards underfoot and how, in a single season, the new orange planks weathered into matching gray.

One day she stood on the beach before a storm, and the water swept so far out from the shore that she could see the foundation and the hearth from an old house that had long since washed away.

Sometimes she watched her little flock and she felt like warning them, *Be careful, you little ones.* This place had a way of grabbing you and holding you. You could spend the rest of your life longing for a single idealized moment that may not have even happened.

By night Alice knitted a scarf for nobody. She'd started it for Riley, and it seemed wrong, somehow, not to finish it. And then, in an odd brainstorm around the second week of August, she decided she'd make it for Emily. Even if she never got up the courage to give it to Emily, a knitter always needed to know for whom she knitted.

23

From That World into This

On the first day of September, a large and handsome face appeared under the trumpet-vine bower. He took up several times the space of her usual guests.

Alice's body froze in a strange position. Helen and Bonnie looked up at him.

'Who are you?' Helen asked, mildly put out that a fully grown stranger should interrupt their drawing.

'I'm Paul. Who are you?'

'Helen,' Helen said. 'I live over there.' She pointed to her house.

Alice watched the realization as it overtook Paul's face. 'Do you really?'

'Yes.'

'How do you like it?' he asked.

'We like to come see Alice,' Helen answered. She was surprised and pleased to see the laugh she got out of Paul.

'Me too,' he said.

'That's Bonnie.'

'Hello, Bonnie,' Paul said.

Bonnie continued scribbling blue for water.

'She's my sister.'

'Wow. Lucky.'

'We know a secret shortcut,' Helen blurted.

And then she looked at Alice, worrying she'd said too much.

'That's okay,' Alice said. 'He knows it, too.'

* * *

Paul sat at the wooden table on the deck of Alice's house and watched the two little blond heads disappear into the phragmite. He could hardly look at Alice sitting there across from him, her feet on the chair, her arms wrapped around her knees, dressed in his favorite cutoff shorts and a white T-shirt that might once have been his. Her colors were coming back. The sun was turning her skin the syrupy orange-tan color that only Alice turned, finding her freckles again, lighting up the bronze and red in her hair, putting the gold back into the green of her eyes. All the burgeoning possibility in her was practically blinding. *But she doesn't even know,* he thought. He could tell by her posture that she had no idea. He could tell by the fray of her fingernails.

There was a familiar feeling he knew he could feel right now. It opened in front of him like a hallway, beckoning him to walk down it. He could resent her for her beauty. He could feel threatened by her again. He could be threatened by the fact that Alice had already won the adoration of two little girls who now lived in his house. His path in life was not exactly original. Who could live next to Alice and not fall in love with her? And she, being so easily loved, did she really need his, too? What could she want with it?

300

What did he have to offer?

It was a familiar urge to want to weigh her down. To demand the return of things he would not properly give. But he would not be conquered by that urge. He would sooner get up and walk down the boardwalk to the ferry and never see her again. He came back once. He came back twice. He didn't deserve another chance. He'd made a promise to himself that he was not allowed in her presence if he couldn't love her better.

He had to trust her. With her gifts, she could have taken what she wanted from the world. She could have stood up and demanded it. But she didn't take; she gave. He had to trust that even with the full knowledge of her powers, she would use them for good.

Hardest of all, he had to trust her to love him. He knew that was not a trial for Alice, who was so gifted at being loved and loving, but rather for him, who was so poor at both.

'Are you staying over tonight?' she asked him.

'I don't know,' he answered. He didn't want to scare her. 'I might stay with the Cooleys or the Loebs. I came over with Frank on the ferry. I gather they've got extra rooms now that the kids are gone. Have you noticed he has a lot of hair growing out of his ears?'

She laughed. When she left off, there was silence.

'Do you want to take a walk with me?' he asked. 'A long, hot, and tiring one?'

She smiled and nodded, but he could see that a question was on its way. 'Why did you come?'

He thought of a few different answers: *I needed to settle some business with the house. Tom Cooley's been bugging me to play in the softball tournament. I had nothing else to do and the weather was good.*

'To see you,' he said.

★ ★ ★

Walking along next to Paul, Alice looked up at him. His posture was a bit straighter. He'd finally gotten a haircut, she saw. A professional one. He looked like a proper grown-up. Like a man. And though his eyes were dark brown like his father's and his jaw was a similar shape, she thought how little Paul looked like the pictures of Robbie.

She was trying to understand his mood. Was he angry? Was he sorry? Was he forgiving? Was this a postmortem? Would she have her whole life to look back on the things they said today and know that it was the final episode?

The way he looked at her, there was something behind his eyes. Some flickering, questioning part of him that wanted to reach out and make contact, she thought. It came and it went. He had a question, but he couldn't ask it.

'A year ago today, I came to find you and you weren't there,' he said as they walked.

Alice nodded. She remembered it for a different reason, too.

'I waited at your house. I went to the Cohens' to see if you were still working. I tried the yacht club, the courts, the fields, the beach. I couldn't find you, and I couldn't find Riley. I sat in your kitchen alone for hours. I just waited.'

She knew something of waiting. It might have been the first time it was him and not her. 'That's where I found you there when I got back,' she said.

He nodded.

'Do you know where I was?' A part of her was still scared of having responsibility for a secret.

'I think so. Now I do.'

'Riley didn't want you to know. I couldn't tell you.'

'I know.'

The sympathy she had compressed and boxed away, but it started to leak out. It was sympathy for him, for being shut off without an explanation. It was sympathy for them, her and Paul, because they loved each other. Trickiest of all to feel, perhaps, was sympathy for herself, for a year of hardship, loss, and atonement. She had thought she could help. She thought she could make it better, but she hadn't.

They walked past Lonelyville, past the shacks and bungalows at odd angles. Of all the towns, this was the one that seemed to stay the same.

He reached out and held her hand. It seemed so strange at first, to be touched by him. It summoned a thousand other times, each of them signifying a different thing.

'We didn't make her sick,' he said. 'I know it felt like that, but we didn't.'

She gripped his hand hard without meaning to. She could hardly see to walk. She swallowed and tried to talk. 'It felt like that.'

'Alice, I know.' He turned to her and took her

other hand. He sat her on the sand and put both arms around her. He held her and patted her. He brushed her hair from her face and wiped her tears like she was his baby. She felt the solidness of his body enveloping hers, and she let him. He tended to her tears, even though he had his own.

'I felt like we left her. We betrayed her.'

He nodded on her head. 'I know.'

'We were punished for it.'

Paul nodded again. She felt the stubble of his chin on her scalp. There was a long quiet except for the waves and the occasional shout of a swimmer. 'Who do you think punished us?' he asked slowly, not like he already knew the answer. 'Was it Riley?'

Alice sat up, displacing his head. 'No, no. It wasn't her.'

Paul had a thoughtful look on his features. 'How do you know?'

'Because she loved us. It scared her a little, she told me once. But she said she always knew.'

'Then who wanted to punish us?'

Alice pushed her hair behind her ears. 'I don't know. God. Fate. Me. Maybe we punished ourselves.'

They sat for a while, watching the water. She leaned her shoulder against his. A dog went by without a leash and so did an all-terrain ambulance. She thought of Riley cursing at the cars on the beach. You couldn't really curse at an ambulance.

Paul stood up first and reached out for her hand to pull her up next to him.

'You're allowed to grow up,' he said.

★　★　★

They resumed walking at Lonelyville, but Alice didn't open her mouth again until they were past the jetties at Ocean Beach and she got in a talking mood. Of all the things she had to tell him, it was odd to her what came out.

'So often this summer I keep thinking: I know I'm holding back. I know I'm waiting. I know I'm afraid to go forward. But I don't know how to get there from here.'

He was quiet, so she kept going. 'Sometimes I see it as a tricky mountain pass between two valleys. Other times, it's like perilous straits connecting two lands. Partly it's the fear of the trip itself, I think, but partly it's the fear that I won't be able to get back. I'll turn around and the clouds will have settled over the mountain-top. Or the waters will have risen and shifted, and there will be no way home.'

Paul nodded. He took her hand again, which she discovered she appreciated.

'But that's not even the real fear.'

He gave her an odd smile. Short on mirth but affectionate. 'What's the real fear?'

'The real fear is that I won't want to go home.'

★　★　★

'They put the house on the market, you know,' she told him somewhere east of Seaview. She hadn't been eager to tell him that.

His face was incredulous. 'Your house? Here?'

'Yes. I'm supposed to be here helping to show

it and settle it, but it's been pretty slow. In a month, one person has come to see it, and she left without looking at the upstairs. She asked whether you could tear it down and build a bigger house on the lot.'

Paul looked as though his whiskers itched. 'I don't understand why they're selling it.'

'Well.' She tipped her head. 'You sold yours.'

'But your house is different. It's really worth something.'

'Tell that to the realtor,' Alice said.

'Realtors never know what things are worth.'

Alice dragged her toes behind her in the sand, making a linked chain of footsteps.

'Are your folks serious, do you think?' Paul asked.

'They don't want to be here without Riley,' Alice explained. 'You must see that.'

'But this place was her life. It's a way to keep her near, I would think.'

Alice considered the days and nights she'd spent here. Riley's absence was acute, and her presence even more so. 'I think I think so, too.' She shrugged. 'But what a choice. You surround yourself with your pain or you avoid it and let it find you when you are trying to do other things.'

'Are those the only alternatives?'

Alice shrugged. 'Can you think of others?'

'Can't you just keep going?'

Alice thought about that as they passed Ocean Bay Park. She'd considered the fact that she never walked into any of these places, only past them.

'Anyway, the woman who looked at it put in

an offer for the tear-down, as she called it, and my parents said no. They said they don't want anyone tearing it down, but the realtor said there's really nothing you can do. She said anyone who would buy the place would probably tear it down.'

Paul shook his head. 'Every year you come back and a few more are gone.'

'I'm almost glad Riley isn't around to see it happen,' Alice said.

★　★　★

At the Point O'Woods beach, Paul thought of a story to tell her.

'My father was friends with a guy who lost his leg in a motorcycle accident. One time when I was very small, I guess four, because my dad was still alive, he came to the house here at the beach, and while my parents were in the other room, he showed me the place where the doctor cut off his leg.'

'God. Why did he do that?' Alice asked.

'Well, I guess he was not a man who lived his life according to good judgment.'

'I guess not,' she said.

'So anyway, I thought about it all the time. For years after, I used to lie in my bed and worry that I would get a motorcycle and get in an accident.'

'I didn't know that.'

'I hated motorcycles. I said to my mother, 'I'll never get a motorcycle.' And she said, 'You never know what you'll want when you are older.'

'After that, the thing that scared me was not so much the motorcycle itself but that I could turn into a person who would want one. I was scared of the idea that I could become an entirely different person, a stranger to myself.'

'I can understand that.'

'So when I was about nine, I wrote myself a letter. When I cleaned out the house in May, I found many things, and that was one of them.'

He loved the look of amusement on her face. 'What did it say?'

'I addressed it to my future self. It said, 'No matter how much you might think you want a motorcycle, please don't get one.' And then I wrote in all capital letters: 'REMEMBER HENDERSON'S LEG.''

She considered this. 'Did you ever want a motorcycle?'

'Never.'

★   ★   ★

'I am going back to school in the fall,' Alice said on the long road of sand leading to the Sunken Forest.

'Are you?' he said. He tried to keep his face neutral. He'd already given himself a lecture on this subject. Part of loving her better was putting aside his opinions and prejudices, and letting her be a lawyer if she wanted to.

'Yes. Riley made me.'

He laughed. 'Did she?'

'She caught me working at the Duane Reade on Eleventh Avenue. She said I was supposed to be the smart one. It really annoyed her.'

'Well, as you've said, you have to be smart for law school.' He tried to make his voice sound game.

'I'm not going to law school.'

'You're not?'

'No. I applied to the School of Social Work at NYU. They were nice enough to let me apply late. I got the letter on August seventh.'

'Wow. How about that. Well, congratulations.' As he tried to keep his opinion about her suitability for a law career to himself, he felt similarly bound to hide his joy about this.

★ ★ ★

'We trusted ourselves when we were younger,' Alice asked thoughtfully, somewhere between the Sunken Forest and Sailor's Haven. 'Didn't we?'

'Riley did,' Paul said. 'And we, to a lesser extent, did, too.'

'We trusted Riley.'

'Yes.'

'We didn't trust ourselves to be adults, though. We thought we knew better then.'

Paul shook his head, thinking. 'The adults we had around didn't offer much promise. They offered us so many things not to do, it was hard to see what possibilities were left over.'

She looked to his face for bitterness or an expression of dismissal, but she didn't see either. 'I know about Ethan and Lia, you know.'

'Yeah. Riley said she told you.'

'I had no idea before.'

She walked quietly along, feeling the sun on the back of her neck, the wet sand twisting under the balls of her feet, the ache of the muscles in her legs. She was struck by an idea that she liked. 'You know what I think?'

'No.' He squeezed her hand. 'Maybe.'

'I think Riley was trying to tell us that she knew we had to go that way but that she thought we'd do all right at it.'

★ ★ ★

'I see the moon,' Alice pointed out when they'd reached Talisman, just before Water Island. It was there that they decided to turn around and walk west. 'But the sun's still hanging on, so I guess that doesn't count.'

'I think we should keep going. I think we should walk all the way to tomorrow,' he said. The sun was starting its descent over the bay in a modest display. It didn't seem a night for showing off.

'We don't have any water to drink,' she said. It was a warm night. She felt the damp sweat on her neck and back.

'That's a point. I have my wallet, though.' It was a stigma of sorts. Only day-trippers carried their wallets.

'We can buy water in Cherry Grove.'

They did better than that. They had two martinis each and watched a transvestite floor show at The Ice Palace with a special appearance by the winner of the Mr. Fire Island Leather contest. 'The featured fetish this year was fangs

310

and biting,' the bartender informed them.

'Whenever you say you go to Fire Island, this is how much fun people think you are having,' Paul pointed out, once they were back on the beach.

'Little do they know,' said Alice.

They were still seven miles from home, the sand was soft, the moon had the sky to itself, and they were both drunk.

'We're breeders. This is uncouth,' Alice said, sinking beside him into the sand by the water.

'It's a tolerant place,' Paul said. He settled her head onto his chest, holding her tight against him as they fell asleep.

★　★　★

When Paul opened his eyes again, the sun was lighting up the surface of the sea, though it remained underwater. For a moment, he had no idea where he was or how he had gotten there. And then he felt Alice.

Alice must have sensed him stir, because she opened her eyes. He loved to watch her. He felt like he had a private insight, watching her pass from that world into this. He felt like he would know her a little better each time. He liked the spot of drool on his clavicle.

'Is it tomorrow?' she whispered.

'It is.'

His body felt sore and nice as they stretched and rose and resumed their walk west, toward home. He reached for her hand. They had nowhere to be, nothing to do, no one waiting for them. The sand stretched out for miles in front of them, but the emptiness that felt like loneliness yesterday felt different today.

It was the same beach, the same ocean, the same sun. The same shirt and pants. The same girl walking alongside him. And yet somehow different.

24

Not Getting a Motorcycle

It turned out someone was waiting for them. Two people, in fact.

'We didn't have breakfast,' Helen said, palms facing the sky. It was unclear as to whether it was a request, a complaint, or merely a statement of fact. 'I think Bonnie's hungry.'

'Oh, good. I'm starving,' Alice said. 'How about Cheerios?'

Helen pointed at Paul. 'He's still here.'

'He is, isn't he?' Alice said, on her way into the kitchen. She brought out four bowls and four spoons in one arm and a cereal box and milk carton in the other. He loved how naturally she provided and mothered. She'd always been that way, hadn't she? From the very beginning. He had to laugh at himself as he thought of it. He'd picked a baby for a mother.

They sat in a circle on the deck, the planks making lines on their legs.

Paul looked up. 'Oh, my God. Look at that. The butterflies are here.'

Both girls scrambled to their feet.

'Alice! Look at your trumpet vine. Have you ever seen so many?'

Alice looked up in genuine awe. There were hundreds of them, all seeming to descend at once. As the four of them watched breathlessly, the beating wings slowed and the butterflies all at once fell into butterfly repose.

The girls were jumping around, trying to see.

'*Shhh*, try to be quiet, so we don't scare them away,' Alice whispered.

It was one of the most glorious sights he had ever seen. The orange flowers enveloped by a cloud of orange butterflies.

'They are monarchs,' Paul whispered to the girls. 'We only see them here once in a long time.'

Paul saw how they were straining to look. It was a disadvantage, sometimes, being under three feet tall. He picked Helen up in one arm and Bonnie in the other. He was touched by the excitement of the girls, and also by how hard they worked to keep quiet.

The butterflies took flight all at once, and he heard Alice let out a little hum at the beauty of it, all of the orange wings against the blue sky. She reached for his hand as all faces turned upward. The girls fluttered away soon after so they could tell their mother what they saw.

After that, Alice and Paul lay for a long time on the deck, sun-tired and deeply impressionable. When he closed his eyes, he saw only wings.

At last he sat up. 'I had the strangest feeling before. Not strange, really. Probably natural. Just strange to me.'

'What is that?' said Alice, sitting up next to him.

'I held those little girls up, and in the time it took the butterflies to come and go, I changed from thinking of them as people I might once have been to people I could one day have. Do you think your past can change into your future that quickly?'

★ ★ ★

Paul slept on the old, familiar couch. He hated it, but he hated for it to be his last time, too.

He couldn't sleep. He went out to the deck. He looked at his old house. He looked for the moon. He remembered the butterflies. Could Alice sleep? He pictured her sleeping. He tiptoed up to her bedroom. Her door was open. His heart rollicked as he crept in.

Her eyes were closed. Her hair covered most of her face. Was it wrong to wake her? But he had something to tell her, and he wasn't going to do the cowardly thing again of saying it when she couldn't hear. He gently pushed some of the hair away from her face. Her eyes opened and she turned toward him.

'Hey, Alice?'

She smiled at him. 'Yes?'

He kneeled on the floor at the top of her bed so his head was even with hers. He wanted to look her in the eyes, and he didn't want her to have to get up. 'I have something to tell you.'

'Okay.' Her eyes blinked away some of the sleep. She looked at him expectantly.

He was making it as awkward for himself as possible, but that was the point. 'Hey, Alice?'

'Yes.' She was being sweetly patient.

'I love you,' he said. For all the millions of

315

times he'd felt it, how good it was to finally say aloud.

She smiled again. 'I know.'

'Okay,' he said. 'Well, good night.' He walked back down the stairs to his couch and lay down on it. Maybe he could sleep now.

★   ★   ★

She crept downstairs before dawn. She had to laugh at the sprawl of him on the couch. He was too tall to fit on it. In her sleeping shirt and bare legs, she perched on the chair across from him and watched him sleep. He'd kicked off the thin blanket she'd found for him, so his chest and shoulders and arms were bare. One arm was turned out, and she saw the fair underside of his forearm and wrist. She saw the faint blue veins running under his skin, and she saw something else, too.

She stood up and went closer to look. She leaned down with the gradual knowing of what it was. On the inside of his arm just above his wrist, he'd gotten a small blue tattoo. It looked new, as though it was still settling, still healing, but she could see clearly that it was a picture of a dolphin.

★   ★   ★

Alice sat on the deck. She sat on a particular part of the railing where you could see past Helen and Bonnie's house to watch the sun rise up out of the ocean. She sat there for a long time, her hands clasped, her feet dangling, the edge of the wood digging into the backs of her thighs. She waited until the sun had freed itself from the water and was fully situated in a blue-turning sky before she went back inside.

Paul had awoken. He sat on the couch, feet on the ground, with his head resting in his hands. She enjoyed the way his hair was flat on one side and stood up on the other. He looked up at her as she walked in.

She came close again. He put his arms out to her, and she slipped onto his lap. They remembered how to do that. She put her head on his shoulder and her arms around him tight. She felt the joy of being held by him again.

With her legs straddling him, it was hard to conceal the state of things between his legs. She wrapped tighter around him and felt the joy of that as well.

'I'm sorry, Alice,' he said, half choked and half laughing. 'I can't help it. You might have to move.'

'I don't want you to help it,' she said. 'I don't want to move.'

She wasn't sure if he remembered it, but this was the last position in which they'd made love more than a year before.

She lifted up so she could pull off his boxer shorts. He slipped her shirt over her head and pressed her naked self against his.

'Can we . . . right here?' he whispered, his eyes endearingly wide.

'I think we should make the best of it before they tear it down,' she whispered back, even

317

though there was no need to whisper.

He had the look of a man who'd gotten ahead of himself, afraid to believe the place in which he had landed. She laughed at his eagerness.

She felt him tugging at her underpants, but then he stopped.

'We don't have . . . '

She didn't want him to stop, but she knew what he meant. She appreciated that he was responsible. 'Wait a minute. Just hold on.' She pried herself away from him. 'I think I might have one.'

'You do?' He looked only half delighted by that thought.

'Yes. From before. You left them.'

'I did.'

She laughed again. 'You used to have them coming out your ears.'

'That's true, isn't it?'

'I'll be right back.' She not only found a condom, but she also took the moment to lock the door to the deck in case any little girls appeared for an early breakfast.

He looked impatient for her return. He grabbed her up as soon as she'd tiptoed back into the room and with ardent determination, he finished the job of undressing her. He lay her on the couch and made love to her with a solemn face and a joyful body.

It was different this time. They'd been stripped down since last summer. She wondered if he felt that, too. Last time, they'd been hiding out in their alternate universe, like fugitives or wary secessionists. It had been a putsch last time.

Now they were with the world again. It was less privileged, maybe, but at least it connected them to the future.

★   ★   ★

He boarded the ferry with Alice. He kept thinking it was the last time for this ferry and this island, but there kept being another, so he decided to leave it open.

It was a customary goodbye boat, Labor Day in the late afternoon. He tried to put himself in the mood of it, seeing all the teenagers hugging and crying.

But this time he had Alice. He held her hand, in a state of near-giddy disbelief that he would get to hold her hand all the way onto the boat and off of it, too. They'd never left the island together before. He couldn't fathom the idea, the pleasure of not having to say goodbye to her. What he most loved about this island he was taking with him. Well, he thought wistfully, one of the two. And with that thought came an ache. Not so much a pressing ache but the kind you got used to.

They climbed to the upper deck and found a seat at the back by the railing. He put his hand on Alice's thigh. He was happy that he got to do that. He looked at the sky, simple blue, and he looked for the frail daytime moon, which he never seemed to notice anywhere but here.

★   ★   ★

319

As the ferry engine revved and the people swirled around them and Paul held her hand, Alice kept thinking about that passage from one part of life to another. She kept thinking, *Is this it? Will I know if it is? Will I be ready? Will I make it across? Will I chicken out? Will I know when I'm saying goodbye? When I look back, will I still be able to see what I've left behind?*

She thought she would know when it happened. But now, as she looked around, she wondered if it was really like that at all. Maybe it happened in a million different ways, when you were thinking of it and you weren't. Maybe there was no gap, no jump, no chasm. You didn't forget yourself all at once. Maybe you just looked around one time or another and you thought, *Hey.* And there you were.

Paul stood, and so did she as the ferryboat churned and began its laborious backing out. Alice watched the teenagers on the boat frantically waving at their friends who were shouting, screaming from where they stood at the edge of the dock.

Paul cradled Alice's hand in both of his hands and held it to his chest. They watched as the cluster of kids who were left on the dock lifted their arms over their heads and dove in.

Acknowledgments

With great appreciation (and some relief) I thank the valiant Sarah McGrath as well as Geoff Kloske and Susan Petersen Kennedy for their patience, talent, and support. I thank Jennifer Rudolph Walsh, my remarkable agent and friend.

I thank my dear friend Elizabeth Schwarz for her wisdom and her guidance.

With love I acknowledge Jacob, Sam, Nate, and Susannah, and, as ever, my wonderful parents, Jane and Bill Brashares.

We do hope that you have enjoyed reading this large print book.

Did you know that all of our titles are available for purchase?

We publish a wide range of high quality large print books including:
Romances, Mysteries, Classics
General Fiction
Non Fiction and Westerns

Special interest titles available in large print are:
The Little Oxford Dictionary
Music Book
Song Book
Hymn Book
Service Book

Also available from us courtesy of Oxford University Press:
Young Readers' Dictionary
(large print edition)
Young Readers' Thesaurus
(large print edition)

For further information or a free brochure, please contact us at:
Ulverscroft Large Print Books Ltd.,
The Green, Bradgate Road, Anstey,
Leicester, LE7 7FU, England.
Tel: (00 44) 0116 236 4325
Fax: (00 44) 0116 234 0205

Other titles published by
The House of Ulverscroft:

SECRETS

Jude Deveraux

At age twelve, Cassandra Madden fell in love with Jefferson Ames, a young man she met at one of her mother's business conferences. To cope with the pain of a cold mother, she always held on to this unrequited love. Years later her heart still yearns for Jeff, and she travels to Williamsburg, Virginia, where Jeff, now widowed, lives with his daughter. Cassandra becomes the child's nanny, but he's yet to even notice her. Then one day she hears shots coming from the mansion of Althea Fairmont, an eccentric woman and great actress. Cassie runs to investigate and suddenly her life is turned upside down. She learns that everyone has secrets — and Cassie must unravel those secrets, if she and Jeff are to find happiness again.

LOVE THE ONE YOU'RE WITH

Emily Giffin

In the diner Leo doesn't see me at first, and that gives me a vague sense of power, which goes when his eyes find mine. He strides toward my table, and I am fearful that he will kiss my cheek. But that isn't his style — Andy kisses my cheek. He looks the same — perhaps bulkier. A stark contrast to Andy's fine features. Andy is easier on the eyes, I think. Andy is easier, *period*. The same way a walk on the beach is easy. A Sunday nap. A square peg in a square hole. 'Ellen Dempsey,' he finally says, staring into my eyes. I couldn't have scripted a better opening line. I stare back into his brown eyes. 'Ellen *Graham*,' I announce proudly.

BLUE-EYED DEVIL

Lisa Kleypas

Hardy Cates is a self-made man who's bent on revenge against the Travis family. Regarding him as the most dangerous man in town, Haven Travis's family struggles against their rebellious daughter's attraction to him. But then the heiress and the bad boy uncover an explosive chemistry between them. Hardy Cates has a history he's not proud of, but now he's trying to clean up his act. He is looking for the perfect society wife, the kind of woman Haven Travis could never be. After a love affair went badly wrong, Haven vows to stay far away from Cates — but the blue-eyed devil is hard to resist. Then a menace from Haven's past appears, and Hardy may be the only one to save her . . .

WEDDING SEASON

Katie Fforde

Sarah is a wedding planner, but she doesn't believe in love — not for herself, anyway. Following another successful wedding, she somehow agrees to organise two more, on the same day and only two months away. And whilst her celebrity bride is all sweetness and light, her own sister drives her mad with her high expectations on a limited budget. Luckily Sarah is helped by her reliable friends Elsa and Bron — who are great at their wedding work, but romance doesn't feature very highly in either of their lives. All three women soon learn that patience is definitely a virtue in their marriage game. And, totally immersed in preparations for wedding of the year plus one, they've got no time to think about love . . . or have they?